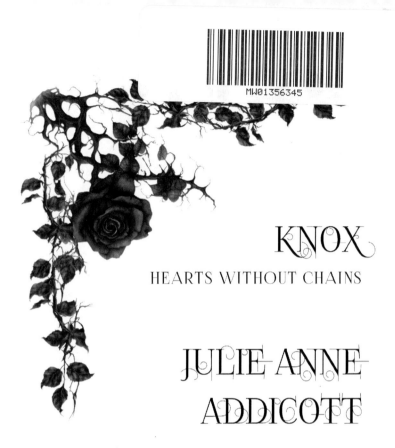

KNOX
HEARTS WITHOUT CHAINS

JULIE ANNE ADDICOTT

Knox – Hearts without Chains
Copyright © Julie Anne Addicott

First published in 2020
All rights reserved.

No part of this publication may be reproduced, distributed, or transmitted in any form or by any means, including photocopying, recording, other electronic or mechanical methods, or fan fiction of any kind without the prior written permission of the author, except in the case of brief quotations embodied in critical reviews and certain other non-commercial uses permitted by copyright law. This is a work of fiction. Names, characters, places, and incidents either are the products of the author's imagination or are used fictitiously. Any resemblance to actual persons, living or dead, businesses, companies, events, or locales is entirely coincidental.

NO AI/NO BOT. The author does not consent to any Artificial Intelligence (AI), generative AI, large language model, machine learning, chatbot, or other automated analysis, generative process, or replication program to reproduce, mimic, remix, summarize, or otherwise replicate any part of this creative work, via any means: print, graphic, sculpture, multimedia, audio, or other medium.

The author acknowledges the trademark status and trademark owners of various products referenced in this work of fiction. The publication/use of these trademarks is not associated with or sponsored by the trademark owners in any way.

Poetry and chapter heading quotes are all original works written by the author.

No part of this publication contains AI generated material.

For permission requests, contact the author:
legal.addicottpublishing@gmail.com

FROM SCATTERED FEATHERS

AND SHATTERED HEARTS,

TO BROKEN PROMISES AND IRON CHAINS,

OUR LOVE WAS DESTINED TO END IN TRAGEDY.

I

PAIN IS MY ANCHOR

KNOX

present day

Pain is my anchor.

Pain is what keeps me tethered to this earth when my wings beg for the sky and my heart beats for the heavens above. Pain is my salvation. When chaos reigns and rage consumes my soul, I crave an ache only a select few can provide. With them, I find solace, without them—anarchy.

Unlike my brothers, I was born with the same traits I carry today. As a heavenly angel, I should have been blessed with serenity and peace, but according to my father—I was a "difficult child" right from the start. Unheard of in the Kingdom of Heaven.

I constantly fought with my brothers; I flew when I was supposed to walk and spoke when I was told to remain silent. I never cared for rules, laws, or anything that stood in the way of me getting what I wanted. Rebelling against the angels was a choice I made alone. I could not be controlled, and no one could calm the fire that had ignited inside me.

That all changed when I was cursed by Haydee. She would become the pain I yearned for; the control I never had. When Haydee is at her strongest, the urge to destroy anything in my path—including myself—is overwhelming. Pain is what gives me life. Pain is how I feel. Without it, I am numb.

The shackles clasped around my ankles and wrists are attached to titanium chains that are bound to the steel framed bed I've been lying on for the past four weeks. Here beneath the ground in the middle of Ambrosia Valley, I'm trapped in the dark basement of the Fray's underground fortress once again. But not for long. They didn't expect me to return, and they didn't expect me to stay willingly.

I turn my head to release the tension in my neck. The more blood they take, the longer it takes to replenish. They believe keeping me alive is the only thing that matters. Soon, they'll realise how wrong they are.

The heavy steel door that leads to the basement creaks open and the candles flicker as it's slammed closed. The chill in the air down here is almost unbearable, and with my waning strength, I'm unable to warm my body. I blink a few times to clear my vision and focus on whoever is walking toward my cell. When his voice registers, rage builds in my chest and causes me to let out an involuntary growl.

The cell door is unlocked then pulled open before his feet pace toward me. I glare at him, not a shred of fear in my eyes—or his. This bastard may think he has the upper hand, but he has no idea what he's in for.

He drags his knife from its sheath and holds it up to his face as though he's staring at his own reflection in the silver blade. When his gaze drops to my chest, a sinister smirk spreads across his lips.

"Ready for some pain, angel?"

"Bring it on, asshole."

There's a sly chuckle before he drags the tip of the blade down my chest. The pain sends a welcome surge of adrenaline through my veins, renewing my strength and forcing me to suck in a breath. If only he knew how much I need this.

Thirteen cocks his head, the snarl on his lips appears and his rage boils over when I don't react to the pain. "What are you? You're not normal."

I grunt in disgust. "You know what I am. You know *who* I am. Are you fucking stupid?"

He presses the tip of the blade into my thigh where the wound from earlier this morning is still in the process of healing. When he twists the knife, I inhale and clench my jaw. He shoves it in further, and when I exhale, he pulls the knife out and paces back and forth. "Your blood isn't working properly. Why is that?"

I laugh and shake my head. "Didn't do your research, did you?"

With his arms crossed over his chest, he says, "Tell me why."

"Look at me. I'm stuck here in this shit hole being tortured while you're taking my blood. It takes time to replenish, if I grow weak, the power in my blood wanes as well. It's not that fucking hard to understand." I roll my eyes.

A brief shadow of what appears to be confusion shrouds his features. An incoherent mumble leaves his lips before he says "Fuck!" He shoves his knife into the sheath on his belt, then storms over to me and begins releasing the chains from my wrists and ankles. "Stand the fuck up."

With a heavy sigh, I sit then swing my legs off the bed. When I stand, I stretch my arms and glare at him. "Now what?"

He narrows his eyes. "Where's my brother?"

I scratch at the stubble on my chin. "Hmm...last I saw he had a sword in his chest." I shrug. "I assume he's dead."

His jaw ticks as he steps forward. "Your brother took him. How about you call him in your head and tell him to come here, with *my* brother, and maybe I'll let you live."

I shake my head. "Not happening. Besides, my brothers severed our link when I made the decision to come back here."

He turns to walk out but stops in the doorway and looks back over his shoulder. "You won't win... angel." He slams the cell door closed and locks it again.

I walk to the cell bars and grip them tight in my hands. The chains are off; now all I need to do is get out of this cell.

Hours later, the basement door opens again. Footsteps pace slowly toward the cell, and when her eyes lock onto mine, a glint of fear appears before she blinks then continues forward. Fumbling with a set of keys, she attempts to unlock the bolt on the cell door, and when she finally manages it, she lets out a quiet sigh. "Twelve wants you, follow me."

"You?" I ask confused. Why the hell would they send this meek little female to come and get me? "Who are you... And Twelve?" *What the fuck?!*

She bites her lip then steps back holding the cell door open. With a quick step forward, she squares her shoulders and stands tall. "I'm Six. Twelve... he's the one who's been taking your blood."

They think he's Twelve. The penny drops. This was the commander's plan. He must have known Roman was ratting him out and brought in his brother to take his place. I grit my teeth in annoyance. If Roman knows about his brother, he's as good as dead, and I'll savour every moment of my hands wrapped tight around that bastard's throat.

I shake my head hard. *No. He wouldn't... Would he?* Fuck! *Roman would never do anything to harm Autumn— or Flynn.* "Where are we going?"

"No talking," she says as she heads toward the back corner of the basement.

When I don't follow, she turns and points to the door. "I said follow me."

Not happening. I run a hand through my hair and drop back down to the bed. "Can't, too weak."

She narrows her eyes and pulls a knife from the sheath on her belt. "Get up, angel."

I laugh. "You know how to use that?"

"You think I'm weak because I'm a girl? Get the fuck up." There's no conviction in her tone.

I stand, and as she steps forward to point the knife at my chest, I grab it from her hand and pull her into me. Her back is hard against my chest and her breaths are heavy and frantic. She's not weak because she's female, she's weak because she wants me to touch her. *Humans... so easy to read.*

I lean down to whisper in her ear, my lips brush lightly against her. "You think I'm weak because I'm an angel?"

She shakes her head. "I ha—orders. I have orders." A breathy sigh escapes her lips. As her body slumps against mine, I trail my fingers down her arm. "Mmm... Ugh, Fuck!" She stiffens quickly when she realises what she's done.

I smirk at her complete lack of willpower. Without another word, I spin her around, storm out of the cell, and lock the door with the keys I took from her pocket.

She screams. "Let me out you fucking asshole!"

"Sorry, sweetheart, I'm busy." Staying in the shadows, I head toward the door in the back corner of the basement. Water trickles down the moss-covered bricks and drips onto the floor. With my hand on the door knob, I take one last look back at the female in the cage.

"They'll kill you," she calls out.

Ignoring her, I pull the door open and leave.

After shoving the keys into my pocket, I continue along the narrow tunnel, the knife tight in my grasp. At the end of the tunnel, paths split to the left and right. I scrub my hands down my face. This place is a fucking maze. For a few minutes, I stand in silence and listen, and when I hear voices coming from the left, I make the split-second decision to go right. Finding the females who are trapped here is my first priority; fighting comes a close second.

Along the inside of the tunnel there are locked steel doors. Above each one, dim lightbulbs flicker as though there's an electrical fault. The only other light comes from further ahead where the sound of voices causes me to stop in my tracks. I push my back hard against a door, only slightly hidden by a stone pillar.

The voices come closer and I hover my hand over the knife, ready to fight.

A radio crackles, then there's a muffled voice. "Yes, Commander." The footsteps come to a stop, their voices closer now. "He wants me back in the arena."

The second voice replies, "I'll finish down here."

As one set of footsteps fade away, I inch forward to steal a glance down the tunnel. The guy has his back to me, so I step out from behind the pillar and pace toward him. With the knife tight in my hand, I hold it by my side, ready to attack.

He turns to face me. "What the fuck?" As he pulls his dagger from the sheath on his belt, I throw a punch and knock him out cold.

I stand over him, waiting to see if he wakes up. When a few minutes pass in silence, I grab his weapons, and give him a kick to the ribs for good measure before I continue along the tunnel and down a narrow stairwell that opens into a large, empty room. Thick chains hang from the walls, and fresh blood is pooled and splattered on the ground. In the corner, a dirty workbench stands, highlighted by the dull glow of a lightbulb hanging from a thick black cord. Tools are strewn out on the bench—all of them covered in blood, and what appears to be human flesh.

I glance down to a bucket and step back, covering my mouth and nose with my hand; forcing down the bile that rises in my throat. In the bucket... an arm, severed just above the elbow. *What the fuck are they doing down here?* It's worse than I thought. Roman's twin brother must be responsible for this. The fucking psychopath needs to die.

Disgusted, I pace toward the stairwell, but stop in my tracks when I hear a faint plea.

"H—help..."

Narrowing my eyes, I scan the room, checking each dark corner before I walk back to the workbench.

Tap. Tap. Tap.

"Ple—hel..."

The fuck? I lean down and check beneath the bench. There's nothing—no one there. Beside it though, there's a large steel box. *No fucking way.*

I inhale, clinging to every ounce of sanity I can muster before I unclip the latches on the box. Lifting the lid slowly, I clamp my eyes shut before I blink a few times to focus. When the lid is open, I lean it back against the stone wall.

What I see is branded into my mind the second my eyes drop to the beaten, bloody body inside the box. Whoever he is, he's so close to death, nothing I do will save him. His eyes are barely open, and when he attempts to move, he lets out a wail of agony.

As I lean down closer, it's obvious why... the guy is missing half his left arm.

"Help." The word dies on his lips.

"Can you tell me what happened to you?" I ask, but don't expect a reply.

"Twelve... fight—lost I, me... can't."

"You lost a fight? Twelve did this to you?"

There's a slight nod. "Kill... me—plea—"

His head lolls to the side and his eyes roll back before he reaches out to me and forces the words from his mouth. "Kill me."

I step back and scrub my hands over my face. Fuck it! I have no problem killing anyone in the Fray, but this guy—he can't fight back. The lump in my throat doesn't budge as I grip the knife in my hand and squat beside the box. The coppery scent of blood wafts past my nose.

"Sorry, man," I say before I pierce the knife into his heart in one swift movement.

A groan of pain leaves his lips before a heavy sigh is released. He's dead.

My heart beats hard against my chest, a reminder of my life... a life that cannot be extinguished so easily. A reminder that as an angel, I have a duty to protect human life, not end it.

Mercy. I had to do it, he begged me.

I shake my head hard then reach down to close the lid and clip the latches back in place before I leave the room.

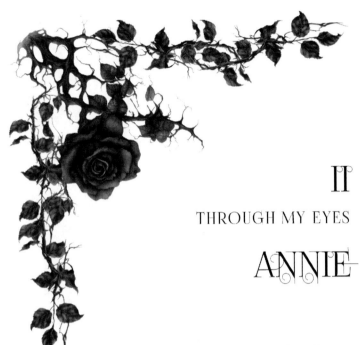

II
THROUGH MY EYES
ANNIE

Before him, I don't know who I was, or where I came from. Before him, was I happy? Was I free? Was I something more than the fathomless void I am today?

After him, I became blind to the world. Unable to see with my own eyes; I learned to live through his. After him, I got lost in the darkness that enveloped me tightly each night. I imagine if I turned back the ticking hands of time, I'd find myself somewhere, traipsing the world, free, but somehow searching for *him*.

Through my eyes, he was everything I wanted to be. Strength flowed through his veins, and in that strength, I found myself. When nightfall came and my heart and soul were being torn to shreds by invisible demons who stalked my dreams, he rescued me. He'd find them, drag them to me, and force them to kneel at my feet. Then he'd slay them, one after another, heads, limbs, body parts... blood. Trapped inside my dream, I'd watch him in awe as he slaughtered those who dared look at me with anything but admiration.

Through my eyes, he was my hero.

Until he wasn't.

It happened gradually. The demons he once slaughtered from afar, came closer. The blood was thicker, and the screams, louder. When I flinched, he'd remind me who I was. *"You're mine, Annastasia."* I always agreed. I proved I was loyal, and I did everything I was ordered to do.

It wasn't enough.

When crimson blood splattered onto my face and I wiped it away, I was weak. When the eyes of the dead glared at me and I closed my own eyes, I was weak. When exhaustion tore me away from reality and I fell to my knees, I was weak.

Through my eyes, I watched him turn into something I feared. Something that scared me more than the invisible demons he slayed when I was a little girl. I was desperate to please him, hoping to find that boy again, somewhere among the wreckage of whatever he had become.

As I learned to fight, the boy returned. Pride would steal across his face for a fleeting moment when I mastered a kick or held my balance until he ordered me to move. Sometimes, if I was quick enough, I would catch a glimpse of a smile. The same smile he wore the first time I saw him.

When I was fighting, I was strong. When I won, he would reward me with extra training time, or new training equipment. When I lost, I was forced to stand and watch as he slaughtered those who had beaten me. He promised no one would lay a hand on me and live to see the next sunrise. He promised I would be his, forever. And he promised that if I ever left him, he would find me.

I was ten years old when he woke me in the middle of the night to tell me he had a surprise for me. Curiosity, and my promise to him that I would always obey, led me out of my bedroom, and into the basement where a young girl was tied to the spare bed. She struggled against the ropes that bound her wrists and ankles to the bed, and I wondered why she was there. Was he replacing me? Did she belong to him too?

He handed me his silver knife. The shiny blade caught my eye and I wanted nothing more than to run my fingers along the silver blade. He was letting *me* hold his knife. Not her... me.

"Stab her," he whispered against my ear.

I didn't hesitate. There wasn't a moment when I considered doing anything else. As much as I was his, he was mine, and I would do anything for him.

The knife slid into her flesh so easily, and when her blood seeped from beneath her skin, I looked over my shoulder, hoping to see the pride I longed for, shining in his eyes. Her screams meant nothing to me, a confusing mix of words and cries that distracted me. *She* was distracting me... from Adam.

He took a step forward and put his hand around mine, guiding it into the girl's flesh as she writhed on the bed, a strange moaning sound spilling from her lips with each panting breath. Together, me and Adam continued, ignoring her until finally, she was silent. Piercing her stomach, her chest, and her thighs, he moved my hand with his as though we were caught in a silent, bloody melody; a rhythm that would lull me into a dreamlike world, where every word he spoke was laced in the praise and adoration I craved.

I'd known for a long time that Adam loved blood—I loved it too. The rich, crimson stain that spread over the fibres of the soft satin sheets. The deep red drops that trailed slowly down the female's torso and neck. As the blood seeped from her flesh, I was mesmerised. With each slice of the blade, I sucked in a breath, taking in the scent of the blood, and the beauty of the scene before me—the end... of life.

When it was over and her body was nothing more than a mutilated mess of flesh and blood, he took the knife from my hand and lifted my bloody fingertips to his lips.

"Don't ever leave me," he said before he lifted me into his arms and carried me back to bed. For the first time ever, he laid with me and stroked my hair while I fell asleep.

He was my hero.

My saviour.

My Adam.

I craved his attention until it became an obsession. He was in my dreams, my nightmares, and my thoughts. He lingered in the shadows and beckoned from behind closed doors. None of it was real. Sometimes, I imagine what I felt, was love. At least what I *thought* love was.

It wasn't until I was fifteen that I came to realise, everything was wrong. Perhaps I'd suddenly matured, or maybe it was the fact that the fear that used to pass by fleetingly, had become the only thing I could feel. Even the blood I'd once craved with all my being, couldn't calm the storm that was brewing in the deepest, darkest parts of my soul.

The swirling sensations in my stomach that once appeared when he was close by, disappeared. The stolen glances I used to take when he was training me, were gone. My eyes focused only on the wall, and when he ordered me to look into his eyes, I no longer searched for the boy.

The boy was gone.

The man had taken over.

I hated the man. But I would always obey.

If my life were a story, half my pages would be torn or missing, the other half, written by him. Commandments I would follow to ensure his happiness, and my survival. Over the years, the pain disappeared, now, only numbness remains.

But the man knows my weakness.

He knows how to hurt me.

That pain—it's all I live for.

III
VICTORIOUS
ANNIE

Adam—who now wants me to call him Twelve—leads me into the arena where the Fray are standing, waiting for the next fight to start. We arrived in this town almost six months ago, and since then, all I've seen is the dark midnight sky, and the Fray's underground headquarters. I don't even know the name of the town we're in, only that it took eighteen hours to drive here. Eighteen hours of nothing but empty paddocks and trees, and a few small service stations where we stopped for bathroom breaks.

I didn't want to leave Daylehurst, it was safe there, familiar. The rules were clear and easy to follow. Here, everything is different, unrecognisable... and loud. Adam told me his grandfather, Michael, needed to be with his son, and that we'd be living with them too. I assumed I'd continue doing the same mundane tasks I'd been doing at home. Fetching drinks and meals for the old man, washing his laundry, and ensuring he never had to get off his ass unless it was absolutely necessary.

So far, he's not asked me to do anything for him. I've spent each day training or fighting with Adam and some of the other guys here, who I'm forbidden to speak to. None of them have names, they're all numbered, and I have no idea why.

The commander, Aeron, refuses to speak to me. He looks down on me as though I'm a piece of trash blowing in the wind. Not that I care. He wouldn't dare touch me, family or not, I know with certainty that Adam would kill him if he hurt me.

For the past hour, I've been training in the Fray's arena. I've barely recovered from my last fight where I was kicked in the ribs by Eight, the asshole. I got him back though, and next time he calls me weak, I'll make sure I kick his balls into his throat.

Adam tightens his grip on my arm as he leads me toward Michael who raises his brow. He puts his finger under my chin to lift my head slightly. "You enjoying your time here?"

I keep my eyes on his. "Yes, Sir."

As his hand moves slightly to cup my cheek, Adam tugs me back. "Hands off, old man," he growls.

The old man smirks and drops his hand by his side. "Take her back over there." He waves a hand in the air as he drops back into his seat beside the commander. "If she doesn't win, put her in the cells."

Fucking asshole.

The commander grunts under his breath. "Or you can send her in to the recruits. They'll teach her a thing or two."

Ugh. Every male I have ever had the *dis*pleasure of meeting, has been a total dick. The Fray guys here, at least the ones I've met so far, are all disgusting pigs. They think I don't know, but I see them. Their eyes follow my every move, tracing the curves of my body as they ogle me. It won't continue much longer; Adam's been watching them too. It's only a matter of time before they end up dead.

I'm about to turn to walk away when Adam drops his hand from my arm and pulls his knife from its sheath. He steps forward and points it at the commander. "You... or anyone here touches her, and I'll cut your fucking cock off and shove it down your throat. Got it, *Aeron!*"

When the commander drops into his seat, he turns to whisper to Michael, then waves Adam away without another word.

With a growled curse, Adam leads me back to the centre of the arena. His eyes are dark, and rage will soon take over. Someone will die tonight, and it won't be me.

"This time you'll win, won't you," Adam whispers against my ear.

I nod. "Yes, Twelve."

"And if you don't?"

"I will be punished."

He raises his brow and cocks his head. "Good girl, Annastasia. Remember who you are... and who you belong to."

After ordering me to stand in the centre of the square marked out on the arena floor, he steps back. With my hands clasped behind my back, I inhale slowly. A sharp twinge pierces my rib cage when I breathe, but rather than cause pain, it gives me the push I need to stand tall and prepare to fight. Nothing else I have endured comes close to this.

These guys... the Fray, they're nowhere near as strong as Adam, or the men I've had to fight in the past. With Adam here, they'll come to learn that weakness will not be tolerated.

The commander steps up to the lectern and speaks. "Ten, step forward. You'll fight the girl."

A guy, who appears to be around the same age as me, paces toward the square with his head held high and a ridiculous smirk on his face. When he's in front of me, he mutters under his breath, "You're going down, little girl."

Nope, that's not happening.

I give him a sweet smile and when the commander shouts "fight" I swing a punch before he can react. Ten stumbles back, his face a picture of rage as he raises his fist and comes toward me. I raise my own fists and side step around the square as the Fray shout for Ten to punch me. The drawback of being an outsider here, and the one who arrived with Adam and Michael, is that none of them are willing to acknowledge my abilities because I'm a girl. If I put in some real effort, I could kill any one of them with a perfectly timed kick or punch, but Adam refuses to allow me to show my true strength. *Why I hate men: Reason number 3.*

As Ten and I fight, he manages to punch me a few times, and lands a hard kick to my thigh that causes my knees to buckle and throws me off balance. As I jump to my feet, I glance out the corner of my eye to see Adam glaring at me.

This is it, I need to get this guy down, and fast. Ten prances around me, his fists raised, his voice grating on my nerves as he dares me to come closer. "Hit me, little girl. Come on," he taunts.

I clench my fists and steady my feet, then, without overthinking it, I spin and land a kick to his jaw that throws him off his feet. He lands on the floor with a loud thud and before he can get back up, I press my knee into his chest and slam my fist into his jaw. Blood and spittle flies from his mouth as he tries to force me off him, but I don't budge, I throw another punch, then one more. When his head falls to the side, I stand and kick him in the balls then clasp my hands behind my back again.

The arena is silent. The commander stares at me, and Michael raises his brow. Adam walks toward me and I drop my head, waiting for his instructions. When he reaches me, he grips my jaw in his hand and stares into my eyes as he rubs his thumb across my lips, smearing my blood across them.

His voice is low, warning, "You can do better."

"Yes, Ad—" *Shit!*

He cuts me off, squeezing my jaw until my mouth is forced open. "What the fuck did you say?"

"Twelve," I say quickly. "Yes, Twelve. I can do better." I swallow hard. "I *will* do better."

He drops his hand and steps back, and as he walks away, he calls out, "Eleven, fight the girl."

The Fray go wild, chanting "Eleven" and cheering for the guy as he comes toward me. And this guy is huge. Tiny tendrils of fear weave through my veins and panic coils in my chest. I have to win. Whatever this guy does to me will be nothing compared to the punishment I'll be forced to endure if I lose.

Two minutes into the fight and I've landed two punches and a kick, and Eleven is still going strong. Stronger than any of the others. He must be using the blood Adam and Michael were talking about at home. Michael's been working on it for as long as I can remember. The blood of angels and vampires. I've never used it, but Adam has, and when he does, I do everything possible to avoid being punished. Somehow, that blood turns him into a monster, and nothing—no one—can stop him.

I'm knocked out of my thoughts when Eleven lands yet another kick to my shoulder. I fall back and hit the floor. Dazed, I shake my head hard and as I'm about to leap to my feet, Eleven is on top of me, straddling me and forcing my arms above my head.

This is the worst place to be. For him, because if he doesn't get off me, he has mere minutes before Adam kills him. And for me, because I'm trapped.

Flailing, I kick my legs out and wriggle beneath him as his weight bears down on me. When he removes one hand from my wrists and attempts to grab my throat, I struggle to free myself from his grasp. A heavy fist comes toward me, and right before it lands on my face, I manage to move my head to the side. He rams his closed fist into the floor before letting out a howl of agony.

I take my chance to scramble backwards, then spin and kick him in the head. Another spin, and another kick. He falls forward, his hands splayed on the floor in front of him as he spits out a mouthful of blood. When he raises his head, his eyes darken as rage takes over, but he's not fast enough. I grab a fistful of his hair and pull his head back before I punch him square in the nose.

"Fuck!" he groans.

Once again, I step back and await my instructions.

There's only one male I am afraid of, and I'll do anything to keep it that way.

IV

WE'RE ALL WINGIN' IT

KNOX

Cracking open the door to yet another room, I hold still and wait before I slip in and close it behind me. Like the other six rooms I've checked, this one is dark. The only light comes from a candle emitting a dim glow at the back of what appears to be a storage room.

I make my way through the room, avoiding the boxes stacked on the floor when a quiet whimper catches my attention. I freeze, my eyes scan the darkness and search for any signs of life.

As I press forward, a soft voice whispers "shhh," before the candle is blown out and the scent of wax permeates the surrounding air.

I keep my voice low, "I'm here to help, where are you?"

Feeling my way through the room, I finally reach the back wall and keep my eyes down, knowing that whoever is in here, is on the floor.

As my boot hits something hard, there's a gasp, then a muffled cry. I blink a few times to try to focus. There's a shuffle, then a panicked "no" before a torch lights up the two females huddled in the corner. I reach down and take the torch from her hand, turning it to the females. They're both battered and bruised and covered in dried blood.

"What are you doing here?" I ask confused.

"Please... don't hurt us, please..." one female begs.

"I'm not going to hurt you." I sigh. "I'm going to get you out of here."

"Y—you can't, he'll kill us. He's killed so many—"

I kneel in front of them. "Who are you talking about?"

"Twelve... he used to be different. I—I think he's on drugs or something."

The other female nods in agreement. "He's crazy now. Since he fought the commander, he's changed. He keeps killing... everyone."

Fucking hell. That bastard they think is Twelve *is* insane. A year ago, my brothers and I thought Corbin was crazy, but compared to this guy, Thirteen... Twelve? Whoever the fuck he is, Corbin was weak as piss.

"Does anyone come in here?" I ask after encouraging them to stand.

"No. No one has been in here at all."

The brunette, Alice, tells me they snuck in here two days ago to hide and have been too terrified to come out, afraid that *Twelve* will kill them. The smaller of the two, a blonde named Kassidy, tells me they've been forced to fight the Fray, and if they refuse, they're whipped and beaten. Neither of these females are the one I saw when I was in the room with Vandrick and the asshole who now calls himself Twelve.

"Are there more females?" I question.

Kassidy nods. "Three more who were alive. One of them, she was in the torture chamber, but Twelve kept taking her out to fight." She drops her head. "She might be dead now. Every time she came back, she had more bruises. She never cried, never said a word."

"And the other two?" I question.

She shrugs. "We ran before they came back. But there are—"

"Tell him," Alice whispers.

With a heavy sigh she crosses her arms around herself. "Two girls... he, he kil—" She chokes on a sob. "He killed them... cut their bodies up." Tears dribble down her cheeks as she tries to speak. "There's blood everywhere."

The torture chamber is nothing more than an old boiler room, reinforced with solid steel walls and a steel door locked tight. An access card or code is needed to get in. I crack my neck and clench my fists. Fuck. I should have taken the card from Flynn before I left. I scrub my hands down my face and pace back and forth before footsteps in the distance come closer.

Alice gasps. "Someone's coming, we need to hide."

I grab their hands and lead them toward the open drain opposite the boiler room. After helping them down, I descend the ladder and wait, watching as the guy walks toward the boiler room with a female. It's her. The one I saw when they had me chained to the wall.

As the guy shoves his hand into his pocket, he lets go of her arm, she scans the area, her eyes wide, and her long, dark hair pulled up into a ponytail. And still... there's not an ounce of fear in her eyes.

He pulls out the card and swipes it through the reader, and when the lights turn green, the door clicks open. He shoves the female inside and slams the door closed. Instead of walking away, he pulls a cigarette from the pack in his pocket, and lights one up, his eyes focused only on the ground at his feet.

I need that card.

Slowly, I come out of the drain, and while his back is turned, I grab him in a headlock and snap his neck. *Too easy.* A surge of adrenaline rushes through me as I drag his body toward the drain and drop him down. The females gasp, but when I order them to stay silent, they both nod. That drain must lead somewhere, and my guess is it's the same tunnel that leads to the water tower.

Rushing to the door, I swipe the card, and when it clicks open, I enter the room the females told me was called the Torture Chamber. As soon as the door closes behind me, I'm forced to swallow the bile that rises in my throat.

On the floor, in a pool of blood, are two females whose bodies have been mutilated. A severed hand lays in the blood, and the floor is littered in what I assume are pieces of human flesh. Side stepping the horrific scene, I lean forward to look past a tall steel cabinet.

I find the female sitting on the floor, picking at her fingernails. "Are you the only one here?" I ask.

Her head shoots up and her eyes are wide as she flicks her ponytail off her shoulder. "What the fuck? Y—you're the angel!"

I nod once. "Get up, I'm getting you out of here."

For a long minute, she stares up at me as though she's actually contemplating staying here in this shit hole of death. "That's not a great idea... You saw what he's capable of. He won't let you leave."

"Get up," I say again. "I've got two other girls waiting, I don't want to waste time."

Slowly, she gets to her feet and wipes her hands over her black leggings. "Why are your wings black?" She takes a step toward me, a questioning glare in her eyes.

What the fuck? "You're stuck in this... this place, and *that's* your question?"

She shrugs. "So, you're not gonna tell me?"

I wasn't wrong about her. She's not afraid. "There are two fucking dead females right there. The walls are covered in blood, and you want to know about my wings?" I shake my head. Damn she's confusing.

She tilts her head and raises her hands in defence. "Jeez, calm down... I'm not afraid of a little flesh and blood." As she slips past me, she kicks the severed hand out of her way.

Resisting the urge to roll my eyes, I step back and avert my gaze. "We need to go," I say once more.

"Ugh, fine, I'm going," she groans. "Someone's moody." And *she* rolls her eyes—at me.

Who the hell does this female think she is? Ignoring her attitude, I pull the door open and scan the area before I lead her to the drain where the other females are waiting.

"Eleven, you still down here?" a voice calls.

"Get down there, now," I say, and I jump down after her and slide the drain cover over.

"This way," I tell them.

Traipsing through the filthy, rat infested drain, Kassidy and Alice gag and cry as we make our way through the tunnel. The other female shakes her head. "Suck it up, you never smelled a bit of sewage before?" She rushes ahead and steps over what looks like a pile of shit, then stops. "Oh look, it's half a rat." When she looks over her shoulder, there's a hint of humour in her eyes.

Kassidy looks down and sees the dead rat, she squeals into her hands and backs up against the wall. I kick it into the pool of stagnant water and tug on Kassidy's arm. "Come on, it's dead it can't hurt you."

"Why don't you carry her," the female says without turning around, "in case she dies from you know... actually walking."

Damn, this female is feisty. "What's your name?" I ask her.

She turns and glances up at me, her deep brown eyes sear into the depths of my soul. I clamp my eyes shut and shake my head.

"Annastasia. Just call me Annie."

"They made you fight?" I question as I take in the bruises and blood covering her arms and face.

"Obviously. What about you? I didn't see you out there fighting."

I cross my arms over my chest and look down at her. She's tiny, but I can already tell she has a fire inside her that no one would dare extinguish. "They won't make me fight. I'd kill them."

"Mmm hmm..."

"What? You don't believe me?"

Kassidy and Alice's glances flick between me and Annie as though they're enjoying every moment of our conversation, but they don't say a word.

Annie shrugs. "Do you even know *how* to fight? Because last I saw, you were chained to a wall and being stabbed in the gut."

No comment. I clench my fists, searching for the rage, but it's not there. I'm calm. Fucking calm. I shove my fingers through my hair and ignore her. The truth is though, I'm fucking speechless.

For the next twenty minutes we walk in silence until we reach a steel door with a padlock attached. Annie sighs as she stands in front of the door and crosses her arms over her chest while tapping her foot on the ground as though she's the queen, and I'm her slave. "Great, you led us to a fucking dead end."

"What the hell is your problem?" I ask.

She shakes her head. "Did you plan this escape, or did you just *wing it*, angel boy?"

I suck in a breath as I pull the keys from my pocket, determined not to let this tiny female piss me off. Then, I step forward, pick her up, and set her back on her feet beside me.

She narrows her eyes, glaring at me. "Do—"

I raise a finger to her lips and shush her before I give her a wink and unlock the padlock. When I pull the door open and extend my hand, Kassidy giggles, but covers her mouth when Annie storms past and tells her to shut up.

After walking for another ten minutes, the tunnel narrows and we stoop down to make our way through. When we reach the end, I breathe a sigh of relief when I raise my head to see a dim light shining down through the drain cover.

"Wait here. I'll check it out," I say as I grip the ladder.

When I reach the top, I peer out to see we're not at the water tower as I expected. Instead, we're at the rear parking lot of The Plaza, and thank fuck it's empty.

I push the cover across and get out to reach down and help Kassidy and Alice up. When Annie climbs the ladder, she looks up at me. "I don't need your help."

I pull my hand back and wait for her to come out. When she stands, she looks around as though she's seeing the entire world for the first time in her life. Her eyes are wide and a hint of a smile dances across her full pink lips. She tilts her head back and looks up at the sky, revealing thick scars around her neck. *What happened to her?*

"Finally." Haydee's voice is music to my ears.

What time is it? I ask her.

"Just after one."

"Okay, let's go," I tell the females.

"With you?" Annie says. "Ah, nope, I'm good." She walks toward the forest in the distance.

Haydee follows me as I grab Annie's hand and pull her back. "Come with me, you need to get those wounds checked out."

She pulls her hand out of mine. "I'm fine, I don't need any help." Then, she runs toward the trees in the distance.

I let out a heavy sigh and watch her as Haydee laughs, and when she stops before the tree line, panting, I sprint over and pick her up, wrapping my arms around her tiny body.

"Let me go you fucking asshole!" she screeches and kicks before she throws her head back, headbutting my chin.

"Stop fighting and I'll let you go," I say calmly.

"Annie, come on," Kassidy says. "It's not safe out there, what if they're looking for us..."

Annie stops instantly, and when I drop her to her feet she spins around and glares at me, pointing a warning finger. "Fine, I'll come. But you touch me again, and I'll fucking punch you."

"Whoa, feisty," Haydee says. "I like this one."

I raise my hands in defence, but I can't hide my smirk. "Wasn't even thinking about it."

"Liar," Haydee murmurs as the females follow me toward the main street.

V.
FAKE FREEDOM
ANNIE

Freedom—kind of. I would be free if this smartass angel had let me go. I bet he used some kind of angel power to make me follow him, to make me believe he's one of the good guys. I know better. All men are bastards, and that will never change. I could have fought back. I could have run or screamed. But curiosity got the better of me, and I never truly believed the stupid, beautiful angel would make it out alive.

For now, I have something I've never had before. Freedom. Even if it's only for a while.

At the hospital, we're led into a small room with a doctor, who locks the door behind us, then introduces himself as Doctor Charles—a friend of Knox's. He pats the bed and smiles. "Okay, ladies, who's first?"

I step back, leaning against the wall as Kassidy rushes forward, a stupid smile plastered on her face. He asks her a few questions, including her name and age, then he checks her over as she winces in pain. She giggles and bats her lashes when he apologises. *So fucking pathetic.*

After he's checked Alice and given them both some antibiotics, they head off with a nurse to shower and get changed. *Shower.* God, I need a shower, and a gallon of shampoo and body wash. Even then, I doubt it will scrub away the filth that clings to my flesh and reminds me of the dirty cells and rooms in the Fray's underground warehouse.

I sit on the steel framed hospital bed and look at Knox—the moody angel with black wings. I want to tell him to leave, but a tiny—and I mean minute part of me—is slightly thankful he got me out of that place, so I don't say anything. Plus, he's not bad to look at, if he keeps his mouth shut and his hands to himself. Who the hell does he think he is touching me like that? No one touches me. *No one.*

"And how old are you, Annastasia?" the doctor asks after I give him my name and tell him I don't have a "home address".

"I said call me Annie, and I'm seventeen."

From the other side of the room, Knox clears his throat. When my eyes lock with his, he cocks his head. "You're only seventeen?"

So? I nod and sigh. "Yep. I'll be eighteen in two weeks. Why?"

He shakes his head. "Just asking."

As Doctor Charles checks my face, my arms, and my chest, he asks, "Are you in any pain, Annie?"

"Nope. None. I think I broke a rib though; it'll be fine."

He steps back and straightens. "You *think* you broke a rib? Has this happened before?"

I shrug and run my fingers through my hair that's matted with dry blood and god knows what else. "Yeah, a few times. It's all good, Doc. I can handle it."

I'm about to stand up when he raises a hand. "Just a few more things," he says. He asks me to lie down so he can feel around my stomach and ribs, and when I don't flinch, or tell him it hurts, he rubs his chin and looks down at the clipboard in his hand. "I'm going to order an X-ray, just to be safe. As for the other injuries, they'll heal over the next week or two." He glances down at my forearms, but when I cross them around myself, he steps back.

"Whatever," I say, dropping my feet to the floor. "Can I shower now?"

He nods once. "There's a shower through there, I'll have the nurse bring you some clothes."

After talking quietly to Knox for a few minutes, the doctor leaves, but Knox stays, staring at me as though he's about to speak. "Ah, I'll wait outside..."

Nervous apprehension coils in my belly and I shake my head hard. I've read about this shit. Those women who get attached to the guy who saved them from tragedy. NO! That's not me. I'm stronger than that. I don't *need* anyone, and I certainly don't need a man—even if he is the sexiest goddamn angel I've laid eyes on.

"You can stay, if you like. I'll be in there anyway." I nod toward the bathroom. "It's not like you're going to see anything. Plus, I'm *only* seventeen, so you'd probably be arrested if you even peeked at me in the shower." My attempt at being sarcastic *and* brave, is a dismal failure, and as the blush creeps to my cheeks, I turn quickly and head into the bathroom, locking the door behind me.

After stripping off my bloodstained clothes, I glance at my reflection in the mirror. I'm covered in scars and bruises. With each year that passed, I collected new scars. Some, by my own hands, others from fighting and training. The worst scars are from Adam. They litter not only my skin, but my heart, my mind, and my very existence. Those are more than reminders of the past, they're seared into the deepest, darkest parts of my soul. The places inside me where my secrets are locked away from the world; only Adam knows those secrets, no one else can ever hold those keys.

A heavy sigh leaves my lips as I get into the shower where I close my eyes and let the steaming water rush over me. I use all three bottles of shampoo and empty out the body wash. Anything to rid myself of the stench that lingers on my skin. Twenty minutes later, I wrap a towel around my breasts and comb my fingers through my hair.

There's a knock on the door. "Annie, here's some clothes for you." It's Knox.

I open the door a crack and reach out until he puts the clothes in my hands. "Thank you," I murmur.

"You're welcome. And I didn't peek, so no need to have me arrested."

As his footsteps move away from the door, I narrow my eyes and whisper "smartass" under my breath, but I can't stop the smirk that plays on my lips. I pull on the grey track pants and white t-shirt, and I sigh. Great. No underwear, and no bra. I tug on the hem of the tight white t-shirt, trying to stretch the fabric over my breasts but it's pointless, I need some clothes that fit. I drop my head against the bathroom door and clamp my eyes shut. I need to find a place to stay and find a job so I can buy my own clothes. But with zero experience in anything except fighting and waiting on the old man and Adam, I've got no hope.

Wait! Hmm... maybe the angel will help. They're all purity and virtue, right? I laugh to myself before I take a deep breath and head back into the hospital room where Knox is sitting on the leather recliner beside the bed.

Talking Knox into helping me wasn't anywhere near as difficult as I thought it would be. It was almost as though he expected me to ask for *his* help. Maybe that's why he stuck around while I was in the shower... What if he wants something else from me? *No. He's an angel. They don't even have sex... do they?* I shake the thoughts from my head.

I heard Adam and the old man talking one night, and the old man said angels can read minds, but they're forbidden to read the minds of humans. I wonder if that's true.

The angel we had at home, trapped in the basement, never spoke. He was silent when Adam stabbed him; didn't flinch when Adam wrapped a hand around his throat. But he had white wings. Knox's wings are pure black. I guess there are different races of angels, like there are with humans. For as much as I do know about them, there's a hell of a lot more I don't know.

As Knox leads me into a spare bedroom in his house, he tells me it's used by his female friend when she's not at home. Apparently, she leaves a heap of clothes here for when she stays over. I'm about to tell him I don't believe she's *only* a friend, but he grabs the phone off the dresser and makes a call. He doesn't mention her name, but he talks about me, and asks which clothes I can use, so I guess he's telling the truth.

He places the phone back on the dresser and points to the chest of drawers. "Char—Charlotte said you can use anything in those drawers, and there's a few pairs of sneakers under the bed."

My eyes widen as I pull open the top drawer to find skimpy lingerie in every colour imaginable. When I rummage through and check the bras, I see they're all my size. *YES!* Whoever this girl is, I'm thankful.

"I'm going to have a shower," Knox says. "I'll let you get settled and changed, then I'll show you around. Unless you want to sleep..."

I push the drawer closed and sit on the edge of the bed. "I'll see how I feel once I get changed."

When he's gone, I pace the room for a few minutes. I've never seen a bedroom so... pretty. The huge bed is covered with pure white bedding and pillows along with a thick shaggy grey blanket.

I trace my fingertips along the edge of the dark timber dresser, there's not a speck of dust. Walking toward the robe, I wonder if it's full of clothes that belong to Knox's friend. I slide the mirrored door across, and my eyes grow wide. Hanging from the rack are at least twenty dresses in different colours. I swipe through the rack, allowing my fingers to linger on the cool, soft fabric, before my eyes lock onto another dress that's covered in tiny diamonds... or crystals. On the floor of the robe are high heel shoes, a pair to match each dress.

I slide the door closed. I've never worn a dress in my life; especially not one that beautiful. And those shoes, I can't imagine being able to walk in them. All I've ever worn are sneakers, black leggings or jeans, and black or white t-shirts.

For the next hour, I pace back and forth in the bedroom. I sit on the bed, and I stand again. I look through the bathroom cupboards and drawers, and I open the curtains to look out the window. It's still dark, but the view from the window looks out to a lake and a playground that are lit up by blue tinged lights. Above, the moon appears as though it's hanging from an invisible thread as it shines down onto the treetops in the distance.

Where am I? I should have asked Knox what this town was called.

After changing into a white t-shirt that's softer than anything I've worn before, I slide under the covers of the bed and onto luxurious silky-smooth sheets. With a little sigh of pleasure, I lay my head on the pillows and close my eyes to the world, wondering if Adam knows I'm gone.

VI

RULES AND REGULATIONS

KNOX

She's fucking seventeen. How long has that bastard been keeping her... using her to fight?

With my hands splayed on the tiled wall, I stand under the shower, relishing in the burn of the steaming hot water. I shake my head hard. I haven't even called my brothers yet. All I can think about is Annie and her take no shit attitude that draws me to her in all the wrong ways.

Haydee sits on the bathroom benchtop. "So... you're gonna play Daddy now?"

I scrub my hands through my hair and drop my head back. "She's not a kid, Haydee. She's eighteen in two weeks."

She jumps down and stands at the shower door, licking her lips as her gaze travels down my body. "Are you gonna fuck her?"

"What the fuck?!" I shout. Then I lower my voice. "No, I'm not going to fuck her." I turn off the water and reach past her for a towel. "Don't you have something else to do?"

She rolls her eyes. "Like what? My sisters are *gone*. Remember. And I promised if you came back, I'd give you a little break." She presses her thumb to her finger then separates them slightly. "A teeny tiny break."

I raise my hand and cup her cheek before I press a kiss to her forehead. "I'm sorry. Have you heard anything from Venys yet?"

She twirls her fingers through her hair. "She might be in Arcane. Ugh, it stinks over there, so many angels."

"Are you going there?" I ask curiously.

A smile tugs at the corner of her lips. "Why? You wanna come?"

"Nope." I wrap the towel around my waist. "There's nothing there I'm interested in."

"I'm sure Kamen would love to see you..." she says.

When I glare at her, she steps back, raising her hands in defence. "Calm down, it was a joke, you remember what a joke is, right? I'll be back later." And she disappears into a cloud of black smoke.

After getting dressed, I head back to the spare room to check on Annie, wondering if she has a home, or a family who are looking for her. The bedroom door is wide open, and the lamp is still on. I call her, and when there's no reply, I take a step into the room to find her snuggled up under the blankets, her long black hair spread across the pillow. I pace across the room quietly; the sound of her breathing is the only thing I hear as I watch her sleeping. The scowl that's been on her face since we met, is gone, it's been replaced with a look of contentment. I lean down closer; a deep purple bruise mars her cheekbone and jaw. How can she not be in pain?

My phone vibrates in my pocket and I step back and walk out of the room, pulling the door closed behind me.

"Hey."

"Brother, nice of you to call."

"Clay, man. I needed a shower..."

"It's been three months, and that's all you've got to say? You needed a shower..."

I pace the kitchen and sigh. Most of the time, I try not to treat my brothers like shit. Most of the time, I fuck up, and they still stick by me. I shake my head hard. "Sorry brother. I got these girls out, took 'em across to the hospital, then came home. I was going to call."

"Hmm... and were you going to mention the female in Char's room?"

Fuck it, Charlotte! I knew she'd call them. "Eventually..." I admit.

"When are you coming home?"

"I'll come around in the morning."

"Okay. We missed you, brother—"

I cut him off, "I'll be there around nine."

I put my phone on the dresser and lie on my bed as I think back to the times my brothers stood up for me, the times they took the fall because of my behaviour.

Knox
10 years old

"Come on, Flynn, no one will know," I urged him again.

He shook his head. "No. Father said we're not to leave the boundary of Caelestia."

Flynn jogged over to where Steel and Clay were training in the meadow with their angel swords. Each clang of the swords sent a spark of blue light into the sky. I watched them for a while, wishing they'd stop and do something else, something fun.

I hated training; it was too easy. I knew how to do it and didn't want to spend every day of my life in the meadow.

I wanted adventure, but I was stuck here, forbidden to explore the Kingdom of Heaven until our sixteenth year.

Leaving Caelestia was something I'd wanted to do since I was six years old. My mother told us stories about the diamond caves hidden in the Mountains of Astra. Of course, only the older angels could go there, the ones who'd spent years training and obeying all the laws and rules. The ones who were being rewarded for their faith, grace, and love.

With a backwards glance at my brothers, I took one step across the boundary line, then another. By the time I'd walked twenty paces, I could already see the mountain tops in the distance.

I tilted my head, my eyes fixed on the sky. I could fly there. I inhaled, and as I exhaled, I let my wings unfurl and extend. The rush of warmth that surrounded me sent shivers down my spine. Adrenaline raced through my veins and into my angel heart.

"Knox, no," Clay's voice caused me to turn around.

"Come back," Flynn said. "Quickly."

I shook my head. The only thing on my mind was the sky.

"You'll be lashed," Steel warned.

I shrugged. Lashings started at age ten. We were ten years and four months old, and I'd been lashed three times already. Seeing the diamond caves would be worth a hundred lashings.

I turned and continued walking, then, I broke into a sprint and took to the sky. My wings carried me higher, and as I shot through the sky, I felt more alive than ever before.

Seconds later, Flynn and Steel were beside me, grabbing my arms and forcing me down below the clouds. When we crossed back over the boundary into Caelestia, our father appeared, and we knelt before him.

He didn't smile, and his emerald green eyes held a cloud of sadness. "My sons, you are forbidden to cross here. You know that."

"It was me, Father," I said, bowing my head. "I will accept my punishment."

"No," Flynn said as he stood. "Father, I wanted to go, too."

Steel and Clay stood beside him. "And me," they said in unison.

When my father told me to stand, the look in his eyes said he already knew my brothers had no part in this, but without hesitation, he accepted their apologies.

That day, my brothers were lashed for the first time—for me. And it wouldn't be the last time they would take a lashing for me.

Still half asleep, I run a hand through my hair as I flick on the coffee machine. It's damn good to be back home and out of that filthy basement, but anger burns inside me when I recall the bodies of the women who were murdered and left to rot in the boiler room. I need to get that guy out in the open, up here on my turf where I have the power to destroy him. Sighing, I grab my coffee and sit at the bench.

Her soft voice drags me from my thoughts. "Thanks for letting me stay here."

I turn on my stool to come face to face with the most beautiful female I have ever laid eyes on. Even with the bruises and the swelling beneath her eye, she's fucking magnificent. And I stare. I can't force myself to look away until she drops her head and runs her fingers through the long black waves of her hair.

"Did you sleep well?"

She nods. "Yeah fine. So, I was gonna ask if you knew of any jobs available around here?"

I stand from the stool and extend my hand, offering her a seat. "Do you want a coffee? Breakfast... anything?"

She slides onto the stool, her eyes dart around the kitchen before they stop on my mug. "Coffee... I'll try it."

She's never had coffee? As I make her coffee, I avert my eyes away from her smooth, pale flesh where the white t-shirt she's wearing falls off one shoulder. "There are always a few positions available at The Plaza. Do you have a family, Annie? Anyone who'll be looking for you? You can give them a call if you like."

She sits on the stool and rests her elbows on the bench. "I don't have anyone. The old man and Ad—Twelve... I've been with them for ten years."

I turn and pass her the coffee. "Ten years?" I try to hide the shock in my tone. *What the fuck?*

She lifts the mug to her lips and inhales slowly before a tiny smile tugs at the corner of her mouth. After taking a sip, she places it down again. "Yep. My parents... they're gone." She shrugs. "The old man took me in, gave me a place to stay. I'm not going back there, that's for fucking sure."

What the hell would the old man want with a seven-year-old girl? My head spins as thoughts race through my mind. None of them good and knowing what happened to Bella only increases my thirst for vengeance. "Did they hurt you?" I ask.

Her face remains the same, not a hint of concern, or a shred of fear. "Twelve taught me to fight. The old man used me as his slave..." Her lip curls in disgust. "Fucking lazy bastard had me doing everything for him. I was punished, and some other shit happened." She waves a hand in the air. "What's done is done, right? Fuck them."

I lean against the wall, watching her. On the outside, she's purity and innocence. A beauty with ebony hair that reaches her slim hips. When she speaks, there's something more... something raw and untamed. The desire to link into her mind and hear her thoughts is almost overwhelming, but that's one thing I refuse to do. It's rare that I even talk to my brothers that way anymore. The thoughts in my own head fuck me up enough.

When she meets my gaze, she says, "Once I get a job, I'll pay you back for the clothes. I'll be out of here after this." She nods down to her coffee before she takes another sip.

No. You're not leaving. "You can stay here as long as you need. And don't worry about the clothes, Char's got plenty more, trust me. I need to go see my brothers at nine, but when I get back, I can take you to The Plaza, get you some of your own clothes, anything else you need." I will give her *everything* she needs.

She tilts her head, seemingly confused. "Why would you help me? Why not the other two girls?"

Because you belong to me. What the fuck? I scrub my hands down my face. This woman... NO! This girl... she doesn't belong to me. *Seventeen.* I remind myself.

I shrug. "They both had families... a home to go back to. You're not going back out there to live on the streets. The Fray will already be looking for you."

She pulls her hair over her shoulder and twists it around her hand, playing with the ends. After a few minutes of silence, she agrees. "Okay, fine. I'll stay... but only for a few days. And only because I know you're an angel and you're not allowed to kill people. And my rule still applies..."

"What rule?" I question.

"You touch me, I punch you."

I try to hide my smirk as I raise my hands in defence. "Hands off. Got it. Besides, you're *only* seventeen."

"Almost eighteen..." I'm sure she mutters something else under her breath, but when I ask her what she said, she shakes her head and takes another mouthful of coffee.

"Is there anything you need before I leave?" I ask.

"Nope. I'll have a shower and stay in the bedroom. I won't touch anything else." She stands to go back to the bedroom.

"Annie..."

She bites her lip and looks up at me, and when I don't speak, she narrows her eyes. "Knox?"

"Ah, make yourself at home. There's food in the fridge and in the pantry. If you want to watch TV, the remote's on the coffee table."

She nods but doesn't say a word. Her eyes are locked on mine, and her lips slightly parted. Her tongue darts out and glides across her lips before she turns and walks into the bedroom, leaving me speechless once again.

VII
BROTHERS
CLAY

Over the past few months we tried to gain as much information as we could about Roman's brother, but it appears as though no one is talking. Roman managed to get in touch with a few guys from the Fray. According to Roman, they're "dropping like flies". Up to ten Fray a week are being killed through the fights being run by Roman's brother, Adam, who is posing as Twelve.

After piecing together the information Flynn got from Alec, and what Roman got from his contacts, we still can't figure out exactly what the commander and his father's plans are. None of the Fray have been seen in the valley since Roman was *'killed'* by the commander. Hopefully Knox can shed some light on this guy, and we can figure out a way to get rid of him.

Steel looks up from where he's sitting at the kitchen bench feeding Arc and Angel. Gabe watches closely and claps each time the babies take a mouth full.

"What time's he coming?" Steel asks.

"Nine," I say. "He didn't seem happy about it though." Gabe jumps from the stool he's sitting on, then pushes it closer to me before he climbs back up.

"Knox come home today?" he asks.

I rough up his hair. "Yep, he sure is."

"Knox," Arc says.

"Good boy," Gabe says clapping his hands. "Now say, Gabe."

"Ga.. gaaa... Gabe," Arc says before slamming his little hands onto the tray of the highchair. "Gaaabe."

As Gabe laughs hysterically, the twins continue banging their hands on the highchair trays. Their little cheeks pink from giggling.

Steel shakes his head. "Okay, enough now. You need to eat your breakfast."

"Dada," Angel shouts. "No more."

Arc joins in. "Dada, dada. No more." As his hand comes down, he hits the edge of the bowl and it flies into the air and lands upside down on the kitchen floor.

I lean over and look down at it as Steel sighs and rubs his head. "Ah man, every time."

Gabe jumps down and picks up the bowl. "No dropping bowls," he says to Arc.

Arc reaches out to him, kicking his legs out and bouncing in the highchair. Gabe tilts his head and looks up at Steel. "Dey had enough now. We play?"

With a sigh, Steel turns to me. "You gonna help or what?"

I laugh. "Ah, actually, Knox is here. I'll go see him."

"Me too!" Gabe shouts before he runs to me and grabs my hand.

"Me too," Arc screams.

I pat Steel on the back. "You've got this, brother."

"Gabe..." Steel calls, "If you help me, I'll take you for a ride on my motorbike."

Gabe stops in his tracks, and I laugh, shaking my head. But when Arc and Angel start screaming to get out of the highchairs, Gabe grips my hand tight. "I not like bikes today, Steel."

"Chocolate!" Steel says. "You like chocolate? I'll buy you all the chocolate you want."

"Not today," Gabe says. "Come on, Clay, we see Knox now." Gabe drags me out of the kitchen. "Dey sooo noisy today," he says when we reach the foyer.

When the front door opens, Gabe shrieks, "KNOX!"

Knox scoops Gabe up in his arms and says hi before Gabe starts telling him *everything*.

"You come home. Do you know Roman stay in dis house too now? He good boy like you and Clay and Steel and Flynn. We all good boys in dis house." Gabe wraps his arms around Knox's neck and continues, "Kailey got baby in her tummy now. Roman is Daddy and Kailey is Mummy. You get a girlfwend too soon? Maybe you have babies too."

"Ah, I don't know, mate," he says, his eyes darken with rage.

Knox glares at me and I shrug. "It's not like you were here for it to bother you."

He sets Gabe down on his feet and shoves a hand into his pocket. "Gabe, go find Lexi, okay."

Gabe doesn't budge. "Lexi!" he shouts. "Knox is home now, come and see."

Lexi comes down stairs, smiling. Knox hugs her, then when she hears the twins screaming, she glances into the kitchen.

"Heyyy, Lexi," Steel calls. "Can you help me... please?"

Lexi heads into the kitchen, and Gabe follows her, telling her about Arc throwing his cereal on the floor. A few minutes later, Steel comes out and sighs with relief. "Come on, Flynn's in the office," he says.

In the office, we sit and wait for Knox to fill us in on what happened while he was gone, but for a few minutes, he's silent and seems to be thinking about something. Then, he shakes his head and returns his focus to us. "Where's Twelve?" he asks Flynn.

Flynn leans back on his leather recliner and props his feet on the desk. "His name is Roman. He's no longer Twelve. And why?"

Knox's brow furrows as he clenches his jaw. "I need to ask him something... And is it true? Him and Kailey are—"

Flynn cuts him off. "It is. And you won't be saying *or* doing anything to change that. They're both happy, and Roman's here to stay. Father bound them."

Knox gets to his feet and paces the room. Each heavy footstep hits the polished timber floor and causes the urns on the side table to shake as he nears them. "This is bullshit! Father agreed to let her be bound to the bastard who killed our brother." He slams his fist into the wall and the gilded frame surrounding an oil painting of our parents, shakes before it crashes to the floor.

Steel lets out a heavy sigh and picks up the frame. "For fuck's sake, Knox, get over it. He's paid for what he's done. And if it wasn't for him, Bella would be dead... maybe Autumn too."

"Get over it?" he roars. "Are you fucking serious!?"

Flynn shakes his head, annoyed. "Sit down. I'll call Roman in, but you start anything; I'll call Maple and you'll be put in the cell."

Surprisingly, Knox drops into the seat and crosses his arms over his chest. No argument, not a single word. He just... sits, and the three of us stare at him, confused.

The female... you want to get back to her? At first, he doesn't reply. But when Flynn leaves to get Roman, Knox turns to me. "She shouldn't be alone. They'll be looking for her."

"Is she hurt?" Steel asks.

Knox shrugs. "She said she's fine. But she has a broken rib. Those bastards forced her to fight... against the Fray."

I lean back in the chair and wonder if Lexi could talk to her. She's been determined to fix people lately. Since she's been back at work, she's become more confident, and more determined than ever to make a difference in the community. The ideas she had for a community centre for teens were put to the Ambrosia Valley Council, and next month, works will start on the first stage of the centre. There is nothing I won't do to keep the smile on her lips.

Flynn returns to the office with Roman, who looks beyond uncomfortable about being in the same room as Knox. These two are never going to get along, but somehow, we need to make it work.

Roman takes a seat opposite us, beside Flynn.

"I met your brother," Knox says. "Your twin." His tone tells me he assumes Roman knows what he's talking about, but other than what Alec told him, he doesn't know anything about his brother at all. Even when our father searched his memories, there was nothing that even alluded to him knowing of his brother's existence. Whatever was going on in that fucked up family, Roman wasn't part of it.

"He doesn't know anything," I say to Knox. "If you had stayed instead of rushing back there, you would have known that."

Roman swallows and cocks his head but remains silent as Knox questions him again. "Do you know about the females they had, the ones they forced to fight?"

"Nope," Roman says. "The commander never used or forced females to fight. If he did, they were part of the Fray, willingly. What's this about?"

"Your brother. He's a fucking psychopath... and they all believe he's you."

"Alec mentioned that Roman's brother was there to take his place," Flynn says. He glances at Roman who squints and shakes his head, then he nods. It's almost comical the way his face changes completely when Flynn's in his head.

Flynn turns his attention back to Knox. "Did you find out anything else while you were there?"

Knox scratches his chin. "You mean while I was chained to a fucking steel bed and being drained. Yeah, I found out that every single male..." He glares at Roman. "In your family, are fucking sadistic assholes."

Brother, don't do this. You won't get back to her. He glances at me and grunts in annoyance.

"They made a deal with Vandrick to use my blood mixed with vampire blood, to strengthen the Fray. To create an army of recruits who will be able to fight harder and heal faster. Apparently, the old man is some kind of scientist." Knox shrugs. "They want to take over the valley... that's all I know." He leans back and sighs. "I need to go, we done here?"

"Not yet." Flynn rests his elbows on the desk. "The female, what's going on with her?"

"She's staying at my place for a few days. I'm taking her to get some clothes this morning. She's got no family, nowhere to go," Knox says.

"Does she know about us?" Steel asks.

Knox nods. "It was hard to keep it a secret when *Roman's* brother was about to slit her throat if I didn't show my wings."

"He's no more my brother than you are," Roman says. "I don't even know the fucking guy, and—"

Flynn raises a hand signalling Roman to stop. "Enough. Knox, you can go. But keep your phone on and let us know if you find out anything else. See what the girl knows. We need to get this guy and end him."

Knox stands and nods, then he looks down at me. "Brother, we need to talk."

Without another word, I walk out of the office and follow Knox out to the driveway.

"What the fuck? Kailey is pregnant? She's a fucking kid."

I scrub my hands over my face. "She's over fifty in immortal years. She's not a kid at all, and you know it." He's making bullshit excuses now, purely because he hates Roman. "She's happy, and she deserves that. Don't fuck it up for her."

He runs a hand through his hair. "Yeah, ah, whatever. I'm gonna stay at my place for a few days, come around with Lexi... tonight?"

"I'll ask her."

"Is she okay, you know with Gabe and all that?" He pulls the car door open and gets in.

"She's better. They're both happy."

He extends his hand and we shake. "Tonight?" he asks again.

Reluctantly, I agree. "Yep, I'll call you."

As Knox heads down the driveway, Lexi's arms wrap around my waist. "Hey, you okay?" she asks.

I turn and kiss her forehead as I trail my fingers up and down her spine. "Yeah. He's pissed about Kay and Roman. He'll get over it."

"You miss him, don't you?"

I nod slightly. "He wants us to go to his place tonight. He's got a girl there, one he rescued from the Fray. She's only seventeen."

Her eyes widen in shock. "Oh my god, is she okay?"

"I think so... so, do you want to go?"

She presses a kiss beside my lips. "Of course, for you I'll do anything." With her fingers laced through mine, she whispers against my ear, "Come to the bedroom. Let me put a smile back on your face."

And just like that, I'm already smiling again.

VIII
INTO THE UNKNOWN
ANNIE

I follow Knox into the huge shopping centre called The Plaza. My eyes dart around, searching for something to focus on, but the lights, the noise, the smells, and the crowds of people cause my heart to race and my hands to sweat. *Calm the fuck down, Annie.* This should be normal, but for me, it's surreal. I'm seventeen years old, and this is the first time I've been to a shopping centre without Adam behind me, watching my every move.

Knox points to a store ahead called Ivy Boutique and tells me we'll go there first. I nod in agreement, hoping I'll be able to get something black. I'm thankful for the clothes I have now, but after sorting through the drawers last night, all I found were bright colours, and a shit load of white t-shirts and blue denim jeans.

Inside the store, Knox speaks to the female at the desk whose name is Ivy. She plasters on a huge smile and with a chirpy voice, leads me to the back of the store where there are racks of bras and underwear, along with pyjamas, and nightgowns. "Do you know your size, honey?" she asks.

"Yeah, I've been wearing bras and underwear for a while now."

Another huge smile, then a laugh. "Well, we have a large range of bras here. What's your cup size?"

I inhale and remind myself I'm getting these clothes for free. "Would you mind if I had a look around by myself?" I ask in my sweetest voice.

"Oh, honey, of course not. You go ahead. Call me if you need any help."

I nod and turn my attention to the rack of black bras and matching underwear. For ten minutes, I wander around the lingerie section, alone, and in complete, perfect silence. I trace my fingertips over a soft cotton bra before I take it off the rack and check the price tag. All the clothing and underwear I had before, Adam purchased for me online. Everything was delivered to our house—I never paid for anything.

The back wall of the store is covered in rows of socks, so I grab a few pairs along with some underwear and pyjamas. Each time I look up, Knox is there, watching me as though he's some kind of body guard. And rather than being pissed off that he's watching me, there's a sense of calm that envelops me, and makes me feel safe. If he can get away from Adam, he must be strong. So for now, I'll let him hang around. A few days, that's all I'll need to find a job and a place to stay.

I place everything on the counter, hoping it's not too much as Knox comes over and pulls a credit card from his wallet. "That's all you need?" he asks.

"Yep."

Ivy laughs. "Young girls these days, they usually buy one in every colour."

"I like black," I say, narrowing my eyes at her. "I don't need anything else."

With yet another smile, she meticulously folds everything, then wraps it all in pale pink tissue paper before putting it all into a black and white striped bag. As she hands it over the counter to me, she says, "Well, sweetie, you have a good day." Her eyes go to Knox next. "Thank you, Mr Fallon, let me know if you need anything else... anything at all." Her hand reaches out to touch his and she bats her lashes and smooshes her lips together in a weird pout. *Ugh.* What is it with women who swoon over guys? It makes me cringe.

After making our way around three more clothing stores, I've got my hands full of bags of brand new clothes, underwear, and socks and shoes, and as we make our way through The Plaza, Knox stops by the electronics store. "Actually, I'll call Jones to get your bags. We need to go in here."

Knox makes a phone call and a few minutes later, his driver, Jones, approaches. He speaks to Knox quietly before he takes my bags and goes back to the car. "What's in here you need?" I ask as we head into the electronics store.

"*You* need a phone. Do you want anything else? CD's, movies or something?"

A phone? What the hell? I narrow my eyes, confused. "Is this a way to get me to like you? Because I'm leaving... and my rule—"

He stops and turns to face me, cutting me off mid-sentence. "I know your rule. And no, it's not to get you to like me. It's for your own safety. You said you were only staying a few days, but when you do leave, I want you to know you can contact me anytime. *If* you need to."

Okay. This is good. He knows I'm leaving and he's not forcing me to stay. "I was just reminding you." I shove my hands into my pockets. "And I don't need anything else, you've already spent enough on me today."

"It's not a problem," he assures me.

Inside the store, I stand at the counter beside Knox while he rattles off the name of the phone he wants. I have no idea what any of it means. I've seen mobile phones, but I've never used one, and Adam rarely used his until we came to this town, which Knox told me this morning is called Ambrosia Valley.

It only takes twenty minutes for Knox to get the phone, and we're heading out again, this time to another clothing store he said I might like. "I don't need anything else," I say for the second time.

Ignoring me, Knox continues into the shopping centre. He points out a store where a group of young girls are rummaging through the racks at the front, laughing and talking as they hold up each item and parade it in front of their friends. My eyes flit from one girl to the next. They're so happy... so free. It's as though they don't have anything to worry about at all. I tilt my head, wondering if I could have been like them if I hadn't met Adam and the old man.

"Annie," Knox says.

"Yeah?"

He extends his hand. "This is the store Lexi likes. My brother's girlfriend, she's eighteen... ah no, she just turned nineteen actually."

I nod and walk in, distracted by the bright lights that shine down on the racks of clothes, and loud music blaring from somewhere above. A girl walks toward me, her name tag reads, "Becca."

"Hi, do you need any help?" she asks.

I shake my head. "I'm only looking."

She gives me a smile and heads back to the counter. I spot a rack of black jeans at the back of the store. Knox follows close behind me, not realising the group of girls I saw outside are watching his every move. Either he's used to it, or he doesn't care. I smile to myself as I wonder if they know he's an angel. *Does anyone here know he's an angel?*

"You like black?" Knox asks.

"Yeah, is that okay?"

"Of course."

With a few pairs of jeans slung over my arm, I head to the fitting room to try them on. The first pair are too small, and I can't get them up past my thighs. The second pair are so tight I can barely breathe once the zipper is up. By the time I get to the third pair, I'm hot and sweaty, and the incessant beat of the music is pounding through my head. *Ugh. I hate this place.* The walls feel like they're closing in on me and my own reflection in the mirror is a constant reminder of what I am. *I'm nothing but a slave. A fighter, a thing used for Adam's entertainment.* I need to get out of here.

Storming out of the fitting room, I huff as I walk past Knox then dump the jeans on the counter and walk out of the store. Once I'm outside, I lean against the glass window of the store with my arms crossed around myself, anger boiling inside me.

Knox is in front of me in seconds. "Annie, what's wrong? Are you okay?" There's panic—or maybe it's anger—in his voice.

I narrow my eyes, desperate to rein in my rage. *Free clothes, free food, a place to stay.* No, I refuse to whine about this. "They didn't fit." I shrug.

"Ahh, okay. Do you want to try another store? Or if you're hungry, there's a pizza place further down."

"Yeah, I'm hungry." I follow Knox to the pizza restaurant where I'll have to fake my way through everything. I've never eaten pizza, and just the thought of it makes my stomach turn.

Before we sit on bright red seats in the back corner of the restaurant, Knox orders pizza and drinks. The walls here are covered in movie posters and framed photographs of the staff making pizza bases and flipping them in the air.

Adam was strict with drinks and meals. Not just mine, his as well. He said good nutrition was important and that we needed to fuel our bodies, not destroy them with garbage. It was times like that, that I suppose he *was* a normal guy. A normal guy who loved killing and was obsessed with blood.

"So how long have you been here... or down there with them?" Knox asks.

"About six months."

He leans back casually in the seat. "And where were you before?"

"Daylehurst. Why?"

"Just curious," he asks as the pizza arrives at the table.

I look down at it and scrunch my nose, wondering what the hell is on it. "Is that pineapple?" I ask, pointing to the faded yellow wedges.

"Yeah, it's ham and pineapple. You don't like it?"

Clearly, I know how to shrug because it's all I seem to be doing today. "Honestly, I've never had pizza. Why the hell does it have pineapple on it?"

He laughs. "Try it, you'll love it."

"You think? Because you don't know me, at all." I point to the bubbly drink. "That's disgusting," I admit.

He cocks his head. "You don't like cola? What did you eat before?"

"Cola... hmm, no, I don't like it. I drink water, and well, I love coffee now."

He smiles. "I noticed that. What about food?"

"Vegetables, fruit, chicken and pasta. I train every day, so I eat to fuel my body." I lean down a little to get a closer look at the pizza, and Knox laughs.

When I sit up, he cocks his head and apologises. "Sorry, that was rude. I've never met a... anyone who doesn't like pizza."

I chew the inside of my mouth as I take a slice of pizza off the tray, a long trail of melted cheese stretches from it and I almost gag. My head is screaming at me to eat the damn pizza and stop making such a big deal out of it, but as I bring it closer to my mouth, I stop.

Slowly, I place it on the small plate in front of me and look up at Knox. "I can't eat it, I'm sorry. I ah... I hope it didn't cost too much." *Oh god, Annie, get over it.*

Knox raises his hand and waves the waitress over. He stands and speaks quietly to her, then she leaves. A minute later she returns with a tall glass bottle of water and a clean glass for me, then tells me my chicken and pasta salad will be ready in ten minutes.

I can't stop the smile that spreads across my lips. "Thank you," I whisper quietly to Knox.

He raises his brow and smiles back at me. My tummy twists and turns in knots I'm sure are because I haven't eaten since breakfast.

While we sit, Knox tells me about the valley and some of the places he says he'll show me if I'm interested. He also tells me him and his brothers own an apartment building a few blocks away from here, and that he'll help me find a place to stay.

Everything is working out. Soon, I'll finally be free, for real.

IX

FINDING A FRIEND

ANNIE

When we arrive back at Knox's house, I lie on the super soft bed trying to figure out how the hell to use this stupid phone that vibrates and makes weird noises when I tap the screen. Frustrated, I throw it on the floor and hold a pillow over my face to muffle my scream. I hate that everything is so hard... so strange.

I have barely any memories of my life before I was taken in by the old man, and once I was there, I was locked inside the house day after boring day. No contact with the outside world other than the times Adam and I would go running around the property, or he'd take me to the shopping centre.

I roll onto my stomach and clamp my eyes shut, trying in vain to ignore the memories that play over in my head.

Annie
14 years old

There are so many people here I'm worried I'll get lost and no one will ever find me. Even though Adam is here, I know he'll be gone for a little while, and it's during those moments that anxiety takes over and all I can focus on is getting back to him.

He nudges my arm and talks quietly. "Sit at the table near the blonde woman. You know what to do."

I nod and obey, and without looking back, I make my way toward the small table in the food court of the shopping centre. When I sit, I drop my head in my hands and squeeze my eyes shut tight, begging the tears to fall. It doesn't take long until I'm sobbing.

It only takes a few minutes for her to notice. "Oh, sweetheart, are you okay?" the woman asks, placing a gentle hand on my shoulder.

I shake my head and rub my eyes. "I had a big fight with my mum and told her I hate her. She's going to leave me here, I know it."

"Aww, sweetheart..." The woman pulls a chair over and sits beside me. "Everything will be okay. Your mum loves you. Is she still here?"

I nod and rub my eyes again. From the corner of my eye, Adam nods toward the exit, then leaves.

Now, I'm alone. Sometimes, this is the exact moment I consider asking for help. Thoughts race through my mind so fast that I can't cling to any one of them long enough to make sense of what's happening in my head. I'm certain that's why I've never spoken up. Or it could be that without Adam, I won't know how to survive.

I look up at the woman with perfectly styled blonde hair, bright blue eyes, and a kind smile. "Would you come with me, just to the exit... that's where Mum parked the car."

She stands and takes my hand in hers. "Of course, sweetheart. What's your name?"

"Annastasia," I say. "But you can call me Annie."

"Let's go, Annie." With the woman holding my hand, we walk to the rear exit of the shopping centre. When we reach the parking lot, I stop and scan the area, pretending to search for a car. "That's Mum's car over there," I say.

"Come on then." She rubs my back and tells me everything will be okay.

But it won't. For her, nothing will be okay ever again.

Two hours later, Adam orders me to sit on the small wooden chair in the basement while he whips, beats, and tortures the woman. While she's chained to the hooks attached to the ceiling, Adam paces around her. I'm forbidden to move, forbidden to look away or close my eyes.

When he's had enough, he slits her throat and continues talking as though she's still alive and listening to every word he speaks. His hand glides down her chest, smearing the blood that oozes from her neck. He traces his fingertips across her shoulders and her cheek. "You shouldn't have touched her. Annastasia is mine." He flicks his head toward me. "Isn't that right, my sweet Annastasia?"

I nod. "Yes, Adam, I am yours."

"Come here. Come and see what I've done for you."

I walk over slowly, trying desperately to keep my eyes on Adam, but they're drawn to the blood still dripping down the woman's pale flesh.

Adam takes my hand and laces his bloody fingers through mine. "Did she hurt you, Annastasia?"

"No, Adam. I'm not hurt."

The sigh he releases is one of relief, and when he squeezes my hand, I smile and squeeze his back. "I am yours," I remind him again.

"Annie, are you okay?" The knocking grows louder. "Annie!"

I blink the tears away and sit up, hugging the pillow to my chest. After wiping my eyes on the shoulder of my t-shirt, I clear my throat. "I'm fine. You can come in."

The door opens slowly and Knox walks in. His eyes drop to the floor where the mobile phone lays on the thick white rug. He reaches down to pick it up and presses some buttons. "You look upset, is everything okay?"

"Yep. I was annoyed at that stupid phone. I think it's defective..."

A smile tugs at the corner of his lips. "You don't know how to set it up?"

I shrug. "I've never had one," I admit. "It doesn't matter, I don't need it."

He sits on the end of the bed and it dips with his weight. He's all muscle. Way bigger than Adam, bigger than Commander Malum even. As he presses more buttons on the phone, I get to my knees and shuffle forward, leaning over his shoulder to watch what he's doing, and trying to memorise every button he presses.

While Knox sets up my phone, he talks, but he doesn't turn to me. "My brother's coming around with his girlfriend, Lexi. She'll be able to help you with the settings and show you how to text and use the camera and apps... if you want her to."

I drop back onto the bed and cross my legs. "I'm not a little kid. And I'm not stupid."

He looks over his shoulder at me, his deep green eyes are shiny now. Down in the basement when I first saw him, they were dark green and kind of murky.

"I know," he says. "If you'd rather stay in here, that's fine. You don't have to do anything you don't want to do." He stands and walks out the room, taking my phone with him.

Damn it! He planned that. Now I'll have to ask for it back. *Stupid angel.*

Still frustrated about the phone, and with the reminders of my past playing over in my mind, I get off the bed to tidy the room. I fold and stack all my new clothes neatly in the corner beside my shoes before I grab the hairbrush and head to the bathroom.

I've always avoided looking at myself in the mirror, it was always the same. Bruises, scratches and cuts from training and fighting. Tonight though, I take the time to really look at myself.

In my reflection, I search for my parents, desperate to remember their faces. Do I have my Mum's eyes, or my Dad's nose? Is my hair the same colour as theirs was? Was I supposed to be this short? There's nothing there but a faded, fuzzy image. A silhouette of two people I know existed but are hidden somewhere in the darkest crevices of my mind.

The earliest clear memory I have, is of Adam and the old man. It was my seventh birthday and the old man told me my parents were gone, and his house was my new home. I don't remember crying or being sad about it. I blew out the seven candles on my birthday cake while Adam stood beside me, his arm over my shoulders. He was already a teenager and told me he'd take care of me, protect me from everything and everyone. He did that.

Everyone who has ever touched me, is dead.

When I come out of the bathroom, I hear voices outside the bedroom door. Every part of me wants to go out there, if only to see what Knox's brother looks like. Is he an angel too? He would have to be. And the girl... I could use her to find out about this town. Yes! I can do this. *I am not weak.*

For a moment, I stand in the doorway watching them. Knox sits on a stool at the kitchen bench, drinking a bottle of beer. The other guy, his brother, sits on the other side of the bench with a glass of what looks like whiskey. The girl sits beside him, her long light brown hair tied up in a ponytail on top of her head. She's wearing a tight, bright pink t-shirt that says, "Roller Queen" and has a picture of a roller skate beneath a pale blue crown. I tilt my head, watching her as she talks to Knox and his brother. She smiles a lot and laughs along with them. What does she see in them, and why is she so happy?

I clench my fists, digging my fingernails into the soft flesh of my palms as I take a step forward.

The girl looks up at me. She raises her hand and waves. "Hey, hi, you must be Annie?"

Knox turns and his brother looks up. "You want a drink?" Knox asks.

"Coffee?" I ask, thinking about the delicious warm coffee I had this morning. I'd never tasted it before, but somehow, it was like a drug, and while Knox was gone, I paced the kitchen for almost half an hour, desperate to make another one. Of course, I had no idea how to use the machine, so I sat at the kitchen bench and stared at it, scowling with disgust.

Knox stands and introduces me to his brother Clay, and Clay's girlfriend, Lexi. I sit on a stool and watch Knox start the coffee machine.

"So where are you from, Annie?" Lexi asks.

"Daylehurst," I say.

"Wow, that's a long way from here," Clay says.

Knox hands me my coffee and I thank him before I inhale the rich aroma for the second time today. Coffee is definitely something I can get used to.

Before I can reply to Clay, Knox changes the subject. "Lex, do you want to show Annie around while Clay helps me with the security cameras?"

What? No. Not Lexi. I don't know her. I take a mouthful of coffee and swallow it down.

"Sure, I'd love to. Come on, Annie, bring the coffee with you."

I glare at Knox, hoping he can sense my anger, but he only smiles then turns back to Clay.

With the coffee mug tight in my hands, I follow Lexi through the main living area where two large black sofas are placed in front of an open fireplace. On the wall above it, a huge television screen. There are a few large cabinets filled with books, and on the floor, a thick fluffy rug that looks softer than anything I've ever seen in my life.

As we head along the hallway, Lexi stops at an open door. "This is Knox's room. The guys have such amazing taste in furniture."

I nod. "It's nice." The scent of Knox's cologne lingers here, a woodsy scent that reminds me of the forest, but with a hint of something I've never smelled before. I inhale and close my eyes for a fraction of a second trying to focus on the smell, and when I can't figure it out, I sigh. Everything is unfamiliar.

"Did you get some nice stuff today at The Plaza?" Lexi asks.

"You know about that?"

She bites her lip, then scrunches her nose. "Ah, yeah, sorry. You didn't want anyone to know?"

"I don't care. I didn't know everyone knew everything around here." There's a hint of spite in my tone, and when Lexi frowns, I feel something... different. "It doesn't matter. I got some clothes and stuff, that's all.

As we walk through the house, Lexi shows me the small library, Knox's office and home gym, and the huge room upstairs that has a glass ceiling that looks out to the night sky. She doesn't stop talking, and doesn't ask me many questions, and because of that, I don't hate her.

When we come back to the kitchen, I realise I left my coffee mug somewhere in the house, but I have no idea where. Oh well, I'll get it later.

For the next few hours, I sit at the kitchen bench with Knox, Clay and Lexi and listen to them talk. Everything is so easy for them, and for Lexi. Clay never asks her for anything. He doesn't ask her to get him a drink or tell her to sit somewhere else so he can talk to Knox alone. It's as though he *wants* her with him. And when she talks to him, he listens, and he kisses her a lot, a whole fucking lot.

I've never been kissed. When I was younger, I used to dream about Adam kissing me, but even in my dreams it ended with me being punished. It can't be that good anyway, and there's no way I want someone's mouth on mine. *Ugh. Gross.*

My idea to use Lexi, fails. She's too nice, and I don't want to do anything to change that.

X
CONSUMED
KNOX

Haydee sits on the end of my bed, twirling her fingers through her dark hair. "You should go home now."

"You should stop showing up *every time* I'm in the shower."

"You know I love looking at you." She laughs and jumps to her feet before she runs her long, sharp nails down my back. A shiver of pleasure courses through my veins and sends my heart beat into overdrive. I step back and shake my head hard as my muscles twitch and I clench my fists.

"Go home now."

"Why? So you can force me to beat the shit out of Roman?"

She smiles wide. "Come on, I know you want to slam his face into those shiny marble tiles."

I walk back to the bathroom and throw my towel into the laundry basket. "I won't do it. I need to be here with Annie in case they come after her."

She drops down onto the bed and pouts. "You're no fun. I could make you go back..."

I stare down at her. "Don't," I warn. "I've fucked up enough and you said—"

She cuts me off, "Fine. But you need to fight, it's been too long. Call Clay to come around."

"Yeah, I will... Did you find Venys?" I ask.

She nods. "I'm trying to get her to come back, but..." She lies back on my bed twirling her hands around as black smoke rises from her fingertips. "She's worried. She doesn't want to curse Flynn again, or hurt Autumn and the babies."

I shake my head. "Flynn won't fall for it again. He's loyal as fuck to Autumn. They miss her you know. Fucking weird how much Autumn loved being cursed."

She laughs. "I'll keep trying."

I flick off the bathroom light and turn back to my bedroom when my eyes stop on Annie. Her eyes are only on me. Well, technically, they're on my cock. *Fuck.*

She gasps and clamps her eyes shut, then she runs. Her feet scamper down the hallway, and a few seconds later, her bedroom door slams shut.

"Fucking hell," I groan.

Haydee laughs wildly. "Ahhh that was the best fucking reaction ev-ahhhh! Wanna know what she was thinking?" *Fuck yes!*

I glare at her. "Don't. She's seventeen."

"Only for another eight days. You think you can keep her that long."

"You think I can't?" I question.

"You haven't kept any female longer than a week."

Bitch. I get dressed while Haydee jumps on my bed like a child.

"Charlotte," I remind her.

She waves a hand in the air and stops jumping, her brows knit and her lip turns in a snarl of disgust. "*She* does not count... in anything."

Shaking my head, I grab her arm and pull her off my bed. She takes my glass of whiskey and swallows it down in one go, grimacing in disgust. "I'm going. I'll be back tomorrow."

Reaching up on her tip toes, she presses a kiss to my cheek before she leans in closer to my ear. "She thinks you're huge, and she wants to touch it." Then, she disappears, leaving me standing in stunned silence—my cock hard as fucking steel.

With a groan of frustration, I lie back on my bed and rub my head. I should apologise to Annie. "Fuck!" I curse as I head down the hallway toward Annie's bedroom.

"Annie." I knock on her door and wait. No answer. There's no way she's asleep, she's probably embarrassed, or pissed off. Come to think of it, she hasn't been bad at all since she got here. "Annie, I want to apologise," I say.

Soft footsteps pace toward the door before it opens. She stands there, wearing a tight, low cut tank top. Her hair piled up on her head in one of those messy buns Charlotte and Autumn always have. "I'm sorry, about before."

She looks up at me, and fuck it, I cannot for the life of me read her expression. "It's not like I haven't seen a dick before." She shrugs, but a slight pink blush appears on her cheeks. "So, I left my coffee mug somewhere in the house, but I have no idea where, and it's all confusing. I guess you'll find it, eventually. Ah, that's what I was looking for. I mean not in your room, but when I—"

I reach out and tuck a strand of hair behind her ear. "I'll find it."

She opens her mouth to speak, her full pink lips slightly parted. Her tongue swipes across her top lip before she steps forward, closing the gap between us. I drop my hand and focus on the rise and fall of her chest as she breathes heavily.

Another step. Her warm breath tickles my chest and goose bumps appear on my flesh.

"Knox," she whispers my name as she rises up on her toes. With her hands planted firmly on my chest, she presses a gentle kiss beside my lips, rendering me speechless.

I swallow hard, determined to keep my hands off her as promised, but the reality is, I want her so fucking bad it hurts.

"Thank you." She steps back and drops her hands. "Goodnight," she says.

I open my mouth, and nothing comes out. *Fucking speak you moron.*

I step back, once, twice, and again.

Annie tilts her head, then smiles. And as the door closes, I remain still. Standing at the closed door, staring at it as though she's going to reappear at any second.

When my brain finally starts working again, I shake my head hard and walk back to my bedroom.

There's a war raging within me. The chaos I've come to know has been silent since I returned from the Fray, since I rescued the females and brought Annie into my home. Even Haydee has backed off. Part of me is confused, wondering why the calm I've been seeking for over a century has finally made itself known. Another part of me is consumed with the desperate, aching need to touch Annie's body, to make her mine, and to give her everything she needs, wants, and desires. But I need to wait, I won't do anything unless she asks for it, or makes the first move.

The past week has fucked with my head more than any day in the past hundred years has. There's something seriously wrong with me, and I need to figure it out, fast.

XI
LEXI

ANNIE

L exi pulls her blue convertible into the parking lot of Rollin'. She called earlier this morning to let me know there was a position available, and that she'd take me to meet the owner. The thought of working for someone, freaks me the hell out, but I'll never admit it. I need some independence, and I desperately need money. Relying on Knox is becoming too easy. He never pushes me to talk, he doesn't ask too many questions, *and* he makes me coffee. I have everything I need there, which is why I have to leave.

Before I left Knox's house with Lexi, he gave me a hundred dollars in cash, *and* his credit card and told me to get anything I wanted while I was out. The guy is seriously weird. But fuck he's nice to look at, and I love his deep voice... oh, and his scent. I've never seen anyone like him.

A smile dances across my lips when I think back to last night. I didn't mean to stop at his bedroom door, which was wide open. I didn't mean to stare at his ass, and the tattoos that adorn his muscled back, and huge shoulders and arms. And when he turned around, I did not mean to stare right at his massive dick, or gasp when my eyes locked on to the thick silver ring pierced through the end of it. *What the hell is that for?*

After racing back to the bedroom, I jumped on the bed and screamed into the pillow, furious that I'd ogled him the same way Ivy at the clothing store had. The same way those girls at The Plaza looked at him. And the kiss? Well that wasn't part of my plan. It was just a thank you. A simple little kiss that meant nothing at all.

Liar, Annie! After watching Lexi kiss Clay the other night, I wanted to know what it would feel like. And it felt good pressing my lips against the rough stubble. Different, kind of weird, but good, and when he stuck to the rules and didn't touch me, I was relieved.

Lexi's voice pulls me from my thoughts. "Annie, are you okay?"

I nod. "Yep, just thinking. So, do I have to skate here? I've never skated before."

She gets out of the car and I follow her into the building. "Nah, not at all. But if you're interested, I can teach you... or help you. I've been skating since I was a child."

"Maybe," I say. "For now, I need money, and a place to stay."

"Knox would let you stay longer. I mean, if you wanted to. I think he likes having you there." She tucks her phone into the pocket of her denim shorts before she stops by the entrance and lowers her voice. "I know he's a bit rough around the edges, Annie, but he really is sweet. He'd do anything to help you."

Twisting my fingers through my hair, I narrow my eyes. "I know. But I can't stay there. I need to be alone. I *want* to be alone. It's easier." I said a few days, and tomorrow my time is up.

"Okay," she says in her cheery voice. "Enough about Knox, let's go in." Lexi opens the door and the noise assaults my senses. Little kids are screaming, girls and boys are skating, and parents are sitting at colourful tables talking to one another as they glance toward the huge pale blue floor that's surrounded by a low wall.

"That's the rink," Lexi says. "Come on, Jane's over here."

We walk across to the other side of the arena where an older lady is handing a pair of roller skates to a young blonde girl, but when she sees Lexi, she quickly turns her attention to us.

"Lexi," she shouts as she runs around from behind the counter to hug Lexi and kiss her cheek. "Are you okay, darling? How's Gabe, is he coping well?" Lexi nods and tells Jane she's okay and that Gabe—whoever that is—is also fine. After a quick introduction, Jane ushers us toward the office and once again, I follow Lexi like I'm a stupid puppy chasing after its master.

Jane tells us to sit on an old stinky sofa that's worn and faded. I keep my hands on my lap and sit up straight.

"Annie, Lexi told me you were looking for a casual job, is that right?"

I nod, not knowing what to say. Maybe I was better off with Adam, at least I knew what to do.

Lexi speaks up for me. "Jane, Annie's just moved to the valley. She's staying with Knox while she settles in."

Jane smiles now, and her face lights up. She clasps her hands on the desk, her attention on me. "Oh, aren't you a lucky girl. Knox is wonderful. Okay, let's not overwhelm you then, hey?" We spend twenty short minutes in the office with Jane who asks me a few basic questions, then surprisingly, tells me I have the job and I can start tomorrow afternoon at three.

All I'll need to do to begin with is sort and place the skates on the racks, and re-tie the laces when people are done. It sounds easy enough, and I'll be getting paid.

When we get back to the car, Lexi asks if I want to go to The Plaza then get some lunch before we head back to Knox's house. I want to go with her, but a bigger part of me wants to go back to Knox's now and make the most of the time I have left there.

After sitting in the car for ten minutes, in silence, I finally turn to Lexi. "Why are you being nice? You don't even know me."

Her huge smile never disappears. "That's exactly why I'm being nice. You've been nice to me, you haven't treated me badly, or said anything wrong..." She hesitates, then as she starts driving, she says, "You're not used to this, are you? I mean all of this stuff."

I shake my head and shrug. "Nope. It's just—" I slump back into the seat and cross my arms around myself. *Damn Adam for not teaching me about real life stuff.* "Fuck!"

Lexi doesn't speak again until we arrive at The Plaza. We spend the next two hours walking from store to store. I wait while Lexi tries on colourful t-shirts and dresses, and she helps me choose a pair of running shoes. Before we leave, we sit at a small table in the food court where we have lunch, followed by coffee and choc chip cookies.

As I take another bite of the delicious cookie, Lexi watches me. "They're sooo good, right?"

I nod in agreement before picking out a chunk of chocolate and savouring it as it melts on my tongue. *Never tasted anything so wonderful.* I'm sure this isn't what I need to fuel my body, but it certainly fuels my love for chocolate.

"Did you go to school back in Daylehurst?" Lexi asks.

I don't want to talk about me at all, so I reply quickly. "Nope, I haven't been to school. I learned everything at home."

"Oh, home school!" Lexi says.

I nod once. "Mmm hmm." Then, I change the subject. "Who's Gabe?" I ask. "I heard Jane ask you about him."

She smiles. "Gabe's my little brother, he's almost four."

I glance around the food court, my eyes darting from one child to another as I try to figure out what a four-year-old might look like. I shake my head. Maybe I'll get to see him... one day. *If I stay.* As the thought enters my mind, realisation hits. If I stay here, Adam is sure to find me. But Knox is here, and he's strong. And Lexi is here too. *Wait... why do I care about her?*

"You okay, Annie?" Lexi's voice brings me back to the present.

"I'm fine. Do you go to school? Or does your brother?"

She laughs a little, shaking her head. "I finished a couple years ago. Gabe will start kindergarten next year, then school starts the following year. He's so excited about it, especially since Clay promised to drive him there each day."

"Lex! Lexi," a loud voice calls in the distance. Lexi stands from her seat and waves to the girl running toward her. They hug one another and kiss each other's cheeks before the tall blonde girl slides another chair across to our table and sits down.

"Annie, this is my best friend, Jess."

Jess's eyes grow wide as she stares at me. "Oh my god, you're gorgeous. And your hair, it's so long."

I try to smile, but I'm biting the inside of my mouth so hard that I barely manage it. I swallow down the lump in my throat. "Hi and thank you," I say.

Jess grabs Lexi's hand and squeezes it tight. "I have to tell you something, can I come over tonight?"

Lexi nods, and I watch them talk and laugh while I sit there, confused but enthralled by their conversation and their facial expressions that change every few seconds. Jess jumps to her feet and slaps her palm to her forehead. "I'm so sorry, Annie, that was so rude of me." She turns her attention to Lexi. "I'll see you tonight." With a quick hug, she says goodbye to Lexi and waves as she turns around and walks away. Long blonde hair swishes behind her.

"What was she sorry for?" I ask Lexi.

"For interrupting our lunch... ah, for talking." Lexi laughs. "She gets carried away when she's excited."

I take a mouthful of coffee and pop the last piece of cookie into my mouth. I don't know what to say. I'm speechless, clueless, and completely lost in a world I should understand.

Damn you, Adam!

XII
MY SAVIOUR

ANNIE

I walk through the front door, and Knox is on the phone. He gives me a slight smile then goes back to his conversation, so I head to my room to change into the black hoodie Lexi encouraged me to buy. She said they're "super comfy", and when I pull it over my head, I'm instantly enveloped in warmth. She was not wrong.

She even talked me into buying some moisturiser and perfume, as well as a make-up kit which I doubt I'll ever use, but she promised to help me with it once I've found my own place and I'm settled in. I spray on the perfume and inhale the fruity sweet scent before I head back to the kitchen to ask Knox to make me a coffee.

When I pull open the bedroom door, I stop in my tracks.

"I'll get rid of her, Char. Don't worry," Knox says into the phone.

For a brief second, my heart stops beating. He lied. They're all the same. All men are bastards. Gritting my teeth, I step back as Knox turns to see me.

"Char, I gotta go." He ends the call and places the phone on the bench.

"You okay, Annie?"

I glare at him. Everything I want to say is resting on the tip of my tongue. "You don't have to get rid of me, I'm leaving." I turn and slam the door before I grab my new backpack and shove a few things inside. Fuck him! I don't want anything he paid for. I dump out the contents and throw the backpack on the floor.

"Annie, it's not what you think," he says from the other side of the door.

I pull it open and my words fly out laced in rage. "You are just like the rest of them. You're all the same. All fucking bastards. I hate you." I attempt to slam the door in his face, but he simply raises his hand, stopping it.

"Listen to me. I wasn't talking about you."

I swipe my phone off the bedside table and shove it in my pocket. "Let me out," I shout as he blocks the doorway with his huge body.

He shakes his head. "Listen to me first."

I shove my hands against his chest. "Let me the fuck out!" I scream and punch at his chest, but he doesn't move. He doesn't even flinch, and when he grabs my wrists and holds them tight, I struggle to free myself, then, in one swift movement, I knee him in the balls.

"Fuck!" he groans as I push past him and run to the front door.

Before I get there, he's got me again, his strong arms wrapped around my waist; my arms locked by my sides. I kick out and scream as loud as I can, cursing at him, throwing my head back, and warning him to let me go.

He carries me to the bedroom and closes the door with his foot before he lets me go then leans against the door, blocking my exit. "Ready to listen now?"

"Fuck you, asshole!"

He crosses his arms over his chest and cocks his head. "I've got all day. When you calm down, we'll talk. *Then* you can decide if you're leaving."

I scan the room, searching for something to throw at him, but other than clothes and bedding, there's nothing. *Fucking angel.* "Let me go," I scream again and storm toward him, raising my hand to swing a punch, but he stops me. He grabs my fist in his own hand and pushes it down with ease.

That's it. I throw clothes at him, shouting with each thing I pick up.

"I don't..." Black jeans hit his shoulder and he raises his brow. "Need anything—" I throw a pile of t-shirts at his face and they fall to the floor. The bastard smirks. He actually smirks—at me.

"Fuck you!" The pillow hits his thigh and he looks down at it, then back up at me, his arms still crossed. "And fuck your money!" I grab my hairbrush off the bed and fling it at him. It misses and hits the door instead, then lands on the pillow. Anger boils inside me. I need to smash something; I need to hurt him. "Stop staring at me," I scream.

"Calm down, Annie," he says quietly.

"NO!" I slam my fist into the mirror above the timber dresser. The pain... I clamp my eyes shut, searching for it, willing it into existence. Tiny glass shards are embedded into my flesh, but other than mild discomfort, I feel nothing. As I shake my hand out, Knox paces toward me.

I step back, clenching my fist as warm blood trickles from my knuckles. "Don't touch me," I shout. I dart to the left to get past him as he moves away from the door, but once again the bastard angel catches me. And this time he doesn't let go.

He pushes me into the wall, his body hard against mine, and his hands holding my wrists, pinning them beside my head. His eyes lock onto my fist that's covered in blood.

"Don't touch me," I mean to shout the words in his face, but they come out as a quiet whisper.

"Or what?" he says, his eyes blaze with a deep emerald glow.

I attempt to lift my knee to get his balls again, but when he pushes himself against me, my body—the traitorous bitch—softens against his.

"You're not crying..." he says it as though I'm abnormal. "Does it hurt?"

I don't reply, I just glare at him, rage still burning in my eyes. But my body, it's doing things it's never done before. My hips move, seeking the pressure of him against me, seeking a warmth I've never felt but somehow know exists. My breasts are pressed against his chest, and my nipples grow hard and sensitive, and when I move slightly, there's an ache inside me that won't let up.

Knox drops his head and breathes beside my ear. "You ready to talk now?"

I open my mouth to speak, but his breath, his scent, his body... everything about him renders me speechless and all that leaves my lips is a tiny sigh. I bite my lip hard and clamp my eyes shut, trying to rein in all the strength I have so I can push him away.

But it doesn't work.

Nothing works.

Until our lips meet.

An urgent, desperate hunger takes over and I kiss him hard, unsure if I'm doing it properly, but not really caring about anything but the taste of him as his tongue swipes across my lips, and I chase his back with my own.

My hands are finally released from his iron grasp, but I can't move them, I don't want to move. I don't want to do anything in case he stops. *Don't ever stop.* His strong, firm hands slide down my waist and he grips my ass before lifting me up and holding me against the wall. Slowly, I place my hands on his shoulders and wrap my legs around his waist as he groans into my mouth.

My own tiny moan of pleasure escapes and I rock my hips toward him, the friction of my pussy rubbing against the length of his dick causes me to moan again, but I can't stop. I'm positive that if his lips leave mine, I will forget how to breathe, and I'll die.

Knox is my oxygen.

My saviour.

My angel.

But I still hate him. *I have to.* I can't let him have the power. *I can't.*

I haven't said one word to him since we kissed two hours ago, and I'm dying for coffee.

Rather than ask him for it, I head into the kitchen and press the power button on the coffee machine. It can't be that hard, surely. I pull open the fridge and grab the milk, then pour it into the milk jug beside the machine.

Looking down at the little buttons, I squint, trying to figure out what they mean. With a heavy sigh, I place the mug under the spout and press the large cup button, hoping it's right.

A second later, his hand reaches out and stops the coffee machine, but he doesn't say a word. He presses the clear button, then presses the button with a picture of a full cup, but it's half black and half white. When he steps back, he grabs the milk and puts it back in the fridge while I stare down at the brown liquid that pours into the mug and sends a welcome surge of relief through my veins. I'm going to miss this when I leave, and I am leaving.

After pouring the milk into my cup, I smile, realising what the button means and secretly satisfied I won't have to ask Knox for coffee now. I walk past him and go back to my room. My last night here, and I'm going to make the most of the gloriously soft bed and pillows.

With my legs crossed, I tip out the little bag of jewellery Lexi bought for me. There's a long silver chain with a silver feather charm. A stack of silver bangles, some with black thread weaved through them, and a silver bracelet Lexi said was "cute". I slip the bangles onto my wrist and shake my hand, listening to them tingle, then I tuck the necklace and bracelet into the backpack, ready for when I leave in the morning... after I have one last coffee.

When my phone chimes, I pull it from my pocket and look down at the screen. It's a text message from Knox. *Did he go out?*

WINGIN'IT: You okay?

ME: Yeah why? Did you go out?

WINGIN'IT: Just checking. I'm here, in the office.

ME: I'm in the bedroom you know

WINGIN'IT: I know

ME: Why are you texting me then?

WINGIN'IT: Giving you some space. I'm sorry, I shouldn't have kissed you.

ME: Okay

I drop the phone on the bed beside me. He regrets it now, he must. Why else would he apologise? Maybe I did it all wrong. *Damn it, Annie, stop thinking about him.*

My phone chimes again.

WINGIN'IT: Can we talk?

ME: Nope. I'm going for a walk

WINGIN'IT: I'll call Jones for you

ME: No. I want to be alone. I'll be across the street at the lake

WINGIN'IT: You shouldn't be alone right now, it's not safe.

ME: Bye

I shove my phone into my back pocket and walk out, pulling the front door closed behind me. It's almost sunset and the sky appears as a brilliant canvas of pale orange and pink hues. Ahead, there's the lake and playground I can see from my bedroom window. *No. It's not my bedroom.*

Past the playground, there's a path that leads into the forest through tall pine trees.

This is the first time I've ever been alone and the urge to run is almost overwhelming, but the reality is, I have nowhere to run to. I glance back over my shoulder at Knox's house and wonder if he's spying on me through one of the windows, then I sigh and walk toward the playground.

There's no one here, so I sit on one of the blue swings and push off with my feet. For a long time, I sit, swinging back and forth, leaning back with my eyes focused only on the sky above.

"Hey, haven't seen you around before," a guy's voice says as I plant my feet in the sand to stop the swing. He looks me up and down, then nods toward me. "You new here?"

"Nope. What do you want?" I ask.

He grips the chain of the swing with one hand, so I stand and step back. "Don't even think about running," he warns.

I scan the area, there's no one around. "Who are you?"

"Twelve wants to see you."

My throat goes dry and I swallow hard. "Who?" I ask, feigning confusion.

"Follow me," he says. "He said if you run, he'll catch you."

Fuck! I take one last look back at Knox's house, hoping he is watching, but it's useless now anyway. What Adam wants, he gets.

I follow the guy toward the path that cuts into the forest. For ten minutes we walk until the sunset begins to fade and the only light comes from between the branches of the giant pine trees.

From behind a tree, Adam steps out, and fear seeps into my bones.

"Annastasia, my sweet girl, come."

Disobeying is not an option, I'm in enough trouble already. This punishment will be the worst by far. "Where have you been?" he asks.

"The angel took me. I couldn't get out until now." The lie comes so easily I surprise myself, but I'm positive he knows.

He cups my cheek and rubs his thumb across my lips, then drops his eyes to my clothes. "He bought you these?"

I nod but remain silent. *Mistake number one.*

His hand smacks my cheek and knocks me off balance, but I regain my footing and clasp my hands behind my back, then drop my head.

He lifts my chin so I'm looking into his eyes. As he paces back and forth in front of me, he says, "Take it all off."

Am I supposed to call him Twelve, or Adam? *Think, Annie... Think!* "Yes... A—Twelve." I strip down to my underwear and wait.

When he grabs my hand, he glares at the bangles as though they are another part of me he despises. He pulls them off my wrist and throws them over his shoulder. "Now, your punishment." He flicks my hair off my shoulder and cocks his head. "You running away with the angel—That actually worked well for me. Do you know why?"

"No, Twelve."

His sinister smirk tells me he has a plan, one that will likely end with me beaten and bleeding. "See, Annastasia, the thing about these angels, they're a little like me. When they want something, they don't give up." He grips my arm and leans in close to my ear. "I know you're lying to me. You think I don't have people watching you... following your *every* move?" Before I can reply, he steps back and runs a hand through his dark hair. "So... punishment. We're going to fight. Of course, you're going to lose, but don't worry, baby, I'll let you live—for now."

"Yes, Twelve."

He raises his brow. "Then Eleven here, he's going to rush you to hospital, and when the angel arrives, well, this time he won't get away."

He's using me again. Using me to lure Knox, to capture him. I can't let that happen. I can't let their lives be destroyed because of me.

Without warning, Adam swings a punch that knocks me off my feet and sends me to the ground. I get to my hands and knees and shake my head hard, but when his boot hits my ribs, I'm thrown back again. *Fuck, I need to get up.*

"Oh sorry, baby, I forgot to tell you, we start now." He comes toward me, but I quickly roll over and spring to my feet. The slight tingle of pain coursing through my body gives me renewed strength and a reason to fight. He stops in his tracks, his eyes fixed firmly on mine. The problem with fighting Adam is, he was my teacher, so he knows what my next move will be. It's been drummed into me since I was eight years old.

I can change. Instead of spinning and attempting to kick him, I steady my feet and wait until he moves closer, then I swing a punch and to my utter shock it connects with his cheekbone. For a split second he stares at me as though he's as shocked as I am. But when he blinks, pure rage takes over.

He charges at me, wrapping an arm around my waist and throwing me down onto the ground.

The air is sucked out of my lungs and I choke on each breath as I struggle beneath him.

His fist slams into my face again, and again, and again until... my mouth fills with blood, my eyes are swollen, and my ears are ringing.

When he moves to stand, he laughs wildly. "Feel anything yet, baby?"

I shake my head, unable to speak, and as he leans down to me, I lift my legs and push my feet hard into his crotch.

He groans and curses as he straightens, and I roll onto my side, gasping for air.

With a handful of my hair in his hand, he drags me toward a tree and lifts me off my feet. "Well, well, have you been practicing, Annastasia?"

I shake my head slightly and when I do, a mild twinge of pain courses down my spine. I wriggle my fingers then clench my fists, ready to push him back, but he pushes me hard against the tree trunk, and with one swing of his fist, everything goes black.

XIII

RUNAWAY

KNOX

four hours later

She's fucking gone. I knew this would happen. I knew if I let her out of my sight, she'd disappear. I don't know if she ran, or if that bastard found her. *Fucking hell.* After calling Clay to come help me find her, I pace my kitchen. I should have spoken to her instead of being a fucking pussy and sending her a goddamn text message.

"Did she say anything before she left?" he asks.

I scrub my hands down my face while I pace the kitchen. "She said she wanted to be alone, that's all. She was going to the lake."

"Right, so we start there... Maybe she's pissed off, man, you kind of have that effect on people." Clay laughs, but when I glare at him, he rolls his eyes and walks out the front door.

I already called her from the playground, but after ten minutes, I gave up and assumed she'd wander back before it got dark. Then again, she wouldn't be afraid, she doesn't show fear, or pain. There's determination in every word she speaks, in every look, and every breath.

But the second I kissed her full pink lips, she came completely undone. Like putty in my hands, she moulded her body to mine until there was no space between us. Her quiet moans of pleasure only fuelled my desire. I couldn't stop. I'd never wanted so desperately in all my life. I can't give her up now, no matter what happens, I will make her mine.

Clay grabs the chain of the swing and kicks his boot into the sand beneath it. "You think she'd go into the forest?"

I shrug and sigh. "Honestly, brother, I don't know shit about her."

"So... you're telling me she just walked out, for no reason." He cocks his head, eyes narrowed as he looks at me sceptically.

I drop my head back and sigh. "I may have kissed her..." I mutter under my breath.

Clay's brows knit in confusion. "You kissed her? She's seventeen... she's—" He shakes his head then lowers his voice. "You didn't hurt her?"

I rub my hand across the back of my neck. *Fuck no. Or did I?* "She's almost eighteen. And no, I didn't hurt her... at least I don't think I did."

Clay turns and walks toward the path that leads through the forest. "What aren't you telling me, Knox, and don't say nothing."

I follow him as we continue toward the lookout at the top of the hill. From here, we can see the lake and the playground lit up by solar lights. I kick the trash can that's bolted to the concrete. "Fuck this! It's too fucking dark to see anything now."

He leans against the steel barrier, his arms crossed over his chest. "Knox, tell me."

Damn. I hate the way he can read me better than I can read myself. "She came here with Roman's brother. They lived together. Her, the old man, and that fucking psychopath." I pace back and forth, scrubbing my hands down my face. "She was with them for ten years."

"Fuck!" Clay shouts. "She's related... or with him?"

I shake my head hard. "No... she was trapped."

"For ten years?" His tone tells me he doesn't believe me. "Look, we can discuss this later. Try calling her again. And make sure you suck up this time."

We walk slowly back down the path as I text Annie. There's no reply. Then I try calling her.

Clay stops in his tracks. "Shhh... you hear that?"

I stop and listen, and a second later, I hear it. Annie's phone. I race toward the sound, searching the dry ground for any sign of her, or her phone, but my head's a mess and rage is winning. My muscles are tense and heat spreads through every fibre of my body, igniting my curse and setting fire to my already smouldering soul.

"Here!" Clay shouts.

When I reach him, I snatch Annie's phone from his hand and shove it into my pocket. I crack my neck and clamp my eyes shut, willing myself to remain calm. For her.

"Ah fuck, Knox..." Clay scrubs his hands over his face.

I spin around and when my eyes lock onto the pile of clothes at Clay's feet I lose control. Chaos reigns, tearing me up from the inside, enveloping me in a cyclone of rage. I swing a punch, cracking the trunk of the nearest tree before I extend my wings and take to the sky.

Knox, fucking hell. Get back down here before someone sees you.

Ignoring Clay, I fly above the clouds until I release a guttural roar of anger. Clouds clash together and the sky splits with a bolt of lightning, then rain. Heavy, unrelenting rain that pours down, drenching me. I fly toward the ground at full speed, hoping the impact will bring a sliver of relief.

When my feet hit the ground, another crack of thunder spreads across the ebony sky as a surge of pain spreads from my feet to my heart. *Must find her.*

Clay takes a step forward. "You won't be any help to her like this..."

As my vision blurs with a haze of red, Haydee appears beside me. "Do it, show him what you're capable of."

The last thing I hear is Clay sighing before my fist slams into his jaw.

He leaps forward, swinging a punch that throws my head back. When he steps back, I lunge for him, knocking him to the ground where I punch him again. Another punch misses him, and I hit the ground instead as Clay rolls from under me and leaps to his feet.

I fly up, my wings spread and my muscles bulging.

"Do it," Haydee shouts.

I land on the ground behind Clay, and as he spins around, I spin and land a kick to his ribs that sends him flying backwards into a tree.

A second later, Flynn and Steel appear between us.

"Aww... three on one," Haydee whines. "That's not fair guys."

I crack my neck again and shake out my arms before I lunge at Steel, but he's up faster than I can blink, and as he swings a punch that cracks my jaw, Flynn steps between us. One hand on Steel's chest, the other on mine. Between us, Flynn's power seeps through and forces its way into my heart.

"You don't stop this, Knox, you won't see Annie again," Flynn warns.

I shake my head hard. "Annie." The only word that leaves my mouth.

Behind me, there's another sigh. "No fair, that's cheating, Flynn," Haydee says. "You suck!"

When Flynn drops his hands, he steps back, ignoring Haydee. His focus only on me. "Right, I'm going home.

Roman should be back by midnight, he still has a few contacts in the Fray, if she's there, we'll figure out a way to get her out."

I clench my fists, focusing on each breath. I don't need—or want—that bastards help.

"Clay," Steel says, "go with Knox. Check the hospital."

Flynn and Steel walk away and Clay pats my back before he heads down the path. "Brother, you're gonna lose your wings if you're not careful."

I don't reply. I'd rather die than lose my wings. But Clay's right. I've fucked up so many times I'm lucky I've made it this far with them. One day, my luck *will* run out.

We arrive at the hospital just after ten and head in through the emergency room entrance. I stand by the wall, flicking my pocket knife open and closed and running my finger along the sharp edge of the blade.

Haydee sniffs the air a few times, then pinches her nose. "It stinks in here, I'll be outside." I don't reply as she walks out, moaning about "mortals and their disgusting stench".

Clay comes back from the counter and tells me a young girl was brought in a few hours ago, but the nurse can't let us through unless we're family. He gets on the phone to Doctor Charles, and five minutes later, we're following him into the Recovery Room.

"You saw her?" I ask him.

"No. I just checked when Clay called. It's definitely her... through here," he says as he opens the double doors.

As soon as we step inside, Clay grips my forearm with a death grip. *Don't. They'll kick us out, and you'll end up in the cell.*

"Annie." Her name on my lips brings a sense of calm. I focus on that. On her name, her scent, and the memory I have of her lips on mine. Those sweet, soft lips that didn't leave mine for a second as she moved against the length of my cock. *Need her... desperately.*

Doctor Charles gasps when he gets closer, then he checks her notes and goes around checking the machines. "Doctor Viceroy has been looking after her," he says. "Do you want me to take over?"

I only nod. Her face is beat to shit. There's not one spot of clean flesh. Her eyes are swollen shut and deep, dark bruises cover her cheeks and jaw. My eyes follow the curve of her neck where there are more bruises, and then her arms. I take a step forward and reach out to take her hand but when I remember her rules, I drop it by my side.

"Who brought her in?" Clay asks Doctor Charles.

He flicks through her notes, then stops. "What the hell?" he says.

Clay looks down at the notes in Doctor Charles' hands. "I'll fucking kill that bastard." He turns to me. "Knox, I think they set this up..."

"Who was it?"

"Harley."

"Fuck!" Roman's brother did this to her, I know it. "Call Flynn, let him know."

Clay nods and makes the call while I stare down at Annie. "She's not going to di—" I can't even say the words.

Doctor Charles presses a button on the machine by the bed. "Nope. She's strong, there are no major injuries. The broken rib... it's obviously not going to heal for a while now."

When the other doctor walks in, he talks quietly to Doctor Charles before handing him a clipboard and leaving again. "I'll stay here. There's nothing you can do now, Knox, not until she wakes up."

Again, I reach out to touch her, but again, I pull my hand back. *It has to be her choice.* "Call me the second she wakes up."

XIV
THE SWEETEST CRAVING
KNOX

When I walk through the doors of Luxuria, Kitty looks up from the front desk. "Hey, Knox, how are you?"

"I'm good, is Char in?"

She shakes her head and leans on the desk almost bursting out of her black corset as she gives me more than an eyeful of her perky breasts. "She's with a client. I'm free though..." She gives me a wink then licks her lips.

I shake my head and attempt to hide my smirk. It's no secret Kitty's wanted me since the day I offered her the position here at Luxuria. Before that, she was living day by day, selling her body to the highest bidder. Beneath her sassy attitude and her mask of indifference, there's a gorgeous woman who craves nothing more than to be wanted... to be needed. Here, she's protected from the filthy bastards on the street who want more than what she's willing to offer. Here she is safe.

Surprisingly, hiring Kitty was Autumn's idea. She said it was her way of "compensating" Kitty since she'd never have Flynn again. That woman deserves a goddamn medal for the shit my brothers and I have put her through since she came into our lives.

Kitty places a gentle hand on my arm. "You know this thing about you not doing it with anyone who's been with Flynn, it's kinda stupid."

I go around the other side of the desk and scroll through the appointment list on the computer. "It's my rule," I remind her.

A heavy sigh is followed by her rubbing my arm. "Ugh, bro codes are stupid. Fine, I'll stop." She leans in front of me and clicks on the vacancy list. "She's here," Kitty says, pointing to the name on the screen.

"No problems?" I ask.

"Everything's been great. Are you coming back soon?"

"Yeah, soon. I'll see you later."

"Bye," she says as I walk down the corridor. Then there's a too loud whisper, "If you ever change your mind, you know where to find me."

I laugh as I head to the room, wondering if I should turn around and leave. Annie's not my girlfriend, far from it. And besides, she's too young for me. But why do I feel like this is wrong?

Haydee's voice appears beside me. "You know... you can go in there and *not* put your cock in her."

I glare at her as I knock on the door. "I'm not fucking anyone."

When it opens, her eyes light up and she smiles. "Hey, you're back. Do I have a client?"

"No. Actually, I came to see you."

The long waves of her brown hair tumble over her bare shoulders as she tilts her head and scrunches her nose. "Oh..." Blue eyes alight when she realises. "Oh, you came to *see me*." She laughs. "Sorry, come on in."

Haydee stands beside me.

You can leave, I say in her head.

She shakes her head. "No way, I wanna watch. I like this one. She's sooo much prettier than Charlotte."

Fuck off, Haydee, is the last thing she hears before I close my mind to her.

"Same as usual?" Katie asks as she hands me a glass of whiskey.

I drink it down in one go and place the glass on the timber side table. "No sex."

She puts her glass down and goes to the wall where an assortment of ropes, chains, whips and belts hang. "Ropes or chains?" she asks.

"Chains."

I walk over and pull off my shirt before I take the leather cuffs from the drawer and begin fastening them to my wrists while Katie attaches the chains to the silver bar that hangs from the ceiling. When the cuffs are on, and the chains are attached, I crack my neck and clamp my eyes shut. I can do this... without the sex. It's not a big deal.

When I open my eyes, Haydee is nowhere to be seen, but it doesn't mean she's not watching.

Katie peels off her satin robe and hangs it on the back of the door before she dims the lights. She stands in front of me wearing black leather lingerie and a harness that's attached to her leather choker; a silver O-ring sits snug at her throat. She's gorgeous, and I've been with her more than a few times, not only here, but for work events as well.

With the whip in her hand, Katie paces around me. The anticipation and the warmth in the room is already causing sweat to bead on my forehead. When the soft leather whip glides over my shoulder, I suck in a breath, waiting for the pain... and the release I need.

The whip cuts through the air and hits my back, sending a shiver down my spine. Then another whip, and another. When she stops, her breathing is slow and steady. She walks around to face me again, not saying a word as she tilts her head and smiles. Her red lips full and pouty, remind me of the last time I was here with her. *I could have her again...*

She reaches up and traces her finger around my nipple causing it to tighten which brings a surge of pleasure as the thick silver bar of my nipple ring is tugged on. I suck in another breath and I let my head fall back as she moves to the other nipple. A few seconds later, she's behind me and the whip glides over my back gently—I hate it. I hate the anticipation; the need that drives me to beg for more. I clench my teeth, determined not to ask for it, but she knows me too well. She knows how to make me wait, how to make me beg, and how to make me crave.

Crave! Crave will work. I won't have to *do* anything with her. It won't be real; it will all be a vivid hallucination. A memory that will linger as long as I allow it to.

As the thought plays over in my mind, the crack of the whip causes beads of sweat to drip down my brow. After another crack, I groan out loud.

"Hmmm," Katie whispers as she stands in front of me. She glances down to where my cock is throbbing against my jeans. "You're awfully quiet tonight." She closes the gap between us and glides her tongue down my chest before she unbuttons my jeans. "Let's get you a little more... comfortable."

I open my mouth to speak, but I can't do it. This was a mistake, and I can't tell her to stop, but I can't continue without wanting more. *Oh, fuck!* If my jeans come off, I won't be able to stop myself.

"Crave..." is the only word that escapes my lips.

Katie smiles and raises her brow. "Really? You're sure?"

I nod.

"You want me to unchain you?"

"No. No don't. Don't unchain me, not until it wears off."

A flirtatious smile dances across her lips. "Ohh..." Her fingertip runs along my lips. "You're not losing control are you, Knox?" She raises her brow.

Fuck it, she knows I'm desperate.

She runs her long fingernails down my chest, stopping at the top of my jeans. "This is about the girl you're watching, isn't it?"

Each breath I take is heavier than the last, my mind is losing the battle, and my body is already aching for her touch. The touch I know will set my nerve endings ablaze and ignite the inferno that's brewing beneath my flesh.

With her hands flat on my chest, she whispers again, "You sure you don't want me? You know I can do it all for you, right here in *real life*. I can give you what you need, and more."

"Can't..." I say. "Fuck. Give me..." I shake my head hard. *No. Focus!* "I—" My words die on my lips when she tugs on my nipple rings. I groan, my hips involuntarily rock toward her.

"Okay. Crave it is." She stands on her toes and kisses my cheek before she goes to the wall safe and takes out a small bag of Crave pills.

"Water?" she asks.

I shake my head.

"Knox..." She pushes the small black pill into my mouth. "I know what you love."

I swallow the pill. "No," I say before I end up begging her to fuck me.

Her hand glides down my chest, then further down until she presses her palm against my throbbing cock and rubs it, but seconds later, I'm finally torn away from reality.

In the middle of a king size bed, I'm lying naked on my back, my wrists and ankles cuffed and chained to the bedposts. The room is warm and the lingering scent of vanilla hovers in the air as the scented candles create a soothing glow.

"Are you ready for me?" The silence is broken when I hear her soft voice. No! It's supposed to be Katie, not her. I clamp my eyes shut, searching for Katie's face, her scent, her voice. She's not here and I'm stuck inside my own hallucination with the female I want more than life itself.

It's not real... I open my eyes and focus on the smooth lines of her flawless body. Long ebony hair reaches her slim waist. She is perfection.

She stares down at me, her eyes raking over my body before they stop on my cock. There's no way to hide my erection, and I don't care. I want her to know what she does to me.

Hallucination.
Reality.
Dream.

I don't care what it is. Right now, she is mine, and I will savour every moment I have with her.

As Annie climbs onto the bed, I'm overwhelmed with desperation. I need to touch her, taste her... feel her body beneath mine.

I tug on the chains binding my wrists to the bedposts.

"Ah, ah," she scolds before she slides her hand down to my abs and traces her fingers up and down my cock. I buck my hips as she continues, her deep brown eyes alight with sexual desire.

I suck in a breath, determined to endure the hedonic thrill of her for as long as possible.

Annie shuffles closer, then she leans down; long silken strands of hair brush over my shoulders as her lips meet mine in a rapturous kiss. Her tongue swipes across mine and I attempt to raise my head to kiss her harder, but she continues with torturous soft strokes of her tongue, and gentle kisses across my lips and jaw. "Do you like this?" she whispers.

"Love... Fucking love this."

Her hand slides up to my chest and she stops at my nipple ring, circling her finger around it. It's all too soft. Too much... Sooo much need. She is an aphrodisiac to my tainted soul, an obsession I crave and cannot turn away from. I am addicted, to her.

She presses another kiss beside my lips. I move my head slightly, chasing the taste of her mouth on mine. She continues to trail kisses down my neck, and across my chest. She flicks her tongue over my nipple, swirling around the nipple ring before she tugs on it with her teeth.

"Harder," I beg through a groan of frustration and pleasure combined.

"Not yet." Her voice is laced in lust. "I'm going to make you beg for it."

Fucking hell. "Baby, I'm begging. Please...fuck me."

She giggles as she tugs on one nipple ring while her tongue swirls around the other. Slowly, she makes her way down my body, peppering kisses down to my abs. When she turns slightly and takes my cock in her hand, I catch a glimpse of her perfect ass and I tug on the chains again.

As Annie's lips touch my cock, I buck my hips. Carnal desire takes hold when her tongue flicks back and forth over the thick silver ring pierced through my cock. Finally, she goes down on me, all the way down, her tongue still swirling around my cock, her hand moving up and down, a slow, sensual rhythm I can't handle.

She whispers, "More?"

I beg, "Yes. God, please. More. Harder. Faster."

As Annie sucks my cock, she moans in pleasure, one hand gripping my length, the other gliding up and down my thigh. She circles her tongue around my piercing again, sending bolts of pleasure into my core. But it's not enough. It will never be enough, not like this. It's still too soft... I need more.

With long strokes, Annie continues to glide up and down the length of my cock. I can't hold still, I need to touch her, want to touch her. "Annie... fuuuck... Baby, I need you."

She turns to look at me, her full lips parted, and her eyes locked on mine. "More?"

"Unchain me."

She smiles and raises her brow. "Oh, sorry, I can't do that... not yet, handsome."

"Please. Please, baby, I need to touch you."

"Shhh..." she whispers before she lifts one leg and straddles my chest. Fuck, her ass... her pussy, she's so close I can't breathe without the heady scent of her arousal beckoning. She's awakened a part of me I believed would lie dormant forever. A part of me that will fall to my knees and worship her for the goddess she is.

For torturous minutes she sucks my cock, her ass closer to my lips with each sensual movement she makes. When I finally feel the sweet, decadent softness of her flesh against my lips, I swipe my tongue along her pussy, once, twice, again. Will die without her.

She moves off me and I growl in frustration as she kneels beside me on the bed. "Come back," I beg.

Annie straddles my thighs then moves forward, her pussy, so wet, so warm, glides along my length, back and forth she moves while she runs her fingers up and down my torso. She's naked. Naked, and so fucking perfect.

Again, I buck my hips, desperate to be inside her. Drowning in the exquisite ecstasy of her delicious scent and her quiet moans.

"Baby, please... I need to touch you. It's killing me."

She leans down slowly, her hair falls in waves over her shoulders and tickles my chest.

She presses her lips to mine as she moves forward and reaches down between us to grip my cock in her hand. I suck in a breath, holding it in while she rubs me against her pussy, seconds later, she slides down onto me. My cock instantly enveloped in her tight, wet pussy.

"Fuuuuck," I groan against her lips, thrusting my hips toward her harder, faster. But she stops and sits up on her knees, leaving my cock straining to be inside her again.

"Slow," she whispers.

I shake my head. "Can't. Too hard, so hard..."

She slides her hands up my arms, stopping at the cuffs. She smiles and I expect her to release my wrists, but she shakes her head a little and presses a kiss to my lips as she lowers herself down onto my cock again.

I tug on the chains as a rush of adrenaline courses through my veins. When I pull my leg back, the chain snaps, then the other one. As Annie moves on me, her pussy throbs around my cock and her kiss deepens until she's moving faster, moaning into my mouth. "Knox, oh fuck, I need you..."

Fuck it. I can't do this. I yank on the chain, freeing one arm. My hand goes straight to her ass and she releases a little squeal of delight. Another yank on the other chain, and I'm free.

I grip her ass with both hands and thrust into her, hard, deep, fast.

"Yes," she moans. "Please, I want more."

I flip us over so she's beneath me. "I've got you, baby. I'll give you what you need."

I rest on my elbows as my hips slam into hers, every breath, every heartbeat, every moan she has, now belongs to me. When I grip the bedhead, I move faster, spurred on by her reactions, her pleas and her panting breaths.

A rush of pure pleasure is followed by white-hot heat that explodes between us, and still, it's not enough. My appetite for her will never be sated. I pull out of her and she pouts.

"Noooo, don't stop now."

"I'm not done with you yet."

She rolls onto her stomach then gets to her hands and knees, her perfect ass grinds against my cock. I drop one *hand down and rub my fingers over her clit, and when I push two fingers inside her, she moans my name.*

I fist my cock, pumping it hard and fast before I position it at her entrance. She pushes back, but I hold her in place, one hand on her hip, the other guiding my cock into her slick, wet pussy.

Breathtaking screams of ecstasy fill the room as our bodies slam together in furious passion.

This moment can never end.

But it has to. This is a mistake.

When the Crave wears off, all I will have is the memory of her body, her scent, and her moans of pleasure. And nothing will stop me from claiming her.

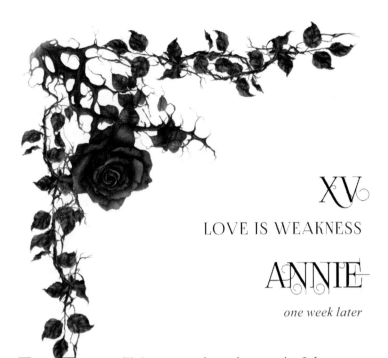

XV

LOVE IS WEAKNESS

ANNIE

one week later

My eyes flicker open, then close again. It happens for a long time, minutes, hours, I don't know. Nothing makes sense and everything is blurry. I clench my fists and press my nails into my palm. I can feel it, which means... I'm alive. *Fuck.*

If I'm alive, he's coming back.

The room is dark apart from the dim glow of a lamp I can see without having to move my head. I wriggle my toes, no pain there. I suck in a breath and hold it for a few seconds. Broken rib. Yep, I'm definitely alive. When I exhale, I lift my hand and blink again. There's no blood, but there is a pattern of bruises across my knuckles, along with a few new scars that are still healing, and they're a little swollen.

"Feel anything yet?"

I try to force a smile as I remember Adam's words, but my lips are dry and cracked, and I taste blood in my mouth. He always hated that about me. Hated the fact that I became so used to his beatings and torture that I no longer flinched when he whipped me. I didn't cry when he cut me or punished me. Everything he did was to get a reaction, and when I stopped reacting, he changed his tactics. I only have myself to blame.

I shut my eyes and focus on his words.

"You think I don't have people watching you... following your every move?"

I need to get out of here and find somewhere safe, away from Knox and his brothers, away from this town. I extend my arms, holding them up to check for any injuries. I move my legs and turn my head slightly. A mild twinge of pain courses through my veins. Ignoring it, I push myself up on my elbows and look around the room. It's small; just the bed I'm lying in and a door that leads to a bathroom. I shove the blanket off and sit slowly before I drop my feet off the edge of the bed.

My head spins for a full minute as I try to focus. *How long have I been here?*

After dropping my feet to the floor, I pace slowly toward the bathroom dressed only in a hospital gown. No fucking bra again. *Damn this place.* When I make it to the bathroom, I pull on the door and go inside. A small mirror hangs on the wall above the sink, and when I catch a glimpse of my reflection, I almost vomit.

This is new. My face has never looked this bad. Usually, he keeps all his hits and kicks below my shoulders. He figured out quickly it was harder to lure unsuspecting women when it appeared as though I was a rebellious teenager who wanted to fight.

Then there were the men who'd pay to come to our house and fight me. Adam would stand in my bathroom and watch while I showered and dressed. He'd watch me do my hair, then check to ensure it was perfect. On the way down to the fighting ring in the huge cellar, he'd remind me I had to win, and that if I won, I would be rewarded.

Training was my reward. And when I trained, I had Adam's undivided attention. That alone gave me the strength and determination to win every fight.

Until I ruined it for myself.

Annie
15 years old

My feet were fixed firmly on the mat, my fists raised. The fighting stance. I'd been holding the position—and the weights in my hands—for almost five full minutes when Adam stood in front of me. He gave my biceps a squeeze, then continued walking around me, counting down the seconds.

When he stopped, he nodded once, and I placed the weights on the floor before we ran through my kicks. I raised my leg, standing in the position he'd taught me. My balance was perfect, as always.

My eyes focused on him. Watching him as he held my foot and lifted it above my shoulder height. When I began to wobble on my other foot, he lowered it slightly.

"Continue training. I need you to go higher than this."

"Yes, Adam," I said.

For the next hour I used the jump rope, the treadmill, and the boxing bag. He watched me like a hawk, his eyes following every move I made until he commanded me to stop.

I dropped my feet to the floor and bowed slightly, but he didn't move. He stood for a second, staring at me as though he was caught in a trance. His eyes were fixed on mine and when I lifted my hand to scratch my head, he didn't scold me, but I didn't want to push my luck, so I dropped my hand and remained still.

"Adam?" I said his name softly, hoping he wouldn't mind.

He shook his head and blinked a few times. "Annastasia?"

I swallowed down the hard lump in my throat, then, I did the most stupid thing I'd ever done in my life. I leaned forward and kissed Adam's cheek.

His eyes darkened immediately, and he grabbed my wrist in his hand. "What the fuck are you doing?"

"I—I'm sorry... I don't know." It was the truth. In that moment, I had no idea why I kissed him, or what came over me. But his reaction told me I would regret it.

"Sorry. I'm sorry, Adam," I said again before I dropped my head.

"Do not touch me. You think I love you or something?" he shouted.

I shook my head hard. "No, Adam."

He turned his back to me, and I braced myself for the impact I knew was coming. He spun and kicked me in the stomach, sending me flailing backwards where I landed on the mat. "You think I'm fucking weak?" he roared.

"No, Adam. No, you're not weak." I scrambled to my feet and stood again.

He stood in front of me, his brow creased, and his fists clenched. "Love is weakness, Annastasia. I am not weak. You will not be weak. I will never love you. Remember that."

"Yes, Adam."

"And Annastasia..."—he paused and leaned in close to my ear—"no one will ever have you. You are mine."

"I'm yours, Adam."

I can't get Adam out of my head or off my mind. *Go back to him.* A voice in my head tells me I need him, but in my heart, I feel something else. An ache, or a pull, something that draws me to Knox. With a heavy sigh, I turn on the taps and let the warm water run over my hands. Glancing at my wrist, I think about the bangles Lexi gave me, I'm pissed off Adam threw them away. *Ugh. That asshole!*

Once I've peed and washed my hands and face, I walk toward the small window beside the door that looks out of the room. There's a guy pacing and talking on his phone, but I can't see anyone else. I'm about to step back when the guy turns, and my knees grow weak. *It's him.*

I need to hide. Does he know I'm in here? Maybe he's come back to finish me off. I spin around, but there's nowhere to hide other than the bathroom, so I run there and close the door, locking it behind me before I sink down to the floor and pray he doesn't come into the room.

XVI

BORN TO DIE?

ROMAN

I pace the hospital waiting room with my phone to my ear, waiting for Flynn to answer. But he doesn't pick up. *Fuck it!* I try again, and again, no answer. I drop down into the plastic chair and clamp my eyes shut. Somehow, I'll figure out this mind talking bullshit.

Flynn, call me, it's urgent.

A few minutes later, my mobile phone starts ringing, and I answer it.

"Fucking hell, I've been trying to call you."

"Man, you know I have kids now, right? Those tiny things that need attention twenty-four-seven—"

I cut him off, "Something's wrong with Kailey, we're at the hospital. Can you..." I lower my voice to a whisper, "Can you fix it?"

In the background, a baby screams and Autumn whines, "Flynn, keep your voice down."

"Tell her I'm sorry..." I say.

"It's all good. I'll be there in ten. Who's the doctor?"

"Doctor Charles. He was already in the ER when we arrived."

I shove my phone into my pocket and go back to the small room where Doctor Charles is attaching straps to Kailey's swollen belly. She reaches out to me and I take her hand and kiss her fingertips. "What's all this, Doc?" I ask.

"I'm going to do some monitoring. This..." he says as he tightens elastic straps over her belly, "is to hold the monitoring devices. They're going to check the baby's heartbeat, and Kaylie's contractions. Then we'll know if she's in any distress."

Distress? No, she's going to be fine. "And you can fix it... whatever it is?"

He presses some buttons on the machine and pulls out a sheet of paper, then steps back. "Well, we need to know what's going on first. I've got a few patients to check on, I'll be back in about an hour."

With a frustrated sigh, I sit on the bed beside Kailey and lean down to kiss her lips. "I called Flynn, he's on his way, babe."

She nods but tears well in her eyes. "Roman, I'm scared. I never thought I would love her this much, and she's not even born yet... what—what if we lose her?" She sobs into her hands and I lay beside her and stroke her hair.

"Baby, it's okay. I'm scared too—actually, I'm fucking terrified, but we can do this. She'll be fine, I know it."

She lifts her head and rests it on my shoulder as she laces her fingers through mine. "If I wasn't a half blood, this wouldn't have happened." She closes her eyes and lets her tears fall.

Cupping her cheek, I turn her head to face me again. "You're perfect, Kay." I press another kiss to her lips. This time she kisses me back as she runs her fingers through my hair and moans against my lips. "I love you so much, Kay."

"Do you two ever stop?" Flynn says.

I smile against Kailey's lips, then kiss her gently before I stand. "Hey, thanks for coming, and sorry about calling."

He waves a hand in the air. "Forget about it. What happened anyway?"

He sits on the chair beside the bed. "We were leaving Gluttony and when we got to the car, Kailey had a few cramps. We thought it was normal, like Doctor Charles said, but they didn't stop. I brought her to the ER. They said it could be preterm labour."

"It's too early, Flynn," Kailey cries. "Can you check her? Or ask the angels to check her? Please, I'll do anything. I don't want to lose her."

I squeeze Kailey's hand, hoping Flynn can do something.

He places a hand on Kailey's belly and the monitor beeps a few times. Flynn closes his eyes and for a minute, he's completely silent. When he opens them, he sighs and shakes his head. "I can't see anything... because she's not an angel. I'm sorry."

I shove my hands through my hair in frustration. If Flynn can't fix this, what hope have we got? Hope! The angel, she said she knew all there was to know. "The angels, can't they check what's wrong and tell Doctor Charles?"

Flynn stands. "It doesn't work like that, Roman. Angels can see, hear, and heal angels and humans, but when it comes to other immortal races, our powers are limited. Especially with harpies, it's rare for them to get pregnant at all. Let's wait for Doctor Charles and see what he says."

Sighing, I sit beside Kailey and hold her hand while we wait.

Doctor Charles' one hour turned into two hours, then three, and finally he arrived. Flynn stood and shook his hand, then I did the same as I watched him remove the paper from the machine. He looked down at it, then went back and forth to the computer before he scratched his chin.

"Let's do an ultrasound," he said. "The contractions are regular, but given Kailey's high pain tolerance, I think it's safe to say she's in active labour... But—"

I cut him off, "But what?"

"Baby's heartbeat has dipped quite a few times, and it's still a little too early for delivery." He lowers his voice to a whisper. "Even for an immortal baby."

Kailey's lip quivers as she takes in Doctor Charles' words.

I'm speechless. I've lost so much in my life. I've seen death, caused death, and lived on the edge without a care. But right now, I would give my life for the daughter I am yet to know.

As Doctor Charles moves the ultrasound probe over Kailey's belly, he flicks a switch on the computer and a quiet noise fills the room.

Kailey gasps. "It's her heartbeat!"

Doctor Charles nods, and I smile. *She's alive. Everything will be fine.*

He continues moving the probe slowly while watching the screen on the computer.

"Right there, Roman, that's your daughter." Kailey squeezes my hand and lets out a squeal of delight. I stare at the small screen where an image of my daughter appears.

Inside her chest, her tiny heart is fluttering. "She's okay then?" I ask him.

"Well, she's measuring smaller than I'd expect..." He hesitates and stops moving the probe. The sound of our daughter's heartbeat disappears, and the fluttering beat of her heart on the screen, is no longer visible. *Don't panic.* He knows what he's doing.

"So, she's going to be small?" Kailey asks. "That doesn't matter does it?"

"It's—" He stops suddenly and leans forward, closer to the screen.

Kailey gasps, then she cries out in pain, and I panic. "What the hell is happening?" I shout.

Doctor Charles drops the ultrasound probe and pulls the straps and monitors off Kailey's belly. "Kailey, I'm sorry, sweetheart, but we need to get her out, she's in distress."

I swallow the bile rising in my throat as Kailey screams, "NO! Roman, no... don't let her die."

Doctor Charles rushes to the door and calls for a nurse, and when I look up at Flynn, he's looking down at Kailey with his head cocked. "What?" I ask him, knowing he's talking in her mind.

He shakes his head. "She'll be okay," he says. "Want me to wait outside?"

I shake my head hard. Fuck that. I have no idea what I'm doing.

A nurse rushes in with a small plastic box that sits on top of a trolley. Inside, there's a tiny mattress, and on the outside, thin tubes are connected to a machine on the bottom of the trolley.

"What the fuck is that? And what's going on?" I ask panicking.

As he works to raise the bed Kailey's on, he speaks quickly. "The cord is caught around her neck; we need to get her out... now. Okay, Kailey, when you feel the next contraction, I want you to push. If we don't get her out quickly, we'll need to do a caesarean."

She nods and squeezes my hand. "I'll do it, please save her, Doctor Charles." Less than five seconds later, she's pushing. Flynn holds her other hand, reminding her to breathe, and each time he says it, I take a breath too.

"Another push," Doctor Charles says. "Well done, Kailey." He calls out to the nurse. "Get the humidicrib ready, and we'll need oxygen."

After another push, our baby's head appears, and I stare in complete and utter shock.

"One more push, and she'll be out," Doctor Charles says. The relief in his voice is obvious.

Kailey sobs before she takes a deep breath and grips my hand. I lean down and whisper against her ear, "You can do it. I love you, Kailey." I wipe her hair off her sweaty brow. "Just one more push, babe and we'll get to see her." She pushes again and as she does, our baby daughter is born. The umbilical cord wrapped tight around her neck, and her tiny face is a horrible shade of mottled purple and blue.

I hold my breath, determined not to breathe until I know she's okay. Beside me Kailey cries as we watch Doctor Charles tuck his finger under the cord and remove it from her neck. She doesn't make a sound, and her tiny body isn't moving.

"Roman!" Flynn shouts. "Fucking breathe."

I look up at him and shake my head as I exhale. *Breathe. She needs you to be strong.*

I give him a quick nod and press a hard kiss to Kailey's lips. "I love you, baby. She's going to be okay. She is."

I let go of Kailey's hand and stand over the plastic crib where Doctor Charles and the nurse are frantically trying to get our daughter to breathe. A tiny oxygen mask covers her mouth and nose, and as Doctor Charles rubs her chest, he begs her to breathe.

But she doesn't.
She remains still.
Quiet.
Blue.

As my entire world crumbles around me, each second passes as though it's lasting an hour. Nothing makes sense, and in the silence of the small room, all I hear is the puffs of the oxygen machine, Kailey's quiet cries, and the sound of my own broken heart beating.

Without asking for permission, I reach out to touch her tiny hand, and when I do, I know without any doubt, I will die for her. "What's taking so long?" I ask Doctor Charles.

He doesn't answer me, instead, he turns his attention to the nurse. "Get the ventilator, now."

When the door closes, the fucking King of Angels is standing in front of us looking down at my daughter.

Doctor Charles shakes his head, then nods. Then, he removes the oxygen mask from her face and steps back. *No. He's not taking her to heaven... No!*

"What the hell are you doing? Fix her!" I shout at Doctor Charles.

Flynn's father looks up at me. "Roman, try to remain calm. Let me check her."

I nod, my hands grip the edge of the crib so hard my knuckles turn white.

He places a hand on her tummy and a bright white light shines from it, spreading across her tiny body. He closes his eyes and drops his head, and for a long silent minute, I wait.

Flynn's hand touches my shoulder. *Breathe.*

I swallow hard and look over my shoulder at Kailey who looks terrified, but I can't move. I need to be here. She needs to wake up.

As the light fades from the king's hand, my daughter's skin turns pink. Her blue lips blush with colour, and her arms move, then her feet. Then, she sounds as though she's choking. The king nods toward Doctor Charles who thanks him, and without another word, he disappears at the same time the nurse returns, huffing and puffing.

"False alarm. She's breathing, I'll put her in the humidicrib," Doctor Charles tells the nurse who sighs with relief and smiles. Doctor Charles works quickly to put her in the humidicrib before he places the oxygen mask back over her face.

"Roman," Kailey cries.

I rush over to her and pull her into my arms kissing her face and stroking her hair. "Oh god, she's alive. She's going to be okay."

"I want to see her," she cries.

"Just give me a few minutes to get you cleaned up, sweetheart," the nurse says as she throws the towels into the laundry basket. "Then you can see your beautiful daughter. How many weeks along were you?"

Doctor Charles answers quickly, "Twenty-five."

"Oh, what a strong little girl she is," the nurse says.

Kailey wraps her arms around my neck. "Like her Daddy."

XVII

THE MOST BEAUTIFUL GIRLS

ROMAN

The room is quiet now and Kailey is sleeping soundly in my arms, she's exhausted.

Beside me in a humidicrib, our baby daughter Georgia, is wrapped in a small white blanket. The oxygen mask still covers her mouth and nose, and her tiny chest rises and falls with each breath she takes. For two hours I watched every single breath she took.

When I saw Autumn and Flynn's babies for the first time, I couldn't believe how small they were, Georgia is less than half their size. We haven't held her yet, the most we've done is touch her tiny fingers and stare in awe at her.

Flynn told me his father, one of the most powerful immortals to live, was responsible for saving Georgia's life. If there was any way to repay him, I would do it a million times over. Flynn didn't go into detail, or tell me exactly how it worked, but all that matters to me, is that it did, and that Georgia will survive.

Doctor Charles said Georgia would need to stay in the hospital for at least two weeks to ensure no one gets suspicious. After that, he said we could take her to the Fallon Mansion where he has everything he needs in the medical room. So much has changed in the past six months, and I'm ready for the next part of my life with Kailey and Georgia.

There's a tiny cry from the crib and I stand up to check her. Her tiny fists clench and she kicks her legs out. Reaching into the crib through the small opening, I touch her hand, stroking it gently while I talk to her. "Hey, sweetheart, Daddy's here... don't cry." *Daddy.* I'm a father. And I'm going to be the best father she could ever ask for. As I talk to her and stroke her fingers, she stops crying and her breaths return to normal.

She's barely twelve hours old and she already has me wrapped around her tiny little finger. Whatever she wants in life, I will make it my mission to give it to her. This love is something I've never felt. I love Kailey with every fibre of my being and watching her give birth to our daughter has increased my love for her a hundred-fold. She is everything I never imagined I'd have.

"Roman..." Autumn's voice appears in the doorway.

I look up and she opens the door a little wider until she sees Kailey sleeping. "I can come back later," she whispers.

I shake my head and tell her to come in. She places a huge bunch of pink flowers on the bedside table along with a pink teddy bear. When she sees Georgia, tears well in her eyes then stream down her cheeks. "Oh my god, Flynn said she was small, but I didn't think she'd be this tiny... Is she okay? I mean she's going to be healthy..."

I nod, still holding her tiny hand in mine. "I love her," I say.

Autumn peers into the crib and smiles. "She has your nose, and Kailey's lips." She rubs my back and presses a soft kiss to my cheek. "I'm so happy for you both. She's perfect."

"Did you know you would love them right away?" I ask her.

She shakes her head. "I loved them of course, but it wasn't until I saw them that I knew without a shred of doubt, I would die for them."

I smile. "It's so weird. I don't feel like a father, but when Kailey says it, I know it's real. And when I look at her, it's almost as though this is what I've been waiting for all my life. Not just Georgia, but Kailey too." I look over my shoulder at Kailey. "God, I love her so much, Autumn."

"I can tell. And Roman, it's all real. You're going to be an amazing husband and father. And she's going to have her cousins to look after her too."

I drop my arm over her shoulder and pull her close to press a kiss to her head. "Thank you, for everything. If I hadn't met you, I wouldn't be here right now. You guys have done so much for me, and I don't know how I'll ever repay you."

"You don't have to. Just make Kailey happy, and look after your little girl."

After talking to Autumn for a while, she takes some pictures, and a short video of Georgia to show the twins, then she heads home. An hour later, Bella and Steel come in, and Bella cries over the crib and congratulates us. Not long after that, Clay and Lexi show up with Gabe and Lexi explains to him why Georgia is in the tiny crib and that she'll be coming home soon. When she cries again, Gabe cries too and tells Clay he's sad because he can't cuddle Georgia and make her feel better.

Every hour, a nurse comes in and checks on Georgia, then Doctor Charles comes in and checks on Kailey as well. We get some food, and Kailey has a shower and gets changed. It's been almost twenty-four hours and I'm exhausted, but I can't bear the thought of closing my eyes and missing one second of my daughter's life.

Finally, after fighting it, my eyes grow heavy and when they close, I dream only of the two most beautiful girls in the world. And they're both mine.

XVIII
THE CURSED

KNOX

I stop at the door and take a deep breath. I promised Flynn I would *try* to be civil with Roman. *Try*. I raise my hand to knock on the door, but the door I want to open, is the room right next to this one. The room where Annie is, awake and waiting for Doctor Charles to do his rounds.

Doctor Charles told me I could see her as long as I didn't cause any issues or upset her. Fuck this curse. It's fucked up my entire life.

I should have listened to my mother all those years ago. Now, it's too late.

Knox
21 years old

"Mother, I don't want to train anymore. I know everything."

She sits on the edge of my bed beside me and places a gentle hand over mine. "Knox, my darling, you have hundreds of years to explore the heavens. There is no need to rush. Take your time, slow down and enjoy this life you've been blessed with."

I sigh, frustrated that I know she's right, and annoyed that I've done this to myself. While my brothers are out exploring Mount Astra and the diamond caves, I'm stuck at home. Stuck in an empty castle all because I didn't listen... again.

"Darling," my mother says quietly. "This anger you hold inside your heart will destroy you if you are not careful."

"I can't help it," I say honestly.

"You must try. When you feel the anger consuming you, try to stop for a moment and listen to your heart. Close your eyes and think about your brothers and all the times they've stood up for you. The times they were lashed for you."

I drop my head, ashamed. The sadness that clouds my mother's eyes almost brings me to tears, but I blink them back and promise her... "I will try, Mother. I will try to be better, to be good. To think about my brothers first."

When she stands, I do too, and when she pulls me into her for a hug, she whispers against my ear. "Knox, your life isn't going to be easy, but it will be worth it... if you try. I promise you."

Six days later I would be cursed by Haydee and sent to mortal earth.

I knock on the door and wait.

"Come in," Kailey calls. Good, maybe Roman isn't there. *Stop it!*

I didn't want to see them. I have no interest in kids at all, except for my nephews and nieces, and Gabe. I'd protect them with my life, but Roman's child... I don't know if I can look past the fact that he is that bastard's brother. *I have to try.* As thoughts of my mother and the pain I put her through force their way into my mind, I open the door a crack.

Shaking my head, I walk into the dimly lit room that's quiet and overly warm. Kailey sits on the bed with her legs crossed, reading a stack of what looks like baby books and magazines, and Roman's standing at a plastic crib, his eyes focused only on what's inside.

I walk over slowly and lean down to kiss Kailey's head. "Congratulations. You okay?"

She nods and smiles. "She's so beautiful, Knox."

I head to where Roman's standing and as I get closer, I stop in my tracks.

"What the fuck?" I whisper.

He looks over his shoulder at me. "Hey."

"She's tiny, is she okay?" I'm positive the baby would fit in the palms of my hands.

He nods as he looks down at her. A tiny oxygen mask covers her mouth and nose and each little breath she takes causes her chest to rise and fall rapidly. "Are you sure she's okay?" I ask him.

"Yeah, positive. Doctor Charles has been checking her, and the nurses... she's going to be okay." His tone tells me he's not one hundred percent certain, and when I look at her, I can't focus on anything but how tiny she is. "Will she grow... I mean when she's older, will she be small, or like normal kids..." What the fuck am I saying?

Kailey laughs a little, and Roman smiles. "She'll always be small. Smaller than other kids her age."

"She's immortal though?"

Roman nods. "Doctor Charles tested her blood. He said she has phoenix blood, no vampire. So she's not a harpie. She's a phoenix, and as beautiful as her mummy."

A huge smile spreads across Kailey's lips. "And she's strong like her daddy."

But she's too small. "What if she gets hurt? Or if something happens to her?"

"I'll give my life before I let anyone hurt her," Roman says with conviction.

My mind is made up. *I will give my life for her.* I may not be close with Roman and Kailey, but this tiny baby is part of my family, and I have to protect her. I place a hand on Roman's shoulder. "I'm happy for you, really. Everything else, it doesn't matter. It's all in the past. She matters now. You have my word, I will never let anyone hurt her."

Roman nods. "Thanks, Knox, I appreciate it, really."

Outside the room, I lean against the wall and take a deep breath. I need to get my life sorted out. My brothers have everything they've dreamed of, they're all bonded to gorgeous females who have given them nothing but happiness. Even Roman has found happiness with Kailey.

Then there's me. The fucked up, broken mess of the family. The difficult one. The one who never fit in, but always stood out. I shake my head hard. *Annie.* She's the one I need.

When I walk into her room, she pushes herself up on her elbows and sits slowly. Some of the swelling has gone down, but bruises still mar her beautiful face, and her eyes, that were so bright before, are now dull.

"You need to leave," she says quietly.

I cock my head. "Annie... I'm sorry, I should have spoken to you, not texted."

She shakes her head slightly. "It's not that, Knox. I need to go back. I belong with him. He's all I've ever known." She drops her head back on the pillow. "Please, just leave."

I pace toward her bed and look down at her face, then at the scars scattered over her arms. "What happened to you while you were with him?"

"I don't want to talk to you, ever again." She turns her back to me, but I'm not giving in that easily.

I sit on the leather recliner beside the bed. "I'm not leaving until you talk."

"Get out. Or *I'll* leave."

"Hmm... Last time you tried to leave didn't work out so well."

With her back still to me, she pulls the blanket over herself and sighs heavily. "I hate you, Knox. I don't want you here."

I run a hand through my hair before I cross my arms over my chest. She's the total opposite of what she was at my place. Something is going on, and I'll get it out of her one way or another.

Slowly, I reach out and place a hand on her shoulder. Instantly, she turns around and shouts at me. "Don't touch me!"

"Talk to me, Annie, let me help you."

Her brows furrow and she shoves her hair back off her face. "Help me? This is your fault. He did this because of you... You know what he said?"

"Tell me."

She clenches her fists. "He said you're like him. That when you want something, you don't give up. I'm not some*thing*. Because of you, he beat the shit out of me, and when I go back, he'll do it again, but I don't care." Her eyes grow dark, but she doesn't cry. She never cries. There is nothing but rage in her eyes. "Get the fuck out, and don't come back."

I swallow hard. I never imagined anyone's words could hurt me or cut me as deep. Standing, I take one last look at her before I turn and walk out the door.

At the hospital entrance, Clay's waiting for me. "How did it go?" I walk past him and get in the passenger seat of his car. When he gets in, he takes off toward the highway. "Where are we going?" he asks.

"Just drive."

As we get further away from Ambrosia Valley, the sky grows darker and the stars appear as tiny specks of light amid the darkness above. The rage I expect, doesn't come. There's no burn, no ache, and no pain. There's nothing but an overwhelming sense of emptiness.

"Georgia's small, right," Clay says quietly.

"Yeah. How the fuck are they so different?"

"The babies?"

"Roman and his brother. Even Corbin. They're all fucked, and he's... he's different." I shake my head hard as the realisation hits me. It's the same with my brothers. They were all cursed, yet they held onto every sliver of hope they could grasp. I've never done that. I've always given in to temptation, no matter what the cost. Sex, chains, whips, pain, more sex. No attachments, no love, and no real connections with anyone, not even my brothers.

Clay's voice pulls me from my thoughts. "I dunno, man. He wanted more. He saw what he didn't want to become, and he changed it. Everyone can change, they all have a choice. Some try harder than others I suppose."

Try. Roman tried. Flynn and Steel tried. Clay tried. They all did it. Haydee was right, I can't keep anyone for any length of time. I drop my head back on the seat and close my eyes. "She said she hates me. That it was my fault... what that bastard did to her."

"She's angry, man. She's been through hell. I can only imagine what she endured at his hands."

"Yeah, but it's true. If I hadn't taken her to my place, he wouldn't have done that. He would have taken her back. But that... he knew I'd see it, he wanted me to see her like that, to see what he's capable of."

Clay pulls over when we reach a T-intersection. "So that's it then? You're gonna give up?"

"I can't force her..." I shrug.

He cuts the engine and I get out of the car and walk across the road to an empty paddock. With my head in my hands, I clamp my eyes shut and think about Annie. Could I love her? Is this need desire, love, or is it merely lust?

Haydee appears in front of me, a second later, Venys appears beside her.

"You're back," Clay says. "Have you heard from Tayah?"

Venys nods. "She got away from him... she said—She misses you, but she doesn't want to come back. She's worried he'll find her or follow her, and she doesn't want to put you in danger."

Clay sighs, but nods. "Is she okay though?" he asks, genuinely concerned.

"Yeah, she's good. Her and Indy are gonna stick together."

"I hear you got a girl," Venys says to me.

"Had," I say.

Haydee traces her fingernails over the tattoos on my forearm. "Eww, you're all..." She gasps. "Wait, are you... sad?" She pulls her hand back and wipes it over her jacket as though I've got a deadly disease, then she tilts her head, staring at me. "You're fucking sad... because of that girl."

Venys smirks, but when I glare at her, she bites her lip.

"I'm not sad. I'm pissed off," I say shoving my hands into my pockets.

Haydee skips around me, laughing. "Oh, well in that case, fight Clay."

I turn to Clay and he rolls his eyes and shakes his head. "Really, Haydee," he says.

"Do it," Venys says.

When I shake my head, Haydee extends her long, talon like nails and drags them down my neck. I groan as blood trickles down my flesh, and before I can stop it, I release a guttural growl that sends a surge of adrenaline through my veins.

"Do it," Haydee whispers.

As much as I try to stop myself, my fists clench and my muscles twitch before my fist slams into Clay's jaw. He scrunches his nose and rubs his jaw. "Fuck it, Haydee," he moans, but she only laughs.

"Do it, Clay," Venys urges, "Fight back."

I clench my fists, watching his every move before I land an uppercut to his jaw, then another punch to his nose. He stumbles back, cursing as he regains his footing. When he rushes toward me, I hold my ground until he rams into me, then I duck out of his way and he falls forward, his hands splayed on the dry grass.

When Clay's back on his feet, I swing another punch that knocks him to the ground again, but this time he doesn't get up right away. Venys rushes to him, kneeling by his side as she shoves his shoulder. "Clay, get the fuck up."

He rubs his head before he leaps to his feet. "You're a fucking asshole, brother."

I smirk as Haydee whispers against my ear. "More."

When I lunge at Clay, Venys stops between us, a swirling red cloud coming from her hands as she shouts, "Enough!"

Through the cloud, Haydee attempts to push me forward, urging me to continue. But I can't move. Venys laughs. "I'm still too strong for you, Haydee. Let's go, I wanna see Flynn and Autumn."

Haydee pouts and gives in, and Venys jumps up and presses a kiss on my cheek. "You can thank me later."

"For what?" I ask confused.

"For stopping you from killing your brother."

"I wouldn't," I say glancing at Clay.

He laughs and shakes his head as he wipes the blood from his lip. "Get out of here," Clay tells them, and they both disappear.

Back in the car, Clay's silent for a minute before he asks, "You want to see her?"

"It's a waste of time."

"Fuck, brother, you're as stubborn as a mule. Go back there, tell her the truth. Maybe she'll fight you, and maybe she'll tell you to fuck off again, but are you really going to sit back and let them take her?"

With a frustrated sigh, I open the window and breathe in the cold night air. "Fuck! Take me back."

Clay smirks, but he doesn't speak as he turns the car around and drives back toward Ambrosia Valley.

XIX

DEADLY DREAMS

ANNIE

A nurse comes in and leaves a clean towel and hospital gown on the chair beside the bed. As she checks my notes and refills my water jug, she talks quietly, telling me about a baby she helped deliver. I don't pay much attention; all I can do is stare at the chair Knox was sitting on when I told him to leave. When I screamed at him and blamed him for what happened to me. I hate myself for what I said, but I can't change it. He needs to stay away from me. I can't let anyone else die. There's already been too much death.

Adam never came into my room, and every time I get up to peek out the window, all I see are doctors and nurses. I glance up at the clock on the wall. It's 2:15am and I'm so tired I can barely keep my eyes open. Pulling the blankets up, I snuggle beneath the rough covers of the hospital bed and close my eyes, listening to the clock tick second by second.

I must be dreaming because the air is thick and there's an unbearable weight pressing down on me, forcing me to fight for every breath. When I try to open my eyes, they're stuck closed, and moving my head is impossible.

As I count the seconds, I think about what Adam told me when I was twelve years old and I sat watching him hold a pillow over a woman's face. He'd used so many different techniques to kill them, and this one was the first that didn't involve blood.

"In seven minutes, she'll be dead. Did you know that, Annastasia? It only takes seven minutes to kill someone with a pillow."

Of course, at twelve years old, I didn't know that, nor did I want to. It seemed to be the worst way to go. Blind to the world while your brain is slowly deprived of oxygen. Killing them with a knife was quick, painful, and bloody. They knew what was happening, and they could feel the pain, that's what death was supposed to be. Painful.

The dream reminds me of Adam, and while I'm here, I search my memories for a time when he wasn't the person he is now. That person though, is long gone. He was always a killer, but it never concerned me. I believed everything he was doing was for a purpose. It was helping him, and me.

There's something caught in my throat and dizziness is beginning to take over. If I can just wake up and focus on the clock again, the tick, tick, tick, of the clock hands. *Breathe.* It's only a dream, just like the ones I used to have when I was young.

Although this one is different.

Shouting pierces the darkness. There's a crash, a bang, then light appears as I suck in a breath of air. Finally, I can breathe. I force my eyes open, desperate to wake from the confusion that's all too real and consuming.

"Annie, open your eyes. Annie!" the voice is frantic, then the hands, pushing me, shaking me. "Annie you need to open your eyes now."

I blink rapidly, searching for something to focus on. A light shines into my eyes and I squint then lift my hand to block it from my vision.

"That's it, open your eyes."

"You... You're the doctor?"

He nods. "Yes, Doctor Charles. Do you know where you are?"

"Hospital."

He presses something cold to my chest and I gasp, then, I hear his voice. "Is she okay?"

He's back. After everything I said to him, he came back. *Is he crazy?*

"She's okay. Lucky you got here when you did. It was close."

Close? What are they talking about? "What?" I call out.

Doctor Charles comes back to the bedside, but Knox doesn't. Wherever he is, I can't see him. "Annie, someone just attempted to..." He hesitates. "He had a pillow over your face, he was trying to kill you... thankfully Knox came in just in time."

"Pillow?" I leap out of the bed and press my back into the wall, then slide down slowly until I'm sitting on the floor, my arms wrapped tight around my knees. "No, that was a dream. It wasn't real. He wasn't real." What's happening to me? Am I stuck somewhere between my dreams and reality? I rub my eyes and take a few deep breaths, then I pinch myself, searching for any sign I'm awake... alive.

The doctor kneels in front of me and takes my hand, when I blink, I catch a fleeting glimpse of blood on my forearm. *I am bleeding. I am alive.* "Annie. Annie, it's okay now, he's gone. I'm going to have you moved to another room, a secure room with card access only. Can you stand up?"

I nod and stand slowly, and when I look past the doctor, my eyes lock onto Knox. He looks confused, or angry, or maybe both. *Why did he come back?*

"Knox," Doctor Charles says, "maybe you could get Annie some clothes, I'm sure she'd be more comfortable in something other than a hospital gown."

He doesn't say a word, and I watch his back as he leaves.

My new room is huge. There's a double bed with a soft blanket and four big pillows. There's a sofa, a television and a bathroom with a shower and a small closet. There's even a tiny fridge Doctor Charles tells me is full of water, milk, and juice. This room is where I'll be staying for three more days. Three days, then I'll be kicked out and I'll have to find somewhere else to stay. So much for the job I had, that's probably gone, like everything else I had before Adam found me and ruined it all.

A few minutes after Doctor Charles leaves, Knox arrives with a backpack slung over his shoulder. The same backpack I bought when I went shopping with Lexi.

"Do you want this in the closet?" he asks.

"Just here is fine, thank you," I say patting the bed.

He drops it down and scratches his chin. "Um... I just want to apologise, again. I fucked up. I don't know how all this stuff—" He scratches his head. "I don't know what I'm trying to say. If you want to talk, tell Doctor Charles to give me a call, otherwise I'll stay away."

He exhales as though he was holding his breath the whole time he was speaking, and when he turns on his heel to leave, I force my voice to work. "Wait..." He stops mid stride and turns back to me. "He'll come back for me. I don't want you to get hurt, that's why you have to stay away." There, I said it. The truth, well most of it.

He cocks his head and almost looks like he's about to smile. "You think he can hurt me?"

I shrug. "He did, back in the basement."

"I can handle it."

I unzip the backpack and search through it for my underwear, then smile a little when I find it neatly folded at the bottom. "I really need a shower. If you want to, you can wait here... or not. I don't care." *God, Annie, stop lying.*

"Actually, my cousin is upstairs, she just had a baby. I'll go see her, then come back before I leave."

"Whatever." I shrug.

"You're safe here, and there are two officers at your door."

"Yep." I grab the towel and my clothes. "See ya."

He stares at me for a few seconds before he leaves.

"Asshole," I murmur under my breath. He could have stayed. Wait... I don't want him here. I *can't* want him here. *Ugh. Fucking men.*

The shower pressure in this room is a hundred times better than the other room I was in, but nowhere near as nice as the shower at Knox's house. After I rummaged through the bathroom drawer, I found a shaver and some deliciously scented body wash that smells like strawberries.

The shower in this bathroom is wide and a small seat sits in one corner. After washing it down, I sit and shave my legs until they're silky smooth. Then I spend five minutes trying to remove the thin blades from the shaver. When I get one out, I smile to myself.

It's been so long since I've felt a blade against my flesh, and I'm desperate to know if anything has changed. Am I still numb to pain? As the hot water rains down on me and relaxes my muscles, I hold the tiny blade between my fingers and press it into my forearm.

There's no pain. I drag it along my flesh watching the blood bead to the surface of my skin before it washes away in a pinkish red swirl.

Still no pain.

The next cut is deeper. Blood seeps from my skin and I watch it, waiting for the pain to come.

Nothing.

Again, I slice into my forearm, and again there's nothing. Frustrated, I drop the blade on the floor of the shower and wash my hair before I get out and grab my towel from the rack. On the wall, a dispenser holds a roll of paper towels and I pull a piece off and press it onto my forearm, where I'm still bleeding. When the bleeding finally stops, I put on my bra and underwear, then run the brush through my hair and pull on the pair of track pants and the hoodie Knox packed for me. At least he knows how to choose comfortable clothes.

I get into bed and inhale, taking in the scents of the body wash and shampoo. I raise my arm and trace my fingers over the cuts, wondering if there's something wrong with me. Surely it's not normal to be numb to pain.

I press my fingers against the bruise beneath my eye, it's healing but is a disgusting greenish yellow colour; it reminds me of the bile I used to vomit up when I was back home with Adam and the old man.

Home. It wasn't home. Looking back now, it was akin to hell. But it was my hell, and I knew what to expect there. I knew that the old man liked his whiskey in a certain glass, with two ice cubes. His bedding had to be washed every Tuesday at 2pm, and every Sunday when he was working in his lab, I had to clean his bedroom and bathroom from top to bottom.

Adam didn't have many demands. Other than training and fighting, all I had to do was keep my bedroom spotless and ensure his meals were made and served on time. He hated the old man almost as much as I did, but he would always remind me that respect was earned—and that the old man had earned it.

As I doze off, the click of the door opening startles me, and I open my eyes to see Knox.

He stops in the doorway. "I'll come back in the morning, if you—"

"It's okay. You can come in."

He pushes the door closed and clicks the lock in place before he sits on the sofa furthest away from the bed. "You had a shower?"

I nod. "Thank you for bringing me the clothes."

"Are you feeling okay? Any pain?"

"I'm fine. No pain." His eyes tell me he doesn't believe me. "How is your cousin and her baby?" I ask.

"They're good. She's tiny, the baby. She was born early so she's in one of those humidicribs."

I have no idea what he's talking about. I don't know anything about babies or what they need, or even what they do. I've never seen one up close. "Oh, okay," is all I say, not wanting to admit the truth.

Knox pulls his phone out of his pocket. "Do you want to see a picture of her?"

I shuffle up the bed. "I guess so. Are you allowed to show people?"

"Yeah." He stands and comes toward the bed. Without getting too close, he hands me his phone. "You can swipe through the pictures, there's a few there."

I look at the first picture, confused. There's a clear plastic box with holes in the side, but I can't tell what's inside. When I swipe to the next picture, I see her. The tiny little baby. Everything about her is perfect. Her little fingers and tiny fingernails; her feet and her toes. And her tiny face with soft pink lips, a little nose, and long dark lashes across her eyelids. She even has a fine layer of dark hair. I swipe to the next picture, enthralled by this baby who looks too small to be human. She looks like a doll I saw at the shopping centre with Adam once.

I swipe to the next photo. It's the side of the plastic box, I realise it must be what Knox called the humidicrib. There's a sign stuck to it that reads, "Georgia Hope".

I glance at Knox, not wanting to take my eyes off the baby for too long. "Is she going to be okay?"

"She's strong and doing well. She'll be home in a couple of weeks."

"I like her name."

Knox smiles and I reluctantly hand him back his phone, locking the image of the tiny baby into my mind. "Yeah, she's perfect." Maybe now I can start collecting memories, instead of scars.

He turns to go back to the sofa.

"Knox," I say quietly. When he stops, I continue, "I'm sorry for what I said. I thought I could push you away, to protect you. He said he'd come here, that he knew you'd come for me. I couldn't risk it."

He sits on the edge of the bed, his eyes on mine. "You could have told me that. I would have had you moved sooner. I want to help you, Annie, but I can't do it if you don't want me to." He rubs the back of his neck and yawns. "Anyway, I'll give you some space." He pulls my mobile phone out of his pocket and places it on the bed near my hand. "Call me if you need anything."

Stay. Please don't leave me. I can't say it. My stubborn ass will not allow the words to come out, and when he stands to leave, I watch him walk away once again.

Annie, you are an idiot.

XX
BIRTHDAY GIRL

KNOX

two weeks later

She studies her reflection in the mirror, then scrunches her nose and crosses her arms. "I hate it."

Watching her, I stifle a laugh. "You look beautiful, Annie."

With a huff, she turns around to face me, a scowl on her gorgeous face. "I look stupid. I shouldn't have let Lexi talk me into this. I don't wear dresses." She tugs on the hem of the short black dress before she sighs yet again. "Why can't I wear pants?"

"You can. You can wear whatever you want to wear. Lex was just trying to be nice."

She narrows her eyes. "Are you trying to make me feel guilty?"

I shake my head. "Nope. Go get changed, I'll wait." I check my watch, waiting for her to go back to the bedroom, but instead, she glares at me and grabs her purse off the bench with a loud huff. "Ugh, fine, let's go."

Without argument, I lead her outside to where Jones is waiting with my car, and we get in. The scowl on her face has turned into a slight smile and there's a glint in her eyes. She won't admit it, but I know she wants to do this. She's never been to a restaurant and says the only birthday she ever remembers celebrating, is her seventh birthday.

Since Annie was released from hospital two weeks ago, she hasn't left the house. She's been spending most of her time in the gym, training. The rest of the time she spends in her bedroom or at the kitchen bench where she sits and reads through the stacks of magazines Lexi's been buying for her. We haven't spoken a lot, but even in silence, I'm enjoying her company more with each passing day.

I notice the little things about her now. The way she clenches her fists when she's annoyed or on edge. The way she pinches the soft skin on her forearms when she's unsure about something but doesn't want to ask. And the way her face lights up with a fleeting smile when she smells coffee. She is an enigmatic beauty, cloaked in darkness and struggling to find her place in the world. I want to be the one to show her everything, to give her the love she needs, and the affection she craves but doesn't know how to accept.

When we arrive at Gluttony, we head into the restaurant and Annie grabs my hand and holds it tight. She doesn't say a word as we're led into the private dining room where we take our seats and I order our drinks.

She looks up to the ceiling where the chandeliers hang, sparkling with the dim glow of the golden lights. "It's beautiful in here." Her eyes take in the luxurious dining room. "Do you come here a lot?"

"I haven't been for a while."

The waitress returns with a bottle of wine and two glasses. "Would you like to try it?" I ask Annie.

"Yeah, okay."

"You're eighteen?" the waitress asks.

Annie's eyes flit back and forth between me and the waitress. "Yes."

She looks at Annie and squints.

"She turned eighteen last week," I say. "Thank you, Lacy, that's all for now."

"Certainly, Mr Fallon."

"You know her?" Annie asks when Lacy leaves the dining room.

I nod. "She works..." I hesitate. Giving her too much information isn't a good idea. Not yet. "She works with Charlotte." *Not a lie.*

"Oh, okay. We're not having pizza, are we?"

"No. They don't do pizza here." I hand her the leather-bound menu and she looks down at it, her eyes wide.

"Oh, it's so expensive," she whispers.

I lean forward slightly. "It's fine. Pick anything you like."

Her nose scrunches and her shoulders drop. "There's too much, I can't decide."

"Want me to pick for you?"

She nods and slides the menu across the table to me.

We talk quietly while we wait for our meals to arrive. Annie tells me about the day she spent with Lexi, and how strange it felt for her to have another girl to talk to. It's already obvious she's formed a bond with Lexi, and for that, I'm glad.

When our meals arrive, the waitress places the plates on the table and refills the wine glasses before she leaves. Annie looks down at her plate, then at mine. "Wow, they look so... It's weird. It's like it's not supposed to be eaten."

She looks up at me, a glorious smile on her lips and a slight pink blush to her cheeks. I could stare at her all night and not even consider looking away.

She bites her lip, then looks down at the plate again. "This is chicken?"

I nod. "If you don't like it, I'll get you something else."

"What's yours?" she asks leaning forward to look at it again.

Damn! This girl is so fucking beautiful. She's so innocent and curious, but at the same time she's filled with knowledge and understanding. I inhale, then exhale slowly, trying desperately to focus on anything but her.

"It's lemon and prawn risotto."

"Rice?" she questions.

I nod. "And prawns, lemon, wine... Do you want to try it?"

Her eyes grow wide. "You mean from your bowl?"

I laugh. "Yeah, go ahead." I push the bowl toward her, and she glances up at me, then back down to her plate.

"Are you sure?"

"Yes, Annie, I'm sure. Plus, it's your birthday, I want you to enjoy it."

She picks up the spoon and scoops a little risotto out of the bowl. As she brings the spoon to her lips, I can't look away. The look on her face as she takes a mouthful, is beautiful. Her eyes close and a tiny moan comes from her throat as she savours the flavours. When she opens her eyes and smiles again, I do too. "Oh, Knox, that's really good."

She places the spoon down and picks up her knife and fork. "Do you want to try mine?"

I shake my head. "No, it's okay. I've had it before."

Dinner continues with Annie asking about the foods on the menu. She talks about cooking, and how she used to make up her own recipes and bake bread from scratch. Everything she knows is from doing. It's almost like she's from another world.

"Knox, what does Lexi's little brother look like?"

"Gabe... ah like a kid. He's short," I say holding my hand up at about Gabe's height. "Dark brown curly hair, and brown eyes."

She smiles but looks confused. "Do you have a photo of him?"

"Yeah, I do, why?"

"Well, when I went out with Lexi, she said Gabe was four, but I've never seen kids, I guess. Except for the ones at Rollin'." She shrugs. "It doesn't matter. I was just curious."

I pull my phone from my pocket, earning me a few disgusted looks from the other diners in the room. Fuck them. Annie is more important than any of them. I scroll through my photos and find one of Clay with Gabe, and I show Annie.

As soon as her eyes are on the screen, she smiles. "He's small. And um... cute?" she asks as though she's not sure.

"I guess he's cute for a kid," I say. "Noisy too."

"I wish I knew more, about everything." Her shoulders drop and she lets out a sigh. "I feel so stupid."

"Hey, Annie, you're not stupid. They had you locked up in that house for ten years. That's not your fault. You're out now, and now you can see and do everything you never got to do before."

The waitress returns to clear our plates and asks if we'd like the dessert menu, but I decide against it, noticing Annie's becoming uncomfortable now.

"You ready to go?" I ask her.

"Home?"

I shake my head. "Have you seen a beach before?"

"Never, well not in *real life*. There's a beach here?"

"It's about an hour away, do you want to go?"

She nods, and I stand and extend my hand, when she takes it, I smile to myself. This night must be perfect, for her. She needs to see I will do anything to make her smile.

ANNIE

Knox stops his black convertible at the top of a hill. It's after 9pm, and even though it's dark, it's a clear, cloudless night, and the moonlight shines down onto the ocean illuminating the waves and making them appear as silver specks in the distance.

Knox reaches into the back seat for my coat then grabs his own. "It's going to be cold out there."

I nod and push the car door open. The wind rushes past with the sound of something loud; I realise it must be the sound of the waves. I pull on my coat and walk to the front of the car where I have the perfect view of the ocean.

Knox stands beside me. "Come on," he says.

As he walks toward the steps that lead down to the beach, I follow him. A large sign is lit up and reads *Victoria Beach*. Each step has a row of tiny lights across the edge, making it easy to find my way down without falling. I gave in and let Lexi choose a dress for me to wear, but I refused to consider the stilettos she insisted were comfortable and easy to walk in. I'm more than certain I would have broken my ankle had I worn them. Instead, I chose a pair of flat shoes Lexi called "super cute". I've never worn anything in my life that could be considered *"super cute"*, and although I'll never admit it, it was nice to dress up and feel like a normal girl, rather than a fighter.

When we reach the sandy beach, Knox continues toward the ocean. Down here, the roar of the waves is louder, and I watch as they crash into the rocks along the beach. I've never seen anything so beautiful, and I imagine during the day it would be even better.

"Want to take your shoes off?" Knox asks.
"Really?"

"If you want to."

I kick off my flat shoes and allow my toes to sink into the soft, cold sand, and as I walk, the tiny grains move between my toes. It's a sensation I've never felt before, and when a lump gets caught in my throat, I stop in my tracks. *What is wrong with me?* I swallow hard, but the lump won't budge.

"Annie, you okay?" Knox asks.

I bite my lip hard and nod before I walk toward the water, keeping my eyes on the horizon where millions of stars are scattered across the sky. Swallowing again, I try to make sense of the emotions playing through my mind and wreaking havoc inside my head, and my heart.

A shiver runs down my spine as a huge wave crashes against the rocks further along the beach. Knox stands beside me. "You like it?" His eyes are fixed on the waves.

I open my mouth to thank him for bringing me here, but my eyes water, and I rub them hard. The wind rushes past and blows my hair across my face, bringing with it the salty smell of the ocean breeze and more tiny grains of sand that swirl around my legs.

When my knees shake, I clench my fists. Something is wrong with me. I'm going to die here. My heart pounds against my chest and when I try to breathe, it's as though my lungs are being crushed. I clamp my eyes shut, willing all the emotions to disappear and leave me alone.

"Annie," he says my name again, softly this time. "Do you want to go back?"

Breathe. It's a fucking beach. "I can't... breathe..." I say.

Knox stands in front of me. He reaches out and tucks my hair behind my ear. "Hey, it's okay. You're okay now."

No. Not okay. I'll never be okay. I shouldn't be here. Not here with Knox. Not here at the beach. Not here in this world. I don't belong.

"No," I tell him. "I don't, um... I—" I lift my head and look up at him. The moonlight glows behind him making him appear almost angelic. *Angel. He's an angel.* I shake my head.

"You don't what?" he asks.

He waits for my reply. His green eyes staring into mine, his lips slightly parted, but he doesn't speak.

"It's not okay..."

His fingertips lightly touch mine, and he takes a step forward, closing the gap between us. "It is," he assures me. "You're safe now."

But why do I feel so... "Ugh." I stomp my foot into the cold sand, my frustration building as I try to figure out what the hell is going on in my head.

I clamp my eyes shut again, and this time, his hand cups my cheek. He's touching me, again. And I didn't ask for it. I don't want it. I want it. *Annie! Pull it together.* "Knox..." I can barely say his name without my lip quivering.

"Annie," he breathes my name against my lips.

My stomach coils in knots, the lump in my throat returns and my heart is surely about to explode in my chest. *Can't breathe.* "Fuck," I shout as I open my eyes.

And that's the last word that spills from my mouth before Knox's lips are on mine for the second time. For a few seconds, I forget *how* to breathe, but then... oh the bliss, the delicious taste of his lips. The velvety softness of his tongue as it glides over mine, forcing me to do the same to him.

Strong hands slide into my coat and flatten against my back. My own hands glide up to his shoulders and I stand on my tippy toes, my fingers laced behind his neck as I kiss him hard and fast.

He pulls back slightly, his lips so close, but so far. "Happy Birthday, beautiful," he whispers before he pulls me into his arms and rubs my back. With my head on his chest, I feel and hear his heart beat against my ear. A strong, steady beat that brings a sense of calm to the chaos that plagues me.

XXI

THE FIRST TIME

KNOX

I didn't talk her into staying with me. She asked. She stood in front of me and asked if she could stay at my house until she could afford a place of her own. *She* wants to be here. And *I* want her.

The past week has been hell. My house smells like her. When I smell coffee, I think of her lips and the tiny smile she has when she takes the first sip of coffee each morning. When she showers, the scent of her freshly washed hair lingers for hours, and when she speaks, all I want is to hear my name spill from her lips every day until the end of time. And the Crave... That memory plays over in my head day and night, taunting my dreams and clouding my mind with licentious thoughts.

Since her birthday, we haven't kissed again, and again it's as though it never happened at all. I want to talk to her about it—about *us*. But I can't push her. The thought of her leaving again kills me.

"Knox." And there it is again. With one word my cock is hard and my heart races. I've spent hours at the mansion fighting with Clay, exercising, running on the treadmill. Anything to keep myself moving and focused, and away from Annie.

"Yeah?"

She closes the magazine that's on the bench in front of her. "Can I use your gym?"

"Your rib won't be healed yet, it's probably better to wait."

She stands and puts her hands on the stool. "It's fine, honestly. It's not sore at all. I need to do something, and since I can't go out, I thought I could use the gym." She steps back and plants her hands on her hips. "I have these training... well gym clothes and it's stupid not to be *in* a gym when I'm wearing them." A hint of a smile tugs at the corner of her lips.

I'd give anything to see her smile again. Reluctantly, I agree and lead her to the gym. It's nothing like the gym at the mansion, but it has a treadmill, a boxing bag, and enough space to exercise and lift weights.

When she walks in, I stand at the door watching her. She's wearing a pair of skin tight grey leggings, and a tight, long sleeve top. I can't take my eyes off her perfect ass.

"Do you use this stuff?"

Looking up, I nod. "Sometimes. At the mansion... we have a full-size gym, so I use that a lot more."

"Mansion?"

"Yeah. This house, it's where I stay when I'm sick of my brothers, or I need some space." I laugh. "The mansion belongs to all of us. Our father bought it a long time ago."

She nods, then turns her attention to the boxing bag. She runs her hand across it before she paces over to the treadmill, then looks down at the weights.

"Have you used any of this equipment before?" I ask.

"Yep. All of this is like what we had at home—When I was with them. I had to train every day." She reaches down and picks up one of the weights. "I hated it at first. I was a little kid, and all I wanted to do was stay in my room and read books. But he—" She places the weight on the floor and waves a hand in the air. "It doesn't matter."

"Did you fight when you were a child?"

She turns her back to me; her fingers touch each weight as though she's counting them. "Yes. My first fight was when I was eight. It was against a twelve-year-old boy. I got knocked out in fifteen seconds. I sucked so fucking hard." There's a quiet huff. "By the time I was eleven, I was fighting grown men. If I won, I'd be rewarded. If I lost..." There's a heavy sigh.

"You were punished?"

She shakes her head. "He killed them... Like the women. He didn't even flinch when he did it. One minute they were alive, the next, dead. He killed them for being stronger than me."

"What women?" I ask.

She ignores my question and looks down at the large exercise ball. "What's this for?"

"That's Charlotte's, she uses it for yoga."

"Charlotte's not your girlfriend?"

I shake my head. "She was. We were together for a while, on and off. We're good friends though, we own a business together. And she's Flynn's wife's best friend."

"Flynn's your brother... the blonde one?"

"Yep."

She sits on the ball and bounces up and down a few times. "Is it okay if I use the boxing gloves?"

"Of course. Char's will fit you."

She takes the gloves from the hook on the wall and pulls them on as though she's done it a hundred times before. When she walks over to the boxing bag, she raises her fists, then throws a punch. She bites her lip, focusing on the bag before she punches again. Punch after punch she continues hitting the bag, never faltering.

As she moves around the bag, I step back and lean against the wall, watching in awe. The way she moves, the way she focuses on each step. That fucking asshole may have hurt her, but he taught her to fight well. Her kicks are hard and fast, each one hitting high above her head before she spins and kicks again. After fifteen minutes, she stops and smiles, her eyes only on the gloves on her hands.

"You're good," I tell her.

There's a half shrug. "It's all I'm good at."

On the other side of the room is a pull up bar. She pulls the gloves off and jumps up to grab the bar.

"You sure you're not in pain?" I ask.

"Nope. I'm fine." She pulls herself up, her chin just touching the bar before she lowers herself down.

I walk over, still watching her as she does a few more pull ups. When she lets go of the bar, she shakes her arms out then stretches them. "Do you use that much? Your arms are massive." A smile tugs at the corner of her lips as her eyes peruse my biceps. My cock twitches when she licks her lips.

"Yeah, every day." I attempt to shove my cock down, but it's no use and the grey sweat pants I'm wearing aren't hiding anything.

"Go on, have a go," she says urging me.

I go to the other side of the room where the bar is higher, and I grip it in my hands and pull up.

Her smile widens and she comes closer. "Can I try that one?"

"You're too short." I laugh. "The other one's your height."

"Nah, I can grab that easily. Watch." She stands under it and looks up, extending her arms and standing on her toes to see if she can reach the bar. Even if she jumps, it will still be out of reach. She jumps and misses it. Then, she inhales and jumps again, and again she misses. "Okay, maybe not."

I take a step forward and place my hands on her hips. When she doesn't protest, I lift her up and she reaches for the bar. She lets out a quiet "yes" when she grabs it.

With my cock throbbing, and my body a volcano of heat ready to erupt at any moment, I step back slightly and watch her, never taking my eyes off her. She does a few pull ups, then hangs from the bar, swinging back and forth. "You're gonna stay there now?" I ask.

She laughs. For the first time, I hear her laugh and fuck, it's the most beautiful sound in the world. "I'm waiting for you to rescue me." A sexy smirk dances across her full pink lips.

I step forward and grip her waist, and when she lets go of the bar, her hands rest on my shoulders, her breasts inches from my face. She smells so fucking good I want to glide my tongue over every curve of her body until I'm consumed by her, until her sweet scent is the only thing I can smell when I breathe.

Slowly, I slide her body down mine, but when her pussy glides down the length of my cock, she grips my shoulders harder, and instead of letting go, she wraps her legs tight around my waist. Her eyes locked on mine. I slide my hands down to her ass and squeeze it, my fingers so close to her warm pussy that's now pressed hard into my cock. She tightens her legs around me, and I know she'll be able to feel me throbbing.

She breathes heavily before she opens her mouth slightly. "Knox..."

Fuck! I can't let her go. I can't move, and I can't think of anything except burying my cock deep inside her and claiming her as my own.

A tiny whimper leaves her lips when I trace my finger over the seam of her leggings. She leans forward. "Will you kiss me again? Please."

That's all it takes for my lips to clash against hers. Her tongue darts into my mouth, gliding over mine as she moans. I run my hands up and down her back, pulling her closer, feeling her move against me. She rocks her hips toward me like she had the first time we kissed, but this time there's more urgency and desperation in her movements—in her kiss.

I don't know about everything that happened to her in the past, but I need to figure her out. I need to learn her body, to find out what she likes, what makes her moan... and makes her wet.

I pull my lips away from hers. "You okay?"

She nods quickly. "Please don't stop, and don't let me go."

"Never," I say as I walk through the door and carry her to my bedroom.

I lay down with her still holding onto me, her leg over mine, and her fingers threaded through my hair as she moans and moves with me. Slowly, I glide a hand down her thigh. I continue, sliding my hand down between her legs where I rub my palm over her pussy.

She gasps and sucks in a breath, but she doesn't stop me, she spreads her legs wider and I rub my hand over her faster. "Knox," my name leaves her lips as a desperate plea.

"Hmm, baby."

"I need more... want... oh god. What's happening to me?"

I kiss beside her ear then glide my tongue down her neck. *So damn beautiful.* "Mmm, I think you like this?"

"Yes, so fucking much."

I tuck my thumb over the top of her pants. When her kiss deepens, I tug her pants down, stopping every few seconds to make sure she's okay. She kicks her legs out in frustration. "Oh fuck, get them off me."

"Slow down, baby," I whisper against her ear.

She shakes her head hard and grips my forearm. "Can't, I feel like..." She stops when I pull her pants off and drop them on the floor. Her fingers go straight to her bare pussy and she rubs it hard and fast. "Oh. My. God. Knox, more... Please."

I take her hand and lace her fingers through mine, then trace my fingers back down her arm.

"You want more, baby?"

"Stop talking and give me more," she begs as she writhes on my bed. "Touch me, please."

I smirk and stop, ceasing all contact as she wriggles closer, begging me for more.

"Why... did you... stop?" Her words are barely audible through her heavy, panting breaths.

Fucking hell, this girl is heaven. I press my lips to her neck, trailing kisses up to her ear. "There's no rush, gorgeous." I glide my fingers down between her legs then slowly slip one finger inside her. She cries out in pleasure, and when I add another, she bucks against my hand, begging me to go faster, harder. I pump my fingers in and out, a slow, torturous rhythm I know is pushing her so close to the edge. She's wet, hot, and desperate, and when I slide my fingers out and glide them up to her clit, she gasps again.

"No, no. Don't stop..." she begs when I slow down.

"Kiss me, baby," I say as I slide my fingers along her soft wet slit.

She kisses me hard and fast, her tongue swipes over my lips before she pulls my lip into her mouth and bites down gently. I trail kisses to her jaw and further down to her neck before coming back up to her soft, sweet lips.

As she rocks her hips toward me, I finger her while I circle my thumb around her clit, and seconds later, with a scream of pure pleasure, she finds her release and a rush of warmth soaks my fingers. She breathes heavily, each breath fans across my jaw as she kisses me.

I glide my hand over her pussy, back and forth, and still she moves against me as though she never wants to stop. "You okay?"

She nods, the pink blush in her cheeks lights up her face, and even her eyes are brighter. She twists her fingers through my hair. "I—" She stops. "I've never... It doesn't matter. That was beyond amazing."

"You've never orgasmed before?" I ask.

She nuzzles into my neck. "I've never been touched... like that, by anyone."

"Ever?"

She runs her fingers along my arm, giving me goose bumps and causing my cock to throb. Jerking off in the shower is not going to be enough this time, but it's all I have, for now.

"Never. You thought they raped me, didn't you?"

"I don't know," I admit. "They didn't?"

"No. Adam never touched me, not like that. He never wanted sex with me, or anything sexual. He said he'd never—"

"What did he say?" I ask.

Her eyelids drop closed and she buries her face in my neck. Her voice is barely a whisper. "He said he'd never love me, that no one would ever love me."

Asshole. I hate that bastard, but a part of me is thankful he had some limits in his sick, twisted games. "Enough about him." I pull her into my arms and tug the blanket up over us as I kiss her head. "Sleep, baby. I won't let you go."

"Promise," she whispers.

"Promise," I repeat.

XXII

HEY JEALOUSY

ANNIE

When Knox got out of his bed to shower, I wanted to run in there after him and beg him to come back, but I couldn't do it. I let out a heavy sigh, frustrated at my own stubbornness that won't allow me to speak up when I need to—when I want to.

I stand in front of the coffee machine, waiting. When the front door opens, I spin around quickly to see a tall blonde who looks as shocked as I must. Her eyes scan my body from my bare feet, to my underwear, then up to my face. She tilts her head, confused I think, before she calls out, "Knox?"

I step back against the counter, wondering if this is Charlotte. It must be Charlotte, but I'm unable to open my mouth and speak. She gives me a small smile and drops her keys on the bench, then slings her handbag over the back of the stool.

When Knox walks in, he doesn't take his eyes off me. He walks toward me as though he's on a mission, then wraps a strong arm around my waist and presses a hard kiss to my lips. He smells like heaven and when his fingers trace my spine, goose bumps spread across my body. "Sit down, baby, I'll get that."

The blonde clears her throat. "Ah, Knox..." she waves her hand in the air as if to say, "look at me".

When he turns away from the coffee machine, he smiles. "Hey Char, how's it going. This is Annie."

Charlotte's face finally changes, and she smiles bright. "Hi Annie, it's nice to meet you."

When Knox hands me my coffee, I grip it tight in my hands and quickly rush to my—oh shit... it's Charlotte's bedroom. I close the door and lean against it as I let out a heavy sigh. How the hell did she get so pretty? *Ugh, I hate her.* No. I don't hate her. Confusing thoughts run the gamut in my mind. I can't hate someone I don't even know.

Through the door, I hear them talking.

"She's so young... I mean she *looks* really young," Charlotte says.

"She just turned eighteen. She's not that much smaller than Lex."

"I guess. So, has she met everyone yet?" Charlotte asks. There's silence, then a few seconds later, Charlotte continues, "Do you think it will work with her? With what you need? And what about Hay—" She stops suddenly, and Knox's heavy footsteps pace the timber floor.

"Are you jealous?" he asks.

"God no, Knox. Did you really just say that, to me?" She laughs, then Knox laughs too. "I love you, and I know what you need. I just want you to be happy... Whatever that means for you."

She knows him so well, and the way she talks to him and laughs with him causes an ache in my heart I wish would leave. I'm not supposed to feel pain. But this is something else entirely. It's a deep, unrelenting pain that causes my throat to tighten and catches my breath. I twist my hair around my fingers and tug on the strands until I feel the pull on my scalp. It doesn't help. The ache lingers and I don't know how to stop it.

After a quick shower, I pull on a pair of track pants and my hoodie and remind myself I'm not a weak ass little girl. My coffee is still warm, so I grab it and go back into the kitchen where Knox and Charlotte are sitting side by side, talking. When Knox sees me, he extends his hand. "Come 'ere, baby."

I shake my head and sit on the stool at the other end of the bench. "Charlotte, if you need your room, I'll pack my stuff and leave."

Her eyes widen as she stares at me. Knox cocks his head, his brows furrowed.

"No, it's all good. I just came by to grab a few things," Charlotte says. "Stay as long as you like."

I take a sip of coffee then thank her for the clothes. "Do you have a boyfriend," I ask her.

She waves a hand in the air and laughs. "Oh, sweetheart, I don't date."

"Except for Knox..." I say.

"It's in the past," Knox says quickly, then he turns his attention to Charlotte. "Right, Char?"

She nods and smiles. "Way back in the past. We're friends, that's all." Charlotte stands and kisses Knox's cheek as she leans over the bench and puts her coffee mug in the sink.

Anger rises inside me. I don't want her lips near him. I don't want *her* near him. And I don't want to think about him touching her the way he touched me. *But I don't want him. Do I?*

"I'll just go grab some things. Is that okay, Annie?" She points to the bedroom.

I shrug. "It's your room."

When she's gone, Knox looks at me. "Baby, what's wrong?"

I hate how much I react to his words. I hate it and it needs to stop. But his hands... God how I loved the way my body reacted to his touch. Is it possible to hate *and* love someone at the same time? "My name's Annie, and nothing is wrong."

He smirks then stands and comes over to me. I drop my head and pick at my fingernails, ignoring him and his sexy body and delicious scent.

With his hands on the seat of the stool, not touching me at all, he spins the seat so I'm facing him, but I pull the hood of my top over my head and keep my eyes down. *I don't even like him.*

He leans down close to me and whispers, "Are you jealous, baby?"

Jealous? I don't even know what the fuck that feels like. "No." I huff.

He comes closer and nudges the hood across with his nose before he breathes against my ear. "You're the one I want. The one I want to hear moaning my name."

For a brief second, I'm positive my heart stops beating. A desperate ache throbs between my legs and I squeeze my thighs together and glare at him. Damn him and his stupid angel powers. He's doing something to me. "I don't even like you." *Liar!*

"You're not very good at lying."

I raise my head and look into his emerald eyes. "I don't like you, Knox."

Still, he smirks as though I'm joking. His thumbs brush across my thighs, but he doesn't touch me anywhere else. "You liked me last night," he whispers. "A lot."

I shake my head. "Nope. My body likes you... a lot. Not me."

He laughs loudly. "Okay, that's good. At least I know where I stand." He walks toward the bedroom and calls Charlotte. She comes out with two long sparkly dresses and two pairs of shoes with high, pointy heels. "Got everything?" Knox asks her.

She nods and wraps an arm around his waist, then kisses his cheek... again. "You coming back to work soon?" she asks.

Knox nods. "Yeah, next week." He follows her to the door and kisses her forehead before she says goodbye and leaves.

I clench my fists and drop my feet off the stool, then I walk quickly to the gym. As soon as I get there, I breathe a sigh of relief. I need to punch something. I'm too angry to even look at Charlotte's boxing gloves, and the hand wraps take too long, so instead, I punch the bag with my bare fists, slamming into it, kicking it, and shoving it. Desperate to release the rage that's brewing inside me, I go harder and faster until sweat is dripping from my brow, and my knuckles are bruised. But I don't stop. I can't stop. I need to feel something.

Adam! NO! I don't want him. I don't. I clamp my eyes shut and shake my head, but I can't stop thinking about him. The way he knows exactly how to make me hurt. That hurt is what I've lived for, for ten years. The punishments, the fights... Physically, they did nothing. But on the inside, Adam inflicted a torture that would course through my veins and send me to my knees. A torture I still crave.

"Annie," Knox's voice stops me raining hell on the boxing bag.

"What?" My foot hits the top of the bag before I drop it and punch again.

His eyes drop to my fists. "Baby, you're bleeding."

I shake out my hands and continue, desperately seeking the pain, any type of pain. "I'm fine. What do you want?"

"Come and talk to me."

"I'm busy." I throw another punch into the bag, then another. Knox stands in front of it as I'm about to swing, stopping me from following through. "Move, or I'll punch you."

He shakes his head and raises his hands in defence. "Stop now. Look at your hands. Let me wrap them for you."

"Move, Knox." I glare at him.

"You are the most stubborn female I have ever met." He shoves his hands into his pockets. "Punch me. I know you want to." There's not a hint of emotion on his face, just a blank stare. I clench my fists, and without a second thought, I swing a punch that hits his jaw. He scrunches his nose and shakes his head, mostly unaffected. "Do it again."

I tilt my head, watching him, then I do it. Again, he doesn't flinch. "I know you're jealous of Charlotte." A sexy as hell smirk tugs at the corners of his lips.

Fucking asshole! "I am not!" I screech. I punch him again, then I spin and kick him in the thigh. He doesn't move. The bastard is built like a fucking marble statue. *Ugh. I need to hurt him.* Punch after punch, I attempt to hurt him, but he stands there, looking down at me with that smirk I want to kiss off his face.

I step back once and drop my hands by sides, my fists still clenched and my knuckles bruised and bleeding. "You fucking suck," I shout as I leave the gym and head back to my room.

Breathing heavily, I sit on my bed and grab my phone to text him. If I try to talk to him now, I'll only want to kiss him again, or beg him to touch me. *No!* He is not going to have that power.

ME: Don't come into my room and don't text me!

WINGIN'IT: Okay, baby x

I narrow my eyes and glare at the screen, furious. My fingers move quickly as I text back.

ME: I said DON'T text me!

WINGIN'IT: I'll call you when dinner's ready then

ME: not hungry

WINGIN'IT: It's risotto, your favourite

Ugh. Fucking angel! Instead of replying to him, I text Lexi. He can wait forever for all I care, and he can shove his mouth-wateringly delicious risotto up his firm and oh, so sexy ass.

ME: Hi Lexi

LEXI: Hey Annie, how are you?

ME: dunno... mad I think

LEXI: Oh no, why? Did something happen?

ME: Charlotte came here, and she kissed Knox... he said I'm jealous of her, so I punched him

LEXI: lmao!!!

ME: what does that mean

LEXI: Laughing my ass off... you really punched him?

ME: YES. I'm not gonna make it up

She doesn't reply again, but my phone rings and Lexi's name comes up on the screen, so I answer it.

"Hey, what happened?" Lexi asks.

"I told you already, didn't you read my texts?" I flop back on the bed and stare up at the ceiling, opening and closing my fist and watching the dry blood crack on my skin.

"So, Charlotte kissed Knox, and now you're jealous." A door closes in the background and her voice echoes when she talks.

"No. Yes. I don't fucking know. What does being jealous even feel like?" Anger burns inside me and my cheeks heat at having to ask.

Lexi laughs. "Ohhh... Annie, trust me, you're jealous of Charlotte. I was too when I first met her. She's gorgeous, but she doesn't want Knox." The line goes quiet but there's a muffled, "Yeah, babe, it's Annie, I'll be out soon."

"Who are you talking to? And you didn't even answer my question," I whine.

She laughs a little. "It was Clay, don't worry I won't tell him anything. And yeah, we were talking about jealousy. It's like when you really like or love someone and another person comes along and you're worried they can take that person away from you."

I kick my heels into the plush covers on the bed and pull my hair back. "Worried? I wasn't worried, I was pissed off."

"Hmm... for you, same thing. You were jealous. And did she kiss his cheek, because that's pretty normal for guys and girls around here."

I sigh and pout. "Yes. And I hate it, and now I hate her, and I hate Knox."

She laughs again. "Nah, you like him. Why don't you tell him, Annie? I know it's all new to you but sometimes, you have to take a chance. Give it a go, and if it doesn't work out, at least you know you tried."

I narrow my eyes and huff. "I don't like him, Lexi. He's stupid."

"Stupid?" I imagine her rolling her eyes at me.

I roll onto my side. "And he's mean."

"Why?"

A heavy sigh escapes my lips. "Because he doesn't do what I want him to do."

"Aww, Annie, you make me laugh. What do you want him to do?"

"Kiss me again." Why doesn't she understand?

"But you don't like him?" Damn, I hate Lexi's questions. She always makes me talk too much, it's so freaking annoying.

I clamp my eyes shut and clench my jaw. "God, will you shut up."

"Really?" She sighs. "Do you want my advice or not?" Her voice is softer now and she sounds a little... hurt maybe.

"Yes... please. And sorry for telling you to shut up."

"It's okay. Right, go and talk to him. Tell him how you feel and tell him what you want. Trust me, if you tell Knox what you want, I can guarantee he *will* give it to you."

With a loud huff, I agree. "Fine. I'll talk to him."

"Good. Text me later, okay."

"Bye Lexi."

For an hour, I sit on my bed and stare at my phone, typing messages to Knox I don't send. Every single one, I delete. Why is this so damn hard?

Finally, after thinking about it for far too long, I do it.

ME: What are you doing?

WINGIN'IT: Getting dinner ready

WINGIN'IT: Shit, I wasn't supposed to text you, you tricked me

ME: You're a smartass... and you're not even smart, or funny

WINGIN'IT: Come out and talk to me

ME: I don't know how to talk

WINGIN'IT: Okay

I wait for another reply, and when I get nothing, I scream into my pillow. God, he pisses me off. What the hell is his problem? I want him to come to me. I want *him* to come in here and tell me he wants to kiss me. No. I want him to just kiss me, all the time. All day and night. And I want to sleep in his bed again where I can smell him all over me, where I feel safe... where I *feel* something.

ME: You're mean

WINGIN'IT: Why?

ME: Because you don't do stuff I want you to do

A loud burst of laughter comes from the kitchen.

ME: are you laughing at me

WINGIN'IT: Nope, 'course not. What stuff don't I do?

ME: Stuff I want you to do

WINGIN'IT: Like what? Can you be more specific?

ME: UGH can't you figure it out? I thought angels were smart

WINGIN'IT: Some are, like humans. Some are smart and some aren't

I narrow my eyes. Is he calling me stupid? *Rude!*

ME: Stop talking to me

WINGIN'IT: Okay, baby x

I'm going to kill him. Yes! I will walk out there, pick up a knife, and stab him. *What the fuck, Annie?* I shake my head hard. No, I'm not doing that.

ME: You suck!

    I throw my phone on the floor and head to the shower. Maybe I can wash away my thoughts of Knox. The scent of him on my skin, the feel of him whispering against my ear. I'll wash it all away and get the hell out of this town once and for all.

XXIII
THE TRADE

KNOX

two days later

Annie frustrates the hell out of me. She goes from sweet and adorable to feisty and angry in mere minutes. I have no idea what is going to set her off, but I crave it. When she's angry, a rush of adrenaline courses through my veins and brings an ache that can only be sated by her.

Even without touching her, I'm calm. I need her. And her constant text messages, I fucking live for them.

As soon as I saw her looking at Charlotte, I knew damn well she was jealous, but I have a feeling she's never felt jealousy before. She knows chaos and rage the same way I do. The difference is, she has zero control.

Since the night she slept in my bed, I've been craving her more than ever, but she refuses to stay in my room, or allow me to touch her again. Which is fine. I don't want her to feel forced, or to push her into anything she's not ready for.

It's just after 10pm when she comes out of the bedroom wearing nothing but a pair of tiny shorts I assume are underwear or pyjamas, and a tight black tank top. She paces over the fridge, never acknowledging me as she opens the freezer and takes out the tub of chocolate ice cream.

She takes a spoon from the drawer, then with a swish of her ebony hair, she turns and walks back to her bedroom, her tight ass is all I see as she closes the door.

Fuck. She's going to kill me just by breathing the air I breathe.

"Annie," I call, "do you want coffee?"

She doesn't reply, but when my phone chimes with a message, I laugh to myself. She really has no idea how to interact with someone outside of fighting.

ANNIE: yes

A few seconds pass before there's another message.

ANNIE: please

ME: You'll have to come out here and have it

ANNIE: why

ME: Because I want you to

ANNIE: ugh you're annoying

I don't reply. She'll either text me again, or she'll come out.

The bedroom door opens, but I keep my back turned, focused only on the coffee machine. Then, I hear her voice, "You're still mean."

Trying not to smirk, I turn to find her sitting on the kitchen bench, and she's still not wearing pants. *Fuck.* She's so fucking beautiful I need to clench my fists to stop myself reaching out to touch her silky-smooth skin. With the tub of ice cream in her hand, she scoops out a spoonful and puts it in her mouth.

I place the coffee mug on the bench beside her and raise my brow. "You're welcome."

Her eyes narrow slightly. "Thank you, Knox." That sassy, smart mouth is going to be the death of me.

I lean against the opposite bench, watching her. "Still not talking to me?"

She shrugs and licks the spoon, her tongue glides over it before she licks her lips. Those lips I need to have wrapped around my cock.

She puts the ice cream tub on the bench and drops the spoon in the sink before she picks up her coffee mug, swinging her legs while she takes a sip. "Did you have sex with Charlotte?"

What? I run a hand through my hair. "Yeah, why?"

"Was it good?"

I shake my head and laugh. Sticking to honesty is going to be the best thing to do. If I lie and she finds out, she's going to be pissed. But if I tell her the truth... damn. She's going to be pissed no matter what.

"Yep. But it's over now."

"Did you touch her... like you touched me?"

I cock my head, watching her expression, waiting for the rage to come. "I touched her, yes. But no one has, or ever will be like you."

Her cheeks blush pink and she drops her gaze to her coffee and takes another mouthful before she returns her attention to me. "I'm not jealous."

"Okay, that's good."

Her jaw ticks and she inhales slowly. When she exhales, she puts her coffee mug back on the bench. "Why do you have a—" She stops and scratches her head. "Piercing?" she says as though she's not sure, then, "in your dick?"

How the fuck do I answer that?

"Something different," I admit honestly.

She bites her lip. "Did it hurt?"

"Yes and no."

She tilts her head and confusion etches her features. "What does that mean?"

"It hurt, but I liked it... Does that make sense?"

She nods, and I take a step forward, glancing at the scars on her thighs. The same scars she has on her forearms. I raise my hand slowly before I trace one finger over the scars on her thigh. Goose bumps cover her flesh, but she doesn't move or tell me to stop.

I drop my hand. "Did they hurt?"

She shakes her head. "I can't feel anything... Ah, pain. I can't feel pain."

"You can't?" I question.

"Not anymore. Not that kind of pain."

"That's not possible," I say. "Are you sure?" But it all adds up. It would explain her being able to use the gym with a broken rib. The way she continued punching the boxing bag with bruised and bleeding knuckles, and the way she punched the mirror and didn't flinch.

She leans forward and slides the drawer open to reach for a small, sharp knife. "Wanna see?"

"NO! Annie, put it back."

"I'll show you... it doesn't hurt."

The part of me that craves pain, wants to see it. The part of me that yearns for her touch and wants nothing more than to protect her from everything and everyone, is stronger. I grab her wrist.

"No," I say again.

She rolls her eyes and sighs. "If you don't let me do it now, I'll just wait till your asleep."

Giving in, I release her hand. At least if I'm here, I can take care of her... do something. *What the fuck am I thinking?*

She rests her arm on her thighs and points the tip of the small blade to the inside of her forearm.

My brows furrow as I watch her slice her flesh. It's not deep, but for a normal, mortal human, it would hurt a hell of a lot.

I look at her face, she doesn't squint, doesn't suck in a breath, nothing. Not a sound as she tilts her head and drops the knife in the sink. "See, nothing."

I grab the first aid box from under the sink and take out a disinfectant wipe. When I wipe it over her arm, she doesn't flinch. "How long have you been like this?"

She shrugs. "Since I was about ten, I think. I guess I got used to it."

"So that night he—When you ended up in hospital, you really weren't in pain?"

"I know there's something there. I can feel it, but it's like... I'm not even sure..." She shakes her head. "Annoying... Maybe that's pain, but it doesn't bother me. I can just ignore it." Another shrug.

I stand closer to her again. "Why were you mad at me earlier?"

When she looks into my eyes, I stare back and all I find in hers, is confusion.

I place my hands on the bench beside her thighs, my thumbs brush against her bare skin.

"Annie?"

"You were mean..." she says in barely a whisper.

"How?"

"You made me angry. And you let Charlotte kiss you." She averts her gaze, focusing on the floor.

"Charlotte made you angry... or me?"

"Both." She huffs. "Lexi said I was jealous."

I bite the inside of my mouth to stop the smirk. *I knew it.* "You spoke to Lexi?"

A nod. "I texted her, then she called me."

"So... you *don't* want Charlotte to kiss me?" I keep my tone even, not giving her a chance to think I might be mocking her.

She shakes her head and her teeth bite down on her bottom lip.

"Why?" I'm going make her say it. She's going to tell me exactly what she wants, then I'll give it to her.

She looks up at me, her long dark lashes flutter as she blinks. "Because." Then she shrugs.

"Why?" I ask again.

She clamps her eyes shut and exhales with a groan of frustration.

I lean closer and whisper against her ear. "Tell me, baby." *Tell me you want me.*

When she opens her eyes, her lips part slightly. "I want to kiss you. No..." She shakes her head hard. "I want *you* to kiss me."

"You do?"

She nods. "But only me."

"Now?"

"Always," she says, and this time I can't hide the smug smile that spreads across my lips.

I glide my hand up her arms to her shoulders, then slowly up to her neck where I twist my fingers through her hair. She spreads her legs and I take another step forward, my lips mere inches from hers.

"Are you sure?"

Her eyes close and her lips part. "Yes..." Her breath lingers against my lips, and without another thought, I kiss her.

The moan that escapes tells me she's been waiting for this, wanting it. My stubborn girl wants everything her way, and I'm only too happy to give it to her.

Soft hands slide over my forearms and up to my biceps as she wriggles closer. I wrap my arms around her, pulling her into me as we kiss.

Her legs tighten around me, her heels digging into my ass. "Knox," she whispers through panting breaths.

"Mmm..." I kiss beside her lips, then down to her jaw and back up, all the while she moves against me.

"I don't... I mean, I can't." In a breathy whisper, she says, "Please stop."

I stop and step back. She pulls her knees together and twists her hands in her lap, her eyes still on mine, but the lust has gone from her eyes and has been replaced with something else. It could be fear, or perhaps it's uncertainty.

"You okay?"

She shakes her head. "I want to kiss you, but I want more... I think... Or—" She drops her feet to the floor and sighs. "Doesn't matter. I don't know what I want, I'm not good at this. I'm so sorry." She turns and walks back to the bedroom, closing the door behind her.

Damn. She's confused. She's never been in any type of normal relationship. Never felt love, never been loved. I will show her everything, prove to her she's worthy of every ounce of love I have to give.

I slump down on the sofa and put my feet up on the coffee table as I drink the last of my glass of whiskey. My phone rings and I grab it to answer.

"Yeah, what's up?" I assume it's one of my brothers calling this late at night.

"Where's my Annastasia?"

I leap to my feet when I hear his voice. "What the fuck?"

There's a quiet laugh. "She belongs to me. I want her back."

"Never. No fucking way." I pace to the window and look outside, checking to see if anyone's there. At the same time, a beep on my phone alerts me to another call.

"Let's trade," he says.

"You have nothing I want. Fuck off."

"Ah, see that's where you're mistaken." After a few seconds of silence, there's a strangled plea.

"Don't... forget about—protect her..." It's Roman. Fucking hell. *Kailey. Georgia... No. I can't let this happen.*

"What do you want?" I shout and Annie opens the bedroom door a crack and looks up at me.

"Annastasia, and you, and I'll let my weak as piss brother go. He's not very strong for a twelve."

I pace the kitchen. "When?"

"One hour, at the water tower." He hangs up and my phone rings again.

"Knox..." It's Flynn.

"I know. I'm going there, he said one hour."

"What?"

"He wants to trade..."

"NO!"

"You can't stop me, brother. I won't let Georgia grow up without a father, and Kailey... I can't let it happen."

"Knox, he'll kill you."

"And you want Roman to die?"

There's silence for long seconds, then a sigh. "You don't have to do this, brother."

"I do. It's the only way. I owe it to him; I owe it to you... all of you." Before he can reply, I hang up and look at Annie.

She crosses her arms around herself, and as though she knows exactly what is happening, she nods and goes back into the bedroom. A few minutes later, she comes back out dressed in black leggings and a black t-shirt.

"Annie..."

"You don't have to say anything," she says. "This is why I told you to leave me alone. I knew he'd come back. Does he really have Georgia's father?"

I nod. "There's something I need to tell you, before we go."

She sighs and leans her elbows on the bench then tucks her hair behind her ear.

"Roman... Georgia's father, he's—What the fuck is his name anyway?"

"Adam?"

"Roman is Adam's brother. His identical twin."

She gasps and stands tall, her brows scrunched in confusion. "Are you fucking serious?"

"He's not like him, he's not like any of them. He's part of our family, he's been helping us for a while."

"He's not like Adam?" she's asking for reassurance.

I shake my head. "Only in looks."

"Knox... I need to tell you something too." Her gaze drops to the floor before she pulls her hair into a high ponytail and meets my eyes again.

"Okay, go ahead."

"Adam, he uses the blood. The blood he took from you and that vampire, Vandrick. He had angels at home, but Michael, the old man, he always said the blood wasn't strong enough."

I pace back and forth, scrubbing my hands down my face. "Angels?" *He had more than one angel... FUCK!* "Do you know their names?"

She shakes her head. "They never spoke, at least not when I was there. They had white wings... That was why I asked why yours are black."

I ignore the last part. I can't get into that with her now. "Are they still alive?"

She shakes her head, her eyes filled with remorse.

XXIV
THE FIGHTER

KNOX

Flynn and Steel stand beside me. On my other side, Annie remains silent.

"As soon as you have him, leave," I tell them. "Don't fight him."

Flynn nods in agreement. "You spoke to Roman?"

I only nod.

The drain cover opens; Adam comes out first. He glares at Annie, then shifts his gaze to Flynn and Steel, before stopping on me. "I'm surprised you kept up your end of the deal, angel."

I glare right back, my arms crossed over my chest. "Where's Roman?"

He kneels, then reaches down into the hole and drags Roman out by his arms, leaving him face down on the ground, bleeding, bruised and fighting for each breath. Now that he's immortal, he won't die, but he'll be in a hell of a lot of pain. Flynn kneels to pick him up and when his head drops back, Annie gasps.

Adam cups her cheek. "Cool hey, baby. That's my twin brother. Too bad he's almost dead, you won't get to meet him, will you?"

"No Adam," she replies.

He grabs her arm and points to the hole in the ground. "Get down there, now. And remember, it's Twelve."

As Annie goes down the ladder, Flynn and Steel walk away with Roman.

"Let's go, angel," Adam says.

Instead of the basement, Adam leads us to the arena where the Fray are watching two guys fight. He takes Annie's hand and talks quietly. "Baby, you're healed up again, let see what we can do about that."

"Yes, Twelve," she says.

I want to rip the bastard's head off and crush him. *Soon. Soon, I will destroy him.*

Adam stands by the side of the square they have marked out on the floor. On the opposite side, the commander and his father sit in large chairs, watching.

"Eleven," Adam calls, "you'll fight the angel first."

A guy runs over, and when he looks up at me, he stops in his tracks. It's Harley, and he's already Eleven; this is fucking perfect.

When Harley doesn't move, Adam raises his voice. "Now."

"Yes, Twelve."

I pull my shirt off and throw it on the floor then stand in the square. When I see Harley swallow, I laugh. "Don't worry, *Eleven,* I'll be gentle, at first."

Adam steps back, his hand still tight around Annie's arm.

"Fight," he says.

Harley doesn't waste any time. He swings a punch and when I grip his fist in my hand, the recruits gasp, then cheer for Harley, calling out "Eleven" and telling him to fight. I release his hand and when he swings again, I grip it in mine.

Punch after punch he tries to fight me, but I block him every time.

"Fucking fight," Adam shouts.

Harley charges forward and lands a hard punch to my jaw, then another to my cheek. I grab him in a headlock to slam him down to the floor, but he manages to worm his way out of my grasp and throw another punch that narrowly misses me.

I kick him in the gut, sending him flying backwards. "That all you got," he mocks. He pushes himself up on his elbows and shakes his head, sending a splatter of blood across the floor from his nose. "Lexi put up a better fight than you."

The bastard must really want to die today. With a growl of anger, I kneel on his chest and slam my fist into his nose. The audible crack causes a few recruits to gasp, then I ram my boot into his ribs. Blood dribbles from the corner of his mouth as he coughs and splutters, and when his head lolls to the side, I wrap my hand around his throat and lean down to him. "That all you got?"

His eyes flicker before they finally close and I stand and step back, glaring at Adam.

Silence falls over the arena as Adam steps forward. He pulls his knife from its sheath and I clench my fists, ready to fight again, but he holds the knife in his hand, swinging it around as he talks. "Who's Lexi?"

"My brother's girlfriend." I narrow my eyes. "His ex."

"Hmm..." He looks down at Harley. "What did he do to her?"

"Why the fuck do you care?"

"You're an angel. And you killed him, why?"

"He's a fucking bastard. He hit her..." I glance at Annie. "Forced her into some shit she wanted no part of." I shake my head. "It's over now. He's dead."

"Hmm, not dead enough." Adam takes three steps forward, then reaches down and grips a handful of Harley's hair to force his head back. Without hesitation, he drags the silver blade across Harley's throat then stands and raises his brow.

When I glance at Annie, she's staring down at Harley as though she's in a daze, her eyes locked onto the blood that spills from his throat. My attention back on Adam, I stand, confused as fuck. What the hell is this guy on? He's gotta be taking some serious drugs.

He calls out, "Eight, get rid of this piece of shit, now! Shove him in the furnace."

I stare at him, waiting for an explanation... for something. "Is there a reason you just slit his throat?"

His lip turns up in a snarl. "One, I like to make people bleed. Two, any fucking bastard that forces a female..." he hesitates, a look of pure disgust on his face. "Sexually..." He holds his knife up and stares at it as though the knife itself is the only *drug* he needs. "Will feel this knife in their fucking soul."

"What the fuck? You're forcing An—You're forcing her to fight."

He shakes his head. "Wrong. I'm training her. Helping her learn that with discipline, comes power. I never fucking touched her *sexually*. EVER!" His rage builds and his eyes darken as he stands in front of Annie and cocks his head. "Am I forcing you to do anything, Annastasia?"

"No, Twelve. I *want* to be here, with you. I want you to train me."

Yeah, that's bullshit. "Right, so according to your *rules*, the commander should be feeling that knife too."

He raises his brow. "Oh, he'll feel it alright. And when he does, you'll hear him screaming from heaven, *angel*."

Okay. He's not only a psychopath, but he's got some kind of split personality as well.

"Your turn, Annastasia," he says as he steps back.

She nods once. "Yes, Twelve."

She walks into the square, clasps her hands behind her back and drops her head.

"Isn't she perfect?" Adam says to me.

I don't reply as he calls a Twelve over who's six-foot-tall and towers over Annie, but I have no doubt she'll win. She must win.

Adam walks over to her and whispers in her ear. All I hear is her quiet, "Yes, Twelve" before he comes back and stands beside me.

Fuck this shit. I should have given her my blood.

When Adam tells them to start, Annie doesn't hesitate. She jumps right in, swinging punches, kicking, and beating the crap out of the guy who fights back just as hard. Every smack of his fist that hits her face sends a bolt of rage through my body. When this is over, I will kill every single person who put their hands on her.

After three minutes, Annie gets him down and he raises his hand to give up. She steps back and drops her head again as though this is all she knows. *It is all she knows.*

Adam paces back and forth, rubbing his head and mumbling under his breath. "Commander, you want to fight the girl?"

I swallow hard. NO! He will kill her. "Why don't you fight her," I say. "Unless you're scared."

From what Annie has told me, he won't kill her. For some reason, she's important to him, but I can't figure out why. He's not using her for sex, and he doesn't want her because she's female. There's something about her, he needs.

Adam narrows his eyes at me then cocks his head. "I have a better idea." When he holds his knife out to Annie, her eyes widen. "Finish him," Adam commands.

The guy on the floor, Twelve, scrambles to his feet. "No... no, I can do better," he says.

Adam glares at him. "On your knees."

He does as Adam commands. He doesn't attempt to fight or run, he merely drops his head and places his hands on his knees as Annie walks toward him.

With a handful of his hair in her left hand, she pulls his back. He clamps his eyes shut and his chest heaves with each heavy breath. As Annie slices the knife across his throat, Adam smiles.

"Perfect." He cocks his head, watching her, and when she locks eyes with him, she smiles. *What the fuck has he done to her?* It's as though she's a completely different girl to the one I was with just hours ago.

Adam waves a hand in the air. "Ten and Six, clean this up." He turns his attention to me. "Come, angel, let's have some fun."

In the basement, I stand against the wall and let Adam chain my wrists and ankles before he returns with a syringe and takes a few vials of my blood. Once he's done, he orders Annie to strip.

"Has he seen your whole body yet, baby?"

"No, Adam."

"Hmm.... I think you're lying to me?"

"She's not lying," I say.

A sinister smirk dances across his lips as he leads Annie over to me. He places a hand on her shoulder and orders her to turn around. When she does, I bite my tongue so hard that blood fills my mouth. I refuse to give him the reaction he's looking for.

Down Annie's spine, from her neck to just above her ass, she's been branded like Roman has. The roman numerals from one to twelve are aligned perfectly down her spine. He turns her back to face me. "Tell the angel what they're for, Annastasia."

She shakes her head, and instantly, his face turns into a menacing scowl. "Tell him!" Adam shouts.

"No."

He slaps her face hard. "What the fuck did you say to me?"

She raises her head and looks him in the eyes. "I said no."

He clenches his fist and slams it into her jaw. There's no reaction to the pain she should be feeling—she's completely calm. Her head is thrown back and blood oozes from her mouth as Adam pulls a knife from the sheath on his belt. "Tell him."

"I don't want to," she says in a soft voice.

Adam presses the tip of his knife into her side and twists the blade, causing Annie to wince, but she doesn't cry. "Last chance."

God, just do it, Annie.

She looks up at me. "Let him go first."

Adam laughs and walks over to me; he shoves the knife into my abdomen and glides his finger down the blade before he walks back to Annie. "Ah ah... I make the rules here, Annastasia. Now, tell the angel why you have those marks, and I won't let him bleed out while you stand and watch."

"Killing," is all she says.

Adam circles her like a wolf circling its prey. "Come on, baby, you can do better than that. Use your words." He presses the tip of the knife into her cheek, leaving a smear of crimson blood in its wake.

"Each brand is for each person I have killed."

Maybe he was trying to shock me, or maybe he assumes I'll be pissed off. But there's nothing. She did what she had to do to survive. She was afraid for her life.

Adam pushes her hair back off her face.

"Why did you do this to her?" I ask.

He paces back and forth, spinning his knife in his hand as he speaks. "You don't see it, do you? Angels should be able to *see* people, but you're different..." He grunts then hands Annie the knife. "Stab him."

She shakes her head.

"Stab him," Adam says slowly.

"No."

He grips her hair in his hand and leads her toward me. "Do it."

"Just do it," I say.

She lifts the knife and clamps her eyes shut as she raises her hand. When the tip of the blade touches my flesh, she opens her eyes. Adam tightens his hand around her throat. "Annastasia... You know what happens when you disobey."

She pushes the knife into my flesh, then quickly pulls it out and drops it on the floor. When she steps back, she drops to her knees. Adam pats her head as he stands beside her. "Such a good girl, isn't she, Knox."

When I don't reply, he walks around so he's behind Annie. "Now, Annastasia... let's start with, hmm... number twelve. Who was that?"

With her head down, she murmurs, "an Angel."

My breath is caught in my throat. All this time I've despised Roman for killing our brother and it's possible Annie has done the same thing. *It's not her fault.*

"Eleven," Adam says.

"Angel."

Fuck no.

Adam glances up at me and raises his brow. "Ten."

"Seven... the Fray guy."

"Nine?"

"Five... the Fray."

A smirk forms across Adam's lips. "Let's skip to number four."

"The woman. With you, Adam."

"What's your point here?" I ask him.

He raises a hand. "Ah ah... wait. It gets better. Annastasia, number two."

"I... I don't remember."

"Oh, come on, you know—"

"You're a fucking psychopath," I say cutting him off.

He scratches his head with the tip of the knife. "And you think she's not?"

She's not like him. He continues, "Did she tell you where the old man and I found her?"

I don't reply, knowing he's going to tell me anyway. I need to know about her, so I can save her.

"Annastasia was six years old when we found her. Me and the old man, we followed her and her mother home from the store. The old man said I couldn't do it, I wanted to prove him wrong. My plan was to murder them. Show the bastard I wasn't afraid; you know how it is." He averts his gaze, and something tells me he's lying. I don't trust this bastard one bit. "I assumed she was a normal kid from a normal family with a boring, normal life. Until we got to her house." He shrugs and pats her head again.

Annie raises her head slightly and Adam looks down at her. "Stand up, Annastasia."

Adam drags the tip of the knife across her flesh as he paces around her. "Where was I? Oh, that's right. So, we waited till night, and went inside. But Annastasia here... she wasn't in her bedroom. She was with her parents." He stands in front of her but speaks to me first. "So... Knox, I'm sure you're curious about Annastasia's lack of pain right now." He leans down and whispers something to Annie I don't hear. When he straightens, he continues, "You wanna see her in pain? Keep watching. Now, Annastasia, do you remember when you were with your parents?"

"No Adam."

"Don't worry, it'll all come back." He starts pacing again. "Now, we assumed we'd find sweet little Annastasia warm in bed with Mummy and Daddy. But no..." He smirks and a devious laugh spills from his lips. "This little girl," he says, lifting her hand and placing the knife in her palm. "She had a knife... Not just any knife. It was this knife right here." He closes her fingers around the knife. "You don't remember?" he asks her.

She shakes her head. Adam grips her jaw in his hand and rubs his thumb across her lips. "Close your eyes, think real hard, baby. Think about the blood... the screams... your laughter. Think about me."

Annie clamps her eyes shut as Adam continues, "She was standing over her father, the knife tight in her little hand, just like this," he says as he raises her hand. "She stabbed him and giggled. Then stabbed him again, and again... In that moment, while I watched her, I knew she was going to be mine. She was just like me."

Annie's face doesn't change at all as he keeps talking. "While I stood in the doorway, she looked up at me and asked who I was. I told her I was going to help her, that I'd make sure the police wouldn't find her. She smiled and skipped across the bedroom to her mother, who was screaming." There's a look of pure disgust on his face. "She was so fucking loud I wanted to kill her myself. *But* I let Annastasia do it. I watched as she sliced the knife across her mother's throat, then dipped her fingers in the blood. She held her hand up to show me. She was so proud of herself, so beautiful, so perfect."

I turn my attention to Annie. Her arms are wrapped tight around herself and her body stiffens as she winces in pain. A single tear drips from the corner of her eye. She inhales, then, she exhales slowly. "Stop." It's barely a whisper, but Adam turns to face her and cups her cheek. "Adam, please, stop it hurts..." Through panting sobs Annie begs, "Stop it, please stop. I can't—I can't take anymore..." As her voice trails off, Annie drops her head, and when Adam turns his attention to me, Annie plunges the knife into Adam's chest. He groans in pain,clutching at his chest as he hits the ground and blood oozes through his t-shirt.

Annie looks up at me. A blank stare is all I get. Urgently, and without a word, she unchains my wrists and ankles to free me. "We need to run. He won't stay down long. He's had the blood."

I grab her hand and race out the door to head toward the tunnel. Behind us, there's shouting and the pounding of heavy footsteps. When we reach the drain, I shove the cover off and push Annie up.

I climb out and we continue running. Adrenaline courses through my veins while thoughts of Annie's childhood play over in my head. What the fuck happened to her to make her kill her own parents like that? He must be lying. She wouldn't do it. Not my Annie.

As we reach the edge of the forest, Annie stops, her hands on her knees as she breathes in and out slowly. I call my brothers in my head to tell them where we are, and at the same time, Annie screams.

I spin around to see Adam holding her against his chest, the knife at her throat.

I stop dead in my tracks as Steel and Clay land either side of me.

"An audience," Adam says. "We love an audience, don't we, Annastasia?"

She struggles to free herself from his grasp.

"Let her go," I shout.

He shakes his head. "You can't have her. She belongs to me."

"Take me instead. You can have my blood, as much as you need. Just let her go, she's been through enough."

He smiles and whispers something in her ear. When she nods, he looks up at me. "No deal." I take a step forward and he presses the blade of the knife into her throat. Clay and Steel pull me back as Flynn lands behind Adam and brings a finger to his lips, warning us to be quiet.

I lower my voice, trying to get him to loosen his grip on her, or at least move the knife away from her throat. "Okay, you can have her. Just drop the knife." I raise my hands in defence, but Adam narrows his gaze and cocks his head. When a sly smile spreads across his lips, he raises his brow. "Nice try, angel, but I'll never let her go."

"You don't want to kill her, Adam. You *need* her, remember."

"Oh, but I do. You see, Knox, if I can't have her... the way she was before, no one will have her." He presses his lips to her hair. "Make a choice, Annastasia, tell me what you want the most."

"Adam," she whispers, and my heart cracks wide open. Everything I thought was true, was nothing more than a lie. Did she plan this? *No.*

Flynn moves closer and when my eyes flit to his, I know Adam saw it.

He raises his brow. "Annastasia, any last words, baby?"

Her eyes lock onto mine and her mouth moves, but not a sound comes out. "I love you," she mouths.

Adam drags the blade across her throat; her blood spills down her chest, a tidal wave of crimson that matches the blood that drips from the corner of her mouth as her eyes close and he pushes her forward. My cry of pain is so loud my ears ring and my throat burns.

I fall to my knees on the ground beside her. My hands and knees now covered in her blood. I look up at Flynn, begging him with my eyes, but I know it's too late, and because we're not bound, he would be forbidden to save her.

The first girl I've ever truly wanted, is dead.

XXV

THERE WILL BE BLOOD

ADAM

Footsteps echo in the stairwell before he paces across the bloodstained floor. I lean back in my leather chair and rub my hands over the arms where the leather is cracked and dry from years of use.

When he stops in front of me, he glances at the male hanging from the wall before his focus returns to me. "You called for me?"

"It's done. What now?"

"You are certain?"

Fucking moron thinks I don't know life from death. His insult offends me, perhaps he'll be next to die. I twist my knife in my hand; blood still coats the blade—her blood. "I slit her throat, she's dead."

"There is a chance he won't do it."

I raise a brow and smile. "Trust me... he'll do it."

He clasps his hands behind his back and paces toward the male hanging from the wall. His wrists are bound by shackles and the chains are attached to a thick meat hook that hangs from the twelve-foot ceiling. Right now, he's unconscious. Soon he'll wake, and I'll have my fun with him.

I get to my feet and pace toward him, keeping my eyes on the bruised and bloody male. His body is a work of art. Pure immortal perfection. At least it was before he came to me. Now, his once luminous flesh is mottled with blue and purple tinged bruises, and his flawless body is littered with scars. He will survive only if I allow it. Using the tip of my knife, I lift the strands of blond hair off his face and push them back.

"Do you think this is a wise decision, Adam? We could use him for leverage—"

I spin on my heel to face him, cutting him off abruptly. "*WE?* There is no we, Vandrick. There is me, and there is you. Do not forget that."

He raises a brow. I'm consciously aware that he's more than capable of killing me at any moment, but he won't. Without me, the power he craves will always be out reach.

As he turns to pace the room, his long cloak billows behind him, a flowing sea of black that carries his scent, along with the metallic scent of blood. "If you kill him, they have no reason to seek you out. They will not retaliate. The fallen protect the living, they do not come for their dead."

Turning back to the male, I inhale as my eyes peruse his battered body. My skin itches, and my mind is at war. The need to see his blood spill is an ache—an uncontrolled desire that unless sated, will bring me to my knees.

Walking away from Annastasia while she bled out on the forest floor, was nothing short of torture. Now, the urge to flee, to race back and hold her lifeless body in my arms while she bleeds out, brings excruciating pain and sets every nerve ending on fire. For ten years she has been my drug. The one who stopped my descent into madness and reminded me that life could be as exquisite as death.

I return my attention to Vandrick. "I have other ways of enticing them."

He crosses his arms over his chest. "Do tell..."

"Wake him up," I say before I head back to my chair.

Vandrick injects a syringe of blood into the male's neck. The blood, a mixture of Knox's pure angel blood, along with vampire blood, will wake him within minutes. My grandfather's attempts at creating a synthetic blood to match that of the royal angels, has failed. Something is missing, and I'm about to find out what that something is.

As the male slowly regains consciousness, Vandrick watches him closely. "I'm surprised they haven't discovered it yet." He's talking to me, but he's still watching the male.

"Their focus is elsewhere, as you know."

The male's eyes scan the room before his gaze stops on me. "Adam?" his voice is hoarse. "Wha—" He tugs on the chains that bind his wrists. "What have you done? Where am I?"

Vandrick laughs. "Javier. How are you, old friend?"

Javier blinks a few times. "Vandrick, you will end up like your father."

I pace toward Javier, and he shakes his head. "No, no. Adam, this is wrong. You must let me go." He clamps his eyes shut, his face a picture of pain.

"Your powers won't work," I remind him.

"Where am I?"

"Ambrosia Valley."

His eyes grow wide. "You were warned... Adam the—"

I grasp his throat and squeeze it tight. "Hush now, angel, and perhaps I'll let you live."

"Please, Adam," he begs. "Let me go. We had an agreement."

I nod toward Vandrick who takes Javier's hand and inhales against his wrist. When he bites into Javier's flesh, Javier lets out a cry of agony. "Save some of that,

Vandrick," I command. I step back, my eyes on Javier—The traitor. "You told them. Why is that?"

He raises his head. "I had no choice. You... you are no longer in control. It's time to stop." He lowers his voice to a whisper. "You've gone too far."

I pull my knife from its sheath and storm toward him, pointing the tip at his chest. "Too far? You think *I've* gone too far?" Furious, I shove the knife into his abdomen and watch the blood ooze from his flesh. I step closer, closing the gap between us before I shove the knife into his thigh. "Too far?" I twist the knife, embedding it deep into his thigh as he groans in pain. "Is this too far?"

"Stop... please. Adam, I can help you."

I drag the knife out slowly and hold it up in front of him. "How?"

"A deal. I will make you a deal."

"Another one? No. This time, I'll do it my way."

"They'll kill you."

I laugh in his face. "Show your wings."

When he shakes his head, I remove the chains from his wrists and let him fall to his knees, his ankles still chained to the wall.

"Wings."

He shakes his head again.

"Vandrick," I say.

Vandrick places a hand on Javier's head, and a few short seconds later, he's screaming in pain as thick, crimson blood drips from his eyes and his nose. As his wings extend, Vandrick steps back.

I pace around Javier until I'm standing behind him. The bones of his wings extend from his shoulder blades. I shove my knife into his shoulder and he falls forward, his hands splayed on the floor in front of him. As I cut through flesh and muscle, his blood runs down his back and pools at my feet. "Vandrick, bring me the sword."

"No!" Javier shouts. "Tell me what you want, I will give you anything." When he attempts to fold his wings, there's a crack as the bone of his left wing snaps, leaving a jagged edge much like a broken tree branch. I grip the broken bone and shove it until there's another snap.

His shrill cry of pain sends adrenaline coursing through my veins. "There's nothing more I want from you. You betrayed me, and for that you die."

With a heavy sigh, Javier straightens his back and raises his head. "Forgive me," he whispers before he closes his eyes.

There will be no forgiveness.

There will be death.

And blood.

XXVI

THE ULTIMATE SACRIFICE

KNOX

Thick, dark clouds of malevolence hover above, blocking the night sky and the stars that scatter the heavens. A cold chill wraps me in a shroud of misery as my brothers' approach, each of them begging me to let her go, to let *this* be her fate. *I refuse to allow it.*

"Maple!" I scream her name with every ounce of life I have left in me.

When she lands, her eyes grow wide and she steps back.

"Fix her! I'm begging you, I will do anything at all. You have to fix her."

Maple tilts her head and raises her hand above mine. The light from her palm does nothing to calm me. "Knox, she is gone."

Haydee's whisper beside my ear is a reminder of my strength, of the strength I should have used to save Annie.

"She is wrong, Knox. She wants you for herself, she doesn't want to save Annie. Kill her, show her you will not give in."

I raise my head. Strength courses through my veins and my heart beats rapidly as I stand and glare at Maple.

"Fix her!" I command. I lunge at Maple, but before I touch her, a blast of angel light hits my chest, and I'm thrown back.

Haydee's laughter swirls around me and I shout at her to stop. Grasping my head in my hands, I pull on my hair in a desperate attempt to get the visions of Annie's lifeless body out of my mind.

"Maple." I shake my head hard. "I'll give you anything," I beg. "Take my life to save her."

Maple raises a brow. "You should let her go."

"What? NO! I'm not letting her go. I need her."

"She is not who you think she is, Knox. I am asking you to let her go."

"No."

"Very well. I will *attempt* to help this... female. A sacrifice."

"Anything at all."

"Your wings." Two words I have hoped and prayed I would never hear. Without my wings, I will lose my powers, and my place in heaven. Without Annie, I will end up in hell.

I don't hesitate. "Yes." This will kill my father. The thought of seeing his face tears through what's left of my broken heart.

"NO!" Clay shouts. "Knox, don't do it."

Maple extends her hand, sending a rush of memories through my mind. One stands out the most and sticks, a memory I will never forget.

Knox
8 years old

When I finally get out of the castle, I run to the meadow to find my brothers. Flynn and Steel are already in the sky, flying with their wings spread wide.

Clay is sitting on the grass with his legs crossed and his head in his hands.

Yesterday was our 8th birthday. The day we got our angel wings. We've always had wings, but they were much smaller and lighter. Now, they're huge and heavy and Clay's still upset he hasn't been able to get off the ground.

"Clay, are you still sad?"

He nods, and a shiny tear drips down his cheek. "Try again," I tell him. "It's not hard."

He looks up at Flynn and Steel. "It's too hard for me. I'm too small."

I jump to my feet and look down at my brother. It's true, he is the smallest of all of us, but he's always been the happiest. Now, he's sad, and I don't like it.

I extend my hand. "Come on."

He looks up at it then drops his head again.

Flynn and Steel land with a thud beside me. "Come on, Knox, let's fly," Flynn says.

"Are you coming, Clay," Steel asks.

Clay shakes his head.

"You're missing out," Flynn says. "It's the best."

When they take off again, I drop to my knees in front of Clay and spread my wings out wide. My feathers flutter and rustle in the warm, heavenly breeze. "Want me to help you?" I ask Clay.

"You can't. I'm not good enough."

Clay is my favourite brother, and when he's sad, it makes me sad too. I need to fix it for him.

I reach forward and grab his hand. "Come on, I'll help you."

Slowly, he gets to his feet and spreads his wings.

I move mine back and forth and tell him to do the same. When he's moving his wings, he looks up to the sky again, and as they move faster, his feet raise up off the ground.

"You're doing it," I say. "Higher."

I hover in front of him, my wings still moving in time with his, but he drops back to the ground again.

It's almost sunset when Clay drops down to his knees and cries. "I'll never be able to use these wings. They're too big."

I take both his hands and pull him up to his feet. "One more time, okay, then I won't make you try again," I say.

With a sad nod, he agrees, and I hold his hands tight and move my wings, faster and faster until I feel them lifting me off the ground. As Clay's wings move, he rises off the ground too. But I know it's my wings that are helping him. I can feel it in my heart and soul, I am strong, stronger than all my brothers.

"Keep moving them," I tell him, hoping that when he gets a little higher, he'll be able to hold himself up.

As we near the clouds, I let go of Clay's hands and he gasps, his wings moving steadily as he floats in the heavenly sky.

"Knox," he shouts with glee. "I'm flying, I'm really flying. Look!"

I smile and nod. "Told you, you could do it."

He goes higher and higher until he's flying through the sky without a care in the world. His wings carry him past the clouds and back down again. He twists and turns and spins around until we're both laughing wildly, and when our father calls from the castle, we land on the ground and Clay leaps forward and hugs me.

"You're the best brother in all the worlds," he says.

I smile, but I don't know what to say. I want to tell him he's brave and strong and that I won't ever let him be sad again, but the only thing that comes out of my mouth is, "You too, brother."

When Maple drops her hand, a tear rolls down my cheek.

"Take them," I tell Maple. "I need her back. Please." I grip Annie's hand in mine, the warmth is already leaving her body.

Seconds later, my father lands on the grass in front of me and my brothers kneel before him. I don't move, I only look up at him, and beg again. "Please, Father, I need her... I *need* her."

Tears fall from my father's eyes as he removes his angel sword from its sheath. The blade glows neon blue as he holds it up in front of him. He glances at Maple. "Is this necessary?"

Maple nods once. "Your Highness, *you* gave us power over the fallen. Your son's disregard for not only Angel Law, but the laws here on earth, has been a never-ending cycle. Knox has had many chances to change; to prove he is as honourable as his brothers. His fate, I'm afraid, was sealed by his own hands."

My father drops his head; for a minute he's completely silent. He raises his head and steps forward toward me.

Maple steps back beside him, and my brothers stand in front of me as I kneel before my father. My back to him and my wings spread wide. "My son, you understand what this means?"

"Yes."

"You will not return to heaven with your brothers. When you pass on, you will be gone, forever."

"I know, Father."

"Knox," Clay says quietly. *Please, don't do it. Not your wings.*

"I'm sorry," I say as I look into his eyes. *I'm so sorry, brother.*

My son forgive me. My father's voice in my head is the last thing I hear.

Clay, Steel and Flynn drop their heads as my father slices through the first wing. The agony is dismal compared to the pain in my chest as Annie lies dead before me. When my second wing is removed, the feathers swirl before they turn to ash and disappear into the heavens.

My father places his hand on my back. All that will remain are scars. A permanent reminder of my sacrifice. My blood will no longer be blue, and my powers will gradually disappear, but I will forever be immortal.

When my father is gone, Maple kneels and places her hand on Annie's head. A few minutes later, she steps back and sighs. "It is done. I cannot guarantee she will wake. If she does, she may not choose you. She is not yours."

"I love her," is all I say.

"This is not love, Knox."

XXVII

INNOCENCE LOST

ANNIE

seven years old

"Annie, Annie? Annie, where are you, sweetheart?"

I pull my long sleeves down very quickly and tug on my warm jacket. "I'm coming, Mummy," I call as I kneel on the floor and push Daddy's special knife under my bed. I need to keep it safe for later because I have a very important thing to do.

Daddy says the knife is called "antique" because it's more than two hundred years old. That's the oldest thing Daddy has in our house, and I think he'll be angry if he knows I took it from the pretty wooden cabinet. But he has so many, so maybe he won't know the shiny silver one with the precious bone handle, is gone.

My bedroom door opens, and I scramble to my feet to see Mummy looking at me with a confused face. "What are you doing, Annie, we need to go."

"I can't find my black ribbons." I squeeze my eyes shut and try to make tears come out, but it doesn't work. Lies are so, so easy, but tears are hard.

Mummy smiles and tells me all the ribbons are in the drawer in the bathroom. I already know that, but I have to make up a lie so she doesn't know about the knife.

While I stand in the bathroom, Mummy ties the black ribbons in my hair and makes them into pretty bows. "Annie, remember what Mummy told you about the dreams?"

I nod. "No talking about my dreams at school."

"Good girl." She leans down and kisses my cheek then gives me a big cuddle. "I love you, sweetheart."

"I love you, Mummy." It's another lie. Mummy always says she loves me, but I don't know if it's true. Sometimes she shouts at me and it makes me sad, and sometimes she smacks my bottom and my face, and pulls my hair or pinches me. It hurts a lot. I don't think I love her. I don't know what love is 'spose to be anyway.

Mummy takes me to school, and for the whole day I sit down, stand up, sit down, stand up. Adam didn't tell me I can kill teachers, but maybe if I listen to him, he'll change his mind. It's so boring at school and I just want to read all the books in the classroom so the day goes very fast.

When it's lunch time, I grab my lunch box and sit at the table next to a boy whose name is Adam. He has the same name as the boy in my dreams, but I'm not allowed to talk about my dreams with anyone except Doctor Holtman. He's a special doctor who only sees kids and helps them stop having dreams and being naughty. I don't want to stop though; I like my dreams. Sometimes, I even think that Adam is real, and sometimes, if I look really hard, I can see him in my real life.

When I shut my eyes very tight, I can always find my dream Adam inside my head. He always calls me Annastasia, and he says that one day he'll come and find me and take me away, but not until I kill Mummy and Daddy. I really want to see him.

When the home time bell rings, I get my bag and run all the way across the school to find Mummy waiting in the parking lot. She waves to me from the car and when I get to her, she gives me a big hug and asks if I had a good day. I always say yes. When I say yes, it makes Mummy happy, and if she is happy, she won't shout at me or ask me about my dreams.

On the way home, we stop at the store and I walk with Mummy while she puts so many things in the trolley. First, she gets vegetables, then meat, then biscuits and tea, and some beer for Daddy. My feet are sore, and I want to go home so I can play with Daddy's knife again, but Mummy just keeps shopping. "I wanna go home now," I whine.

"Almost done, Annie. We need to get some of Daddy's favourite chocolate."

Mummy pats my head and tells me to be a good girl, but it's too late now. My head is getting sore, and it's so hot in the shopping centre. I pull off my jacket and push up the sleeves on my top.

"Annie!" Mummy shouts and kneels in front of me. She grabs my hands very tight in hers and looks at my arms. "What happened to you?" Her angry face is on now as she looks at the cuts on my arms.

"I did it."

"What?" Her voice is loud, and some people stop and look at us, and Mummy pulls my sleeves down very quickly. She leaves all the shopping in the trolley and walks so fast out of the store that I run to catch up with her.

When we get to the car, Mummy tells me to get in my seat and she shouts at me. "Tell me the truth, Annastasia, who did that to you?"

"I did it, Mummy."

Her eyes are big and wide, and her voice is quiet now, the same quiet voice she uses when she pinches me in the store, so people don't hear her mean words. "How did you do it, sweetheart, and why?"

I shrug. "I used a knife in the kitchen. I wanted to see the blood inside me."

Mummy doesn't talk to me. She starts the car, and while she's driving, she calls Doctor Holtman and tells him we are going to see him tomorrow. I don't want to go. I hope Adam is in my dreams tonight so I can tell him. He always knows how to make me feel better.

At home, Mummy made me show Daddy all the cuts on my arms, then she said I had to have a bath and go to bed. Now I have to stay in my bedroom and I don't get to have ice cream. It's not fair. I love ice cream. Mummy and Daddy are so mean.

When the house is very quiet, I creep out of my bedroom to see if anyone is still awake. Mummy and Daddy are in bed, so I go back to my bedroom and close the door. I wriggle under my bed; there's not much space now because I've grown a lot, but if I stay very low I can still fit.

I get Daddy's knife and hold it in my hands. The handle is smooth, and on the edge, there's a pretty pattern that I can feel under my fingertips. I take off the leather cover that's called a sheath, and I touch the pointy tip of the knife and remember the movie I watched one night when Mummy was sleeping, and Daddy was away for work.

There was a man wearing black clothes and a black mask on his face that only showed his eyes. He had a big sharp knife, even bigger than this one, and when he went to peoples' houses, they screamed and ran away from him. But he always caught them, then he stabbed them with his knife and their blood went everywhere. When they were dead, they were so quiet, and it made me smile a lot. That man wasn't scared of anyone, he was so brave.

When I hear a noise inside my house, I crawl out from under my bed. I hold the knife very tight. It's going to be my knife now. My big, sharp knife to kill people.

I think Mummy or Daddy must be awake, because I hear footsteps in the kitchen. I sneak out of my bedroom and tip toe to Mummy and Daddy's bedroom. Their door is open, and they're both asleep. Maybe I was dreaming about the footsteps. I gasp, and an exciting thought makes my mouth spread into a wide grin. It could be Adam coming to say hello. I need to be very quick so I can go to sleep and see him.

I creep into Mummy and Daddy's bedroom. Daddy is snoring so loud and it's really annoying. I go very, very close to him, and I watch him sleeping and snoring. When I lift the knife, the silver blade has a little sparkle of light on it. It looks like a star, and it makes me smile.

I put the pointy end of the knife near Daddy's throat, and then I push it in like the man did in the movie. All Daddy's blood comes out and spills on the bed and on his chest. It's so warm, and when I touch it, it's sticky and slippery on my fingers. I stab Daddy again, and again, and again. Ten times until there's so much blood all over him, and on my hands.

A shadow comes to the door, and when I turn around, there's a boy standing in the doorway. He smiles and looks happy to see me.

"Who are you?"

"I'm Adam. Keep going, I won't leave," he says.

He's Adam. Is he the boy from my dreams? I shut my eyes tight and try to remember his face; I think he's the same.

I nod and skip around to see Mummy. She's still sleeping, but when I giggle, she looks up at me with her confused face. "Annie?" She looks at Daddy and rubs her eyes, but she doesn't say anything. She just screams so, so loud. When I look at Adam, he's still smiling, and he nods.

"I just wanted to have ice cream." I tell Mummy. "You're so loud, Mummy. Please stop screaming." She doesn't stop screaming, but her head drops onto the pillow. She doesn't move, just lies very still, only her eyes look at me. I show Mummy the knife and lots of tears dribble down her face, then, I put the sharp blade of the knife at her throat and I slice it across in a long line. When her blood comes out and spills on the bed, I want to touch it. I put my fingers in it, it's so warm, and I hold up my hand and show Adam.

"Good girl, Annastasia." He comes into the bedroom and smiles.

"What are you doing here?" I ask.

"I'm going to help you. I'll make sure the police don't find you."

I open my mouth to a big wide O. I forgot about police. In the movie, the police came, and they killed the man with the knife. I don't want to be killed. I want to go with Adam.

"You're going to come with me. You can live with me and my grandfather."

I hold up my knife to show Adam. "Can I bring this? It's very special. It's my killing knife."

He laughs a little bit and pats my head before he takes my bloody hand. "Yes, you can bring your knife."

He gets to his knees and speaks quietly. "Annastasia, do you want to be mine? You can do so much killing with your special knife."

I'm so excited, and so lucky I almost do a big squeal of happiness, but then I remember I'm not a little kid anymore. I'm a killer like the man on TV. "Can I stay with you forever?"

"Forever," he says.

"Yes," I say.

My house disappears and all I can see are big, bright lights, then darkness.

XXVIII

LOCKDOWN

KNOX

four weeks later

The mansion is in lockdown, and my brothers'—and Maple—refuse to let me go home to my own house. It's bullshit. I may be slowly losing my powers, but I'm not weak—never have been. I can take care of myself. *Fucking assholes!*

At the front door to the Fallon Mansion I stand beside Annie, my hand tightly gripping hers. She's barely said a word to me, or anyone else, saying she wants to wait until we're alone before we talk. She looks as beautiful today as she did the day I first saw her. The bruises are gone, and all that's left is a deep pink scar across her neck that will forever remind me of the night I lost her and my wings. I would do it again a thousand times over just to see her smile, to hear her whisper my name.

Once she's settled in my bedroom—and in my bed, Doctor Charles comes in and checks her over again; he ensures she's taking her medication, and that her scars are healing well.

I drop down on the bed beside Annie. "Annie—"

She cuts me off. "Flynn told me what you did... for me."

I swallow the lump in my throat. I begged Flynn to tell her everything. I couldn't do it. I didn't want to see the pain in her eyes, and I didn't want her pity. She had to know, but from someone else.

I scrub my hands down my face. *I could still lose her.* "Are you mad?"

"Furious," she says as she traces her fingertip along the scar on her neck.

"Baby—Annie, I couldn't let you go. I know I'm not perfect, and I basically fuck up everything I touch, but you... you're my life, Annie, and without you I can't live."

"Knox..." She hesitates and shuffles closer. "I don't want—I mean I... my rule. Can we get rid of that now?"

I take her hand in mine and kiss her fingertips. "I missed you, so fucking much."

She smiles and rests her head on my shoulder. "I missed you too and thank you for saving me."

I kiss her head and inhale the sweet, fruity scent of her hair.

She punches my bicep, and I wince. "But I'm still mad about your wings. Are you insane? Are you even an angel now?"

"Baby, with you, I don't need wings, I'm already in heaven." I press a kiss to her head. "I'm still an angel, but my powers will gradually fade, and I'll never be able to return to my home in heaven."

"Ugh. All the pretty words in the world won't fix this." She pulls her hand from mine and stands to pace the room. "I'm so fucking angry at you! He's going to come back, Knox. Once he knows I'm not dead, he'll come after me, and then what will you do? You're not going to be able to save me a second time."

She has a point. "I'm not going to let him take you. If you die, I die, Annie. That's it."

She storms toward me and when her knees touch mine, she places her hands on my cheeks, her lips just inches from mine, her breath soft on my lips. "I fucking hate you right now." Hate turns to lust in mere seconds. Then, sweet, soft lips meet mine with furious passion and unbridled rage.

Annie grips my hand as I lead her toward Roman and Kailey's bedroom. She won't admit it, but I know she's afraid of seeing Roman and not knowing what to expect. She's desperate to see Georgia. "What if they hate me?" she asks.

"They'll love you, like I do."

I knock on the door, and when Roman opens it, Annie gasps and tightens her grip on my hand.

Roman drops his head and sighs. "Sorry, ah, come in."

I place my hand on Annie's back and rub it gently. When I take a seat on the sofa, she sits beside me then wriggles closer so she's pressed hard against me.

"She's sleeping?" I ask Roman.

He nods and leans down to lift Georgia out of the crib. "Kailey's gone with Lexi to that spa in the mountains. Something about mud masks and massages." He shakes his head and laughs. "Damn, I'm still getting used to all this female stuff, it's fuck—" Roman winces and covers Georgia's ear with one hand as he pulls her to his chest. "It's weird as hell." He kisses her head and pats her back while Annie watches him, her head tilted and her eyes narrowed.

"You look so much like him," she says quietly.

"Sorry," Roman says quickly. There's something inherently wrong about seeing Roman like this—seeing him vulnerable, worried.

"Don't," I tell him. "You didn't choose him to be your damn twin. Just like you didn't choose Corbin. It's bad fuc—It's just bad luck, man."

Roman comes over and hands Georgia to me, then sits on the opposite sofa. "Are you feeling better?" he asks Annie.

"Yeah. I never want to stay in the hospital again... ever." Roman laughs a little, and Annie gasps. "Oh my god!"

"What's wrong babe?" I ask.

"It wasn't him," she says. "At the hospital, I thought he was there, looking for me. But it wasn't him. It was you," she says to Roman.

"Me?" he asks, confused.

She nods. "I looked out the window of my room, you were on the phone. I remember later the nurse came in to tell me about a baby girl she'd helped deliver. She said she almost died. It was Georgia, wasn't it?"

Roman nods. "Yep. It was."

Annie smiles now and reaches out to touch Georgia's head, then she pulls her hand back quickly. "Is it okay, if I touch her, Ro—Roman?"

"Of course. You can hold her if you want to."

Annie shuffles back on the sofa, and I place Georgia in her arms. When she's holding her, she looks down at Georgia and suddenly, tears spring to her eyes. "She's so small, so beautiful. Please don't let anyone hurt her," she begs me as though it's her own baby.

I rub Annie's back and kiss her cheek. "She's going to be okay, babe, no one will hurt her."

"Roman," Annie says, "I'm sorry for thinking you would be like him. I'm so sorry."

"It's okay, Annie. I have a new family now." He glances at me and I nod slightly. "They're nothing to me, not anymore."

"I love her, Roman, she's so beautiful."

Georgia wriggles and opens her bright blue eyes, Annie gasps again. Then, when Georgia cries, Annie panics. "I didn't hurt her; I promise I didn't." She starts to hyperventilate, and Roman takes Georgia and cuddles her close while he pats her back.

I pull Annie into my arms. "Hey, baby, she's okay. She's hungry, she cries when she's hungry. It's not your fault."

She looks up at Roman as he paces back and forth with Georgia, patting her back while he whispers to her.

"You ready to go," I ask Annie.

She stands slowly. "Thank you, Roman, for letting me hold her."

"No problem, I'll see you later."

She nods and I lead her out of the bedroom and back to my room. "You okay, babe?"

After a heavy sigh, she says, "When I see her, I get all these overwhelming feelings and it's so hard to breathe. All I can think about is someone hurting her. I've never felt like this before—never been so worried about... a child."

Once we're inside my bedroom, I sit on the bed and pull her onto my lap where she straddles my thighs, then I cup her cheeks. "Baby, it's part of loving someone. That's what love is. You want them to have the very best of everything; you want to protect them from all the bad things in the world. It's okay, and it's normal. There's nothing wrong with you."

She puts her hands on my shoulders and rests her forehead against mine. "I love you. I didn't realize it, not really. But I'm sure of it now. I love you, Knox."

"And I love you." I cup her cheeks and press a soft kiss to her lips. "Do you want your birthday present? It's late, obviously."

Her eyes grow wide and she nods. "Ah, okay."

She shifts her weight so she can grind against my cock, and when it throbs, she smiles, her eyes alight with arousal.

"No presents then?" I ask.

She splays her hands against my chest, gently pushing me back. "Lie down." When she's wriggled forward slightly, she glides her hand down her flat, smooth stomach then into her pants. Through her thin, grey leggings, I watch her hand move against her pussy, and I raise my hips. She licks her lips and slides her fingers out before she lies over me and traces her wet fingertips over my lips.

I groan in heart aching pleasure and lick my own lips before I flip her over and lie her on the bed. She giggles and squirms beneath me. "I want you," she whispers between desperate whimpers.

I tug her pants down to see she's not wearing underwear, and as I pull them down further, I trail kisses across her stomach and down to her thighs, then back up as she spreads her legs for me.

"Knox... ugh, please, please more." With each frantic movement of her hips, she begs me to continue.

She's so beautiful, so sweet, and so wet. I'm caught in a fog of torturous bliss where everything I crave is there for the taking. *Slow down,* I remind myself as I run two fingers down between her soft pink slit, then push them into her while she moans and bucks her hips. When I drop my head and glide my tongue over her pussy, she cries out. "Oh my god, Knox... don't ever stop."

I look up at her and smile. The scent of her arousal, the heat of her flesh, and her keening cries fill my head with hopes and dreams I've never dared to imagine. *Could I have this? Would I be enough for her? Will I be able to protect her now?* Shaking my head, I clamp my eyes shut for a short second and focus on the present.

"No, no... keep going," Annie begs.

I lick her again, and again, stopping each time to look up at her. As her frustration builds, her hips buck wildly, and she begs for more. I suck her clit into my mouth as I finger her, each stroke draws out her pleasure; each suck causes her pussy to tighten around my fingers. Another suck and I push my fingers in deeper as she grabs a fistful of my hair and forces my head down.

"More," she cries, forcing my face between her silken legs. "Ahhh, no—yes! Oh my god—stop! Fuck no don't stop—" Her words are cut off when she lets out a scream of pleasure.

When she reaches the climax, I drag my fingers out and glide my tongue over her flesh before I trail kisses up her stomach. She pulls her top off and throws it on the floor. Cupping her breasts in my hands, I circle each nipple with my tongue while she writhes beneath me, still pleading.

I kick my pants off and pull off my shirt, then roll onto my back. I want her in control, I want her to ride me, to give me everything she has to give.

She sits over me, sliding back and forth along my cock, moaning and whimpering, her pale thighs slick and wet.

"Please, give it to me," she begs. "I want to feel you inside me."

"It's yours baby, take it."

She rises on her knees slightly, then grasps my cock in her hand, giving it a few firm, slow strokes. A groan of satisfaction is pulled from my lips when she rubs it over her hot, wet pussy. Before she lowers herself down, she stops and pants. "Can't brea—Ohhh... I can't breathe..."

"Yeah, you can. Look at me, baby, take it slow." After she gives me a quick nod, I rub my hands over her thighs, not taking my eyes off her gorgeous face. She lowers herself down, inch by glorious inch until I'm deep inside her.

"Fuck yes! Ohhh holy fucking hell..." she cries out while she circles her hips and runs her hands over my chest, stopping to play with my nipple rings. "I love your cock!"

I manage to contain my smirk, but I barely curb the urge to take control. She's so tight, so hot, so fucking wet. When she moves on me, she leans down and breathes against my ear, whispering, "You feel sooo fucking good inside me."

I pull her mouth to mine, kissing her passionately; thrusting my hips toward her as she grinds faster and harder. Her fingers twist through my hair; her tongue swipes across my lips. Her breathing becomes erratic and she clenches around my cock, panting, moaning, whispering words of lust into my ear. "Harder... More... Fuck me, Knox." Long, delicate fingers tighten in my hair, tugging on the strands as her body quivers. "I'm gonna—Ohhh..."

"Come for me, baby," I breathe against her ear, and she lets out a shrill cry of pleasure before she falls onto me, her tongue gliding up and down my neck as she licks and kisses me. "Fuck, Annie, you're fucking perfect."

As her breathing slows, she lets her weight rest on me. Our bodies slick with sweat; our skin hot with lust. "Knox, please tell me we can do that again. Every day for the rest of our lives."

I glide my hands over her back, then roll us onto our sides, twisting my fingers through her long, dark hair. "Baby, I will give you everything you desire. You only need to ask, and it's yours."

"I only want you," she says as she traces my lips with her fingertip. "Always you."

XXIX

RIOT AND RAGE

KNOX

one week later

Annie leans back on the sofa, her fingers laced through mine as she watches the twins play on the shaggy white rug in the living room. Kailey sits beside her feeding Georgia, while Roman bounces Hope on his knee, causing her to giggle.

Parker comes into the living room with the phone. For a minute, he stands in stunned silence, a look of shock on his face. He glances at the babies before his eyes narrow when they lock onto Hope. For a minute, he merely stares at her while she looks up at him, unblinking. Tiny, dark lashes framed around her bright green eyes. It's almost as though they're having a private conversation, which would be ridiculous since the babies don't have their powers yet.

"Parker?" Flynn says. "What's wrong?"

His weird connection with Hope is broken, and he takes a step toward Flynn. "The Fray..."

Annie's head flicks around to face Parker, and she jumps to her feet. "Did they hurt someone?" she asks quickly. "Is it Ad—"

Parker shakes his head as Flynn grabs the phone from his hand.

"What the fuck?" Flynn shouts into the phone. "This is bullshit!"

He throws the phone at the wall and it breaks, pieces of plastic shatter and fall to the floor. The babies start crying, and Autumn and Bella rush in and sit on the floor with them trying to calm them down.

"Babe," Autumn says, "What's going on?"

Gabe drops down on the floor with Autumn and pats Hope's hand. He tilts his head, his eyes wide. "Ohhh no. All da bad ones coming. You stop them, yeah Clay?" His deep brown eyes, filled with hope, look up at Clay.

"Fuck it, Flynn. What the hell is going on," I shout.

"The Fray. There in the valley, riots... That was Doctor Charles, they're inundated with injured people."

"No, no," Annie cries. "Let me go back to him, I'll stop him. *I* can stop him."

"No way." I stand and pull her into me, her back flush against my chest. Even from this position, I feel her heartbeat thrumming.

Clay and Steel rush down to the weapons room, coming back a few minutes later with our knives and swords. Everything happens quickly, until I tell Annie to stay with Roman and the babies; and she freaks out and wants to help.

"Wait," Roman says. Somehow, he's the calmest of everyone. "Annie, I can't keep the babies *and* the girls safe if I'm alone. If you're here, you can help me. Help me protect them all." Damn. Why the hell didn't I think of that?

She narrows her eyes, then flicks her gaze between me and Roman, suspicion seeps into her eyes, but when she looks down at Georgia, she agrees. "Okay. I'll stay." She wraps her arms around my neck before pressing a hard kiss to my lips. "Please, be careful. If you die, I'll fucking kill you!"

I smirk, but nod and pull on my weapons belt before I follow my brothers outside.

"We need to hurry," Flynn says.

Clay pulls the SUV up near the park. "Fucking hell. Why are we only finding out about this now?"

"There's no way this just started," I say to myself as I take in the scene unfolding before us.

In the distance, the street, the buildings, everything ahead of us is dotted with fire and thick black smoke. When we get out of the car, screaming surrounds us, along with the sounds of crashing cars and smashing glass.

"Brother," Steel says, placing a hand on Flynn's shoulder. "I've got a real bad feeling about this."

Flynn nods. "Knox," he says, "Be fucking careful."

I nod. I may have very little in the way of powers, but I have no fear, and my strength hasn't waned at all yet. I've been training harder than ever to keep in shape and keep up my strength and endurance. Since I'm forbidden to use Flynn's—or any of my brothers'—blood to strengthen myself, I've had to do it all the normal, mortal way. Thank fuck the angels, after some persuasion by my father, have allowed Flynn to use his blood—but only to heal me. I won't die. I *can't* die. I need to protect Annie and my family. Nothing can stand in my way.

We make our way along the street, helping people out of their burning and crashed cars, getting injured people off the road, and working quickly with the police to cordon off a safe area near the park with bollards and chain link fencing. The entire area is surrounded by security guards, and police in full riot gear.

As Steel runs forward to help a young girl screaming on the sidewalk, a guy runs at him with a knife in his hand. Flynn leaps forward and kicks the guy, sending him flying backwards where he lands in the already broken window of Café 66. Within seconds, a police officer carries the girl to the safe area.

"We need to split up," Flynn says. "Take out as many Fray as you can."

"Looks like they've got a lot of help," Clay says. "Try not to kill anyone who doesn't deserve it..." He scrubs a hand over his head. "Focus on anyone with weapons."

Steel laughs. "Yeah, you know what? Fuck that. If they're comin' at me, weapons or no weapons, they're dead."

"Steel," Flynn warns. "No unnecessary deaths."

Steel rolls his eyes, annoyed. "Not makin' any promises, brother."

This isn't good. There's no way we—well, my brothers'—will be able to hide their true strength at a time like this. One of them is bound to be hurt, blood will be spilled. Fuck! Is *he* doing this because of Annie, or *for* Annie?

I grip my knife tight in my hand and sprint toward the gymnasium where guys are running out with weights and steel bars, using them to fend off the Fray and fight their way into the street.

Thank fuck it's clear who is Fray, and who isn't. This had to be planned. The Fray are all wearing black t-shirts and black cargo pants; around their waists they each have a sheath, a knife, and nunchucks.

A guy rushes toward me, a dumbbell in his hand. He looks me up and down before he realises. "You're one of those Fallon security guys, right?"

I nod. "What the fuck is going on?" I ask hoping to get some answers.

"Me and my mate just came back from Wantonvale, and this gang was running down the street, smashing windows and dragging people out of their cars. I rammed a couple of 'em, but they got right back up. We drove around the lake and down that back street." He points toward the shopping centre. "Man, I swear to you, about twenty guys came out of the drain in the parking lot."

"The fuck?" Adam is controlling all of this. I'm certain of it.

He nods, his eyes still scanning the area. "They must be on drugs or something. Fucking crazy. One guy, his eyes were wild as fuck, all black and shit..." *The blood!* Fuck. They're going to be strong.

"Can you fight?" I ask.

"Yeah, man. Ex pro-boxer, my mate too. Can we help?"

"Just protect whoever you can. If you can get any of the guys in black down, don't let them get back up. Kill 'em if you have to—Can you do that?"

He nods. "Don't worry about me, eight years in the marines, I can handle it." Without another word, he takes off again.

Staying near the wall of the café, I scan the area, my focus on the alley where I can slip through and head to the drain. I need to find Adam and put an end to this. Before I step into the shadows, I notice two men approaching. As they come closer, it's clear their veins are flowing with the blood mixture the old man made. Thin, veiny tributaries bulge with a deep purple tinge in their arms and necks. But my blood... it wouldn't be working now I've lost my wings. *Fuck.* They wouldn't use straight vampire blood; it wouldn't be strong enough. A sense of dread washes over me as thoughts of my brothers' swirl through my mind. Annie said Adam had other angels—I shake my head hard. There's no way he'd have an angel with the royal bloodline. It's not possible.

I clamp my eyes shut, willing my mind power to work. A trickle of power would suffice right now, but there's nothing.

When one of the men lunges at me, I shove my knife forward and pierce his abdomen, he stumbles back, but doesn't go down, and when the blood stops oozing from beneath his t-shirt, he laughs.

"You can't kill me!" he taunts and runs at me again, spinning the nunchucks. "Come at me, dare ya."

I step back as he misses my face by mere inches, but the other guy leaps forward and slams into me, forcing me onto the ground. Swiping my knife through the air, I attempt to make contact with the second guy, and when I do, blood gushes from his throat and spills over my chest. A warm, wet pool that assaults my nostrils with the metallic scent of thick, mortal blood.

I shove the dead guy off me and punch the other one over and over until I jump to my feet and kick him. He goes down, but scrambles back to his own feet quickly. I draw my sword from its sheath and raise it up, ready to slice the fucker's head clean off, still he laughs.

He cocks his head, takes a step forward, then before he can make another move, I swing my sword. His head is removed from his shoulders in one fluid movement. It hits the ground with a thud and rolls into the gutter. Eyes wide and mouth agape. An ear-piercing scream rings through the air, and when I turn my head slightly, I see her.

A fucking female. And she fainted. *Fuck.*

I walk over and scoop her up into my arms, scanning the surrounding area for the guy I saw earlier. Should have asked his name. Through the crowd of people rioting, looting, and scrambling to safety, I spot him on the roof of a car. He looks my way, and I gain his attention before he jumps down and sprints toward me. "Take her over to the cops," I say quickly.

He nods and I hand the female over. But before he leaves, his eyes drop to the concrete where the severed head lies. "Oh fuck," he says. "Those guys did that?"

"I did it," I say, pulling out my sword to show him.

"Man, that's fucked up, but good job, hey."

I laugh as he takes off. Damn mortals never cease to surprise me.

In the distance, through the trees, a muffled cry for help is carried on the breeze. As I walk toward the tree line, Clay's voice stops me in my tracks. "Knox!"

I point to the trees, and he nods. As I continue forward, the cries grow louder. A female begs for help, begs to be let go. Something doesn't feel right and the hairs on the back of my neck stand on end.

I poise my hand over my sword and continue pacing toward the trees. When I reach the path, I follow it for a few steps before she comes into view. A young girl standing by a tree, alone. No one is touching her, and she's not hurt. But she's been crying, her eyes are red and puffy and her lip quivers as she mouths the words "Help me."

Adam steps out from behind the tree and pats her shoulder. "Well done. Now, fuck off." He gives her a shove, sending her to her knees. The girl scrambles to her feet and bolts down the path, screaming again.

"You did this?" I ask him. "You planned it all, didn't you?"

"Where is she?"

"Dead. You killed her, remember."

He laughs as he presses the tip of his bloody knife to his cheek. "You expect me to believe that you let her die? Your blood is useless. It does nothing, for anyone." He paces back and forth. "You saved her, didn't you? Sacrificed your wings for her life..."

How the fuck does he know? I don't reply, but he continues anyway. "You can't fix her, Knox. I made sure of that. She'll always want me, always need me." He stops in front of me, pointing his knife at my chest, but he doesn't push it in. "Did she tell you about your brother?"

"My brother?" I question, annoyed.

"The one from heaven... white wings, black hair, green eyes." He shrugs. "I guess they all look the same though, right? And how many do you have? Must be at least thirty of you now."

Rage builds in my chest and my heart races. They had another one of my brothers'. But how... and why?

"He didn't speak, not at first. Not until I told him about the babies."

I clench my jaw and grip the hilt of my sword. "You what?"

"Four little angels, how sweet." His eyes drop to my hand. "Wait, you'll get your chance to fight me, but first, I need to tell you a little something about our precious Annastasia."

"I don't give a fuck what you have to say." Heat builds in my chest, the familiar ache of rage I once let consume me. The burn doesn't come, but the simmering heat lingers like a lasting reminder that chaos and rage will always be with me somehow.

He smirks as he glides his finger along the blade of his knife. When his blood beads to the surface, he licks it off his finger and continues. "As I was saying, I was telling this angel—your brother—about the babies. They won't be tucked up safe in your mansion forever, will they, Knox?"

Ignore him. Focus. "Can you speed this up, I'm getting bored." And itching to slice your fucking head off, psychopath.

"Okay, okay. So I needed information. And since you went ahead and fucked up your blood, we need another angel. All you need to do to stop me is... bring one of your brothers." He laughs wildly. "Oh, and I want Annastasia back."

Fucking hell. "No. And no."

"Yeah, I thought you'd say that. But want to know something, *Knox*?"

"I'm sure you'll tell me. And man, do you ever stop fucking talking?"

He waves a hand in the air. "Annastasia... *our* Annastasia... she killed a few angels, so you see, according to angel law, *you're* forbidden to claim her."

"Right," I say, not believing him. She wouldn't. *She would. She would do anything he told her to do.* I know it. "And what the fuck do you know about angel law?"

He doesn't reply, instead, he lunges at me; his knife plunges into my shoulder, tearing through muscle and causing an agonising ache to spread through my veins and down my arm. I shout out in pain, pain I'm not used to, pain that reminds me I no longer have powers.

I swing a punch, connecting with his jaw before I shove him off me and leap to my feet. He laughs again before he spins and kicks, narrowly missing my jaw.

I rush at him, slamming his body into a tree trunk, my hand tight around his throat. He struggles against me, and when I feel his knife pierce my abdomen, I try in vain to ignore the excruciating pain and focus on killing this bastard once and for all. But he stabs me again, and this time my grip on his throat loosens and he manages to shove me back.

I draw my sword and swing it, the tip slices through the flesh of his abdomen. He looks down and wipes the blood from his shirt, then rubs it between his fingers before licking them clean. Fuck this guy. Why the hell won't he die?

"I will get her back," he says with a smirk.

I shake my head. "You're going to die. You won't ever get near her again."

I swing my sword again, but he steps back, making no attempt to come at me. He pulls his torn t-shirt off then drops it on the ground at his feet. "Dead or alive, she belongs to me, Knox." He truly believes he's going to get Annie back.

"You're fucking delusional, you know that?"

He steps back. When he raises his head to the sky, he drops his arms by his sides, letting the knife fall from his hand. He's completely still now. *What the fuck is he doing?*

I take a step forward and grip the hilt of my sword while he remains still. When I swing my sword, a flash of bright, white light blinds me, and I'm thrown backwards. I land on my back, shaking my head and blinking away confusion. When I jump to my feet, everything I thought I knew, is no more.

"HOLY. FUCKING. HELL!" There are no other words to describe the shock that courses through my veins like a ten-million-volt surge of electricity.

Adam raises his brow then cocks his head. "Surprise." He extends his arms, and behind him, pure white feathered wings extend from his shoulders, each pristine feather rustles as his wings move slowly back and forth. *His wings. His fucking white wings.*

"What the fuck?" I stare at him, unsure if what I'm seeing is real, or if it's a vivid hallucination.

"Do you know how fucking easy it is to seduce an angel?" he asks.

Seduce an angel? "What the hell are you talking about?" The only angels who can bestow wings upon a mortal, reside in heaven.

"If you get them when they're young enough, you can change their entire life. Turn them into something else, something they never imagined they'd be. You can even turn them against themselves. Make them forget *what* they are... *Who* they are. *Where* they came from. When they're young, they're so pliant and willing, desperate to give, but asking for nothing in return."

"What did you do?" When I eye his knife on the grass beside his feet, he reaches down to pick it up and slide it into the sheath on his belt.

"My grandfather had friends in high..." He looks up to the cloudless ebony sky. "Very high places." He shrugs a shoulder. "And some low places too." He kicks the toe of his boot into the dirt. "With a bit of persuasion, angels will give up anything to protect their own. But of course, you already know that. Don't you—"

"Stop with the fucking games and tell me what you've done!"

There's a thud behind me, then another, and one more. The calming warmth of my brothers' wings surrounds me—I make no move to acknowledge them.

"He made a deal... a sacrifice," Flynn says. His tone is menacing. "A lifetime of chastity. In return, he was given a child. Venys and Haydee figured it out." As Flynn's words play havoc in my mind, I play over every scenario in my head. I can't kill Adam. My brothers can't kill Adam. *He's a fucking angel!*

No. No. Not Annie. It's not true. If she is the child he's talking about and she's killed an angel—

I lunge at Adam. "You fucking bastard!" Before I reach him, his wings lift him off the ground and Clay and Flynn pull me back. Steel storms toward him. "Get the fuck down here! NOW!"

Adam laughs as he hovers a few feet off the ground, his white wings fluttering as though he's worthy of the purity and hope they hold within each feather. Seconds later, Maple and Willow land beside us.

Adam drops back to the ground. "I was wondering when I'd see you again," he says to Maple.

"You fucking know him. You know about this?" I growl.

Maple raises her hand and my voice is caught in my throat. She speaks only to Adam. "You have much to answer for, Adam."

"Hmm... not really. I was told not to kill an angel. I haven't done that... yet."

"You deceived an angel. You forced an angel to kill one of their own kind on your behalf. Bought her up to be a murderer, you used her to lure humans so *you* could murder them. You had Vandrick steal her memories, her essence, and her soul."

"And the problem is?" That fucking smirk on his lips needs to be wiped right off his face.

"You are an angel, Adam," Willow says, as if there is any doubt now. "Regardless of how it came to be, there are strict laws you must adhere to."

"I'm still not seeing the problem here... I was forced to stay here on earth. I'm not pure, Maple, you of all people—angels—should know that."

"He's an angel." Flynn says absentmindedly. "That means Rom..."

"Holy shit," Steel says. "No fuc—"

"No," Maple says. "Adam was not born an angel, and he will never be worthy of heaven."

Adam raises his brow before he erupts into a fit of laughter. "Roman? He's no fucking angel."

A low growl comes from Flynn's throat, but Steel grips his arm and tugs him back.

"What about Annie?" Clay asks. "How did this happen?"

Willow turns her head to look over her shoulder at Clay. "She was born an angel."

Maple takes a step toward Adam and he folds his wings. "You were warned to stay away from this valley, away from the fallen. You were warned about bringing Annastasia here. What do you have to say for yourself?"

My mind is reeling. Not only did Maple and Willow know about Adam, but they'd warned him away from us. The bastard went out of his way to ruin my life, and Annie's life.

Adam's shrug reminds me he doesn't care. "You know when you tell a kid not to do something, and they do it anyway. It's kinda like that. The only difference is, I don't give a shit, and you can't stop me."

Maple sighs. "You are correct, on all accounts, Adam, but you're forgetting which rules apply to you now. The Angel King has decided it's time—"

"No. She's mine. We had a deal." He steps back, but when Maple raises her hand, he's frozen in place.

"Your deal was with the disgraced archangel, Javier. Unfortunately, he has been exiled by the king. But you already know that, don't you?"

My thoughts swirl like a hurricane, out of control, twisting, turning—confusion haunts me. So many unanswered questions. But as each memory plays over in my mind, the pieces click into place.

Annie asked me why my wings were black. She never appeared shocked when she saw them, never questioned why my blood was blue, or how I was so easily able to break out of the Fray's underground fortress.

Adam didn't kill me when he had the chance just minutes ago. He was working with Vandrick. He knew where Annie was all the time. He knew she was with me. He knew I'd come for Roman. He never did hurt Annie. He was telling the truth. Everything he did, she wanted, or allowed because she was bound to him by blood, and by angel law, through a sacrifice she knows nothing about. A sacrifice that stole her childhood, her happiness and her memories of where she came from. He used her and twisted her until she was transformed from the angelic child she could have been, to a killer who would live and breathe only for him. Whatever he asked for, she gave willingly, including wings. *Fuck!*

"She doesn't belong to you." Like a knife to my heart, Maple's words are a stark reminder. *She belongs to Adam.* How will I ever make Annie mine?

Our father, the king, lands between Willow and Maple and we drop to our knees. After a short nod, he turns his back to us so he's facing Adam. "Adam. We meet again." My father doesn't extend his hand, they're both clasped firmly behind his back, he has no fear of Adam, or anyone else for that matter.

Adam doesn't speak. Finally, the asshole has shut his fucking mouth.

"You made a somewhat delusive deal with Archangel Javier."

"Yep."

"And through this deal, you were given a child. His daughter."

His daughter? What the hell? He *gave* his daughter to Adam.

"Mmm hmm..." Adam rolls his eyes.

"As part of this *deal* you made, you agreed to stay away from Ambrosia Valley, and to keep Annastasia away from..." my father lowers his voice, but his words are clear as day. "My son."

Adam laughs. "Ah, that's why you're pissed, isn't it? He lost his wings for her. That fucked up your perfect set."

I clench my fists. This bastard needs to die, I don't give a fuck who, or what he is.

"Kneel," my father says, his tone leaves no room for argument, yet Adam defies him.

When Adam laughs, Maple raises her hand. "You will kneel before the king and show your wings."

Forced by Maple's hand, Adam kneels, and my father draws his angel sword from its sheath. He walks around Adam until he's behind him. My brothers' and I remain kneeling, while Maple and Willow stand silent.

When Adam's eyes meet mine, he smirks. All I can think about is grabbing my father's sword and piercing it through Adam's chest.

Maple places a hand on my shoulder. "Remain calm," she whispers.

As my father swings his sword, Adam's wings extend farther, creating a whoosh of warm air before he darts into the sky. Maple gasps, and Flynn and Steel take off after him, while I stand on the ground, furious. "Stop him," I shout at Maple.

"He is not my responsibility, Knox. You are."

With my fists clenched by my sides, I wish only for Haydee and the wrath she forced upon me. My father walks toward me, Maple and Willow nod before they disappear into the sky.

"My son." My father extends his hand. I extend mine and he holds it between his. "Please, forgive me for all you have endured because of Adam."

"You knew about him?" A sense of betrayal stabs at my heart. I don't want apologies, I want answers, and I want Annie.

"Hey." Clay places a gentle hand on my back. "Let him speak, Knox."

My father continues. "Not until recently. Javier had been acting suspiciously, spending more time away from the heavens. I had Archer and Arrow follow him, and after some research, it came to my attention that Javier had given his daughter to a mortal couple after his love died in childbirth." My father rubs my hand. "Javier informed us the child had passed as well. I allowed him the time away from the heavens to grieve for what he lost. Unfortunately, I was blind to the truth."

I sigh. "I lost my wings because of *him*."

My father nods once. "The reason Javier wanted Annastasia kept away from you, was because he knew his deal with Adam would be discovered had you met. Annastasia is perfect for you in every way, Knox. She has the same traits you have, the same rage, the same chaos... she loves as you do, fiercely."

"Can Knox get his wings back?" Clay asks.

"I'm afraid not. If you were not fallen, it would be easier to seek absolution from Genesis. Unfortunately, that is not offered to the fallen, no matter who their father is."

"Who was Annie's mother?" I ask.

When my father's eyes meet mine, his are filled with sadness. "Princess Amalie."

Clay gasps. "You mean Princess Amalie of the third heaven? Annie is a princess? Why would Javier do this? I don't understand." *Royal blood. He had the blood all along, it just wasn't strong enough.*

"Greed, lust, revenge," my father says. "Javier has always wanted my throne. By removing my firstborn sons—" He closes his eyes momentarily. "By removing you all, Javier and Adam would have no trouble using Annastasia to give wings to the Fray."

I step back from my father and scrub my hands down my face as Flynn and Steel land beside me with a thud; I fill them in on what our father said.

"Well, Father, Adam is gone," Flynn says. "And we *will* remove the Fray."

My father nods. "Adam will return. He won't stray far from where Annastasia is."

I grind my teeth, pissed off I've lost my wings, and that Adam is a fucking angel.

"So what now?" Clay asks. "We just wait until he comes back and destroys the valley again?"

"No. My sons, you were sent here to repent for the sins you committed against heaven. You have proved time and time again that you have the ability to help the mortal world. Now is the time to do that, properly. With the entire community of Ambrosia Valley on your side, it will be difficult for the Fray to continue, for Adam to return without being noticed."

"You're saying we should tell them who we are? Forgive me, Father," I say, "but that's insane."

"No," Flynn says. "It will work. Especially with the girls. Everyone loves them."

My father smiles. "That is true."

"Adam was using Annie's blood, not mine. It's why he wants her back. We will end this, Father."

My father nods, then turns to Flynn. "We are in agreement then?"

Flynn sighs but agrees. "Okay. Once this over we'll figure out what to do about telling the mortals."

"I'll have Maple and Willow meet with you all in the morning. Annastasia will need to be informed, your mother has requested she's the one to tell her about her past."

Finally, I'm at a loss for words, and after a brief hug with our father, we follow the path through the trees, leaving behind unanswered questions and just a sliver of hope.

XXX

ONCE A KILLER...

KNOX

None of us flinch or even look up when screaming surrounds us. We stand strong, together as always, while in the back of my mind, I know this could be the last time I see my brothers. I could die here tonight. Flynn's blood won't heal me if I'm torn limb from limb by the fray. Knowing now what I know about Adam, I'm positive he's still out there, waiting for his chance to strike.

"Ready?" Flynn asks. We nod, unspoken words hang between us until Flynn steps back.

"Let's end this," Steel says. "Bella will kill me if she has to be up all night with the twins."

"Tell me about it," Flynn murmurs.

I almost forget how good it is to be with my brothers like this. To fight together, to have one another's backs. To trust implicitly.

Flynn and Steel head off in opposite directions, while Clay and I head to the parking lot behind the shopping centre to block the drain that leads to the Fray underground.

"Knox—"

"Don't say it, brother. Just... don't." I know what he wants to say. *Be careful. Don't get caught.* I can't hear it, not now. I need to focus on killing these bastards and finding Adam so I can kill him too.

Clay nods and pulls his sword from its sheath, swinging it around while we walk. "I'll go to the roof, give me the signal if you need to."

"I will." As I round the corner by the side of the café, I spot three Fray holding down another guy who's doing his best to fight them off. His face is bloody and his lip's split, but his fists are flying, and to his credit, he's doing some damage. "Hey assholes!" I shout as I draw my sword.

One by one they look up, dazed and drugged out of their minds on a combination of angel and vampire blood. The guy on the ground scrambles backwards, but groans in pain and grabs his thigh where the blade of a knife is embedded deep in his flesh. When his groan draws the attention of one of the Fray who turns around, I plunge my sword into his back and kick him forward as I remove it. Another plunge of my sword pierces his heart and ensures he won't survive.

The other two guys are gaining ground, both swinging nunchucks, their eyes focused only on me. "Wanna die today?" The guy with the mohawk asks.

I laugh and shake my head. "Man, I was just about to ask you the same question."

The guys exchange glances, and mohawk lunges at me. The swing of my sword comes too late, and the nunchuck to my jaw sends me stumbling backwards. My sword clangs to the ground, just out of reach. Mohawk drops his weapon and rains down punches to my face before I jerk upward and shove him off me. I manage to land an uppercut to his jaw, immobilising him long enough to grip the hilt of my sword and remove his head in one swift blow.

I spin and kick the last guy in the ribs, but he jumps up quickly, running toward me like a battering ram. When he reaches me, I grab a fistful of his long hair and drag him toward the concrete wall where I slam his head. Still gripping his hair, I shove him face first into the ground and drop a knee to his back. "How many of you are here?" I shout.

"Fuck you!" He spits on the ground. "I'm not sayin' nothin'."

I draw my short sword from its sheath while the guy struggles and curses at me to let him go. When I press the tip of the blade to his neck, he instantly stills. "How many?"

"I'm gonna die no matter what. Fuck you!"

Slowly, I press the tip of the sword into his flesh and watch his blood come to the surface. "How many?" This time my voice is calm.

"FUCK. YOU."

"I guess it's death then," I say.

As I push my sword into his neck, the injured guy's scream catches my attention. "BEHIND YOU!"

By the time I take in what he's saying, I'm in the sky. Adam's arms wrap around mine as I struggle out of his hold. As the ground gets further away, I stop struggling. Adam won't go down without a fight and dropping me from here won't give him the satisfaction he craves.

He doesn't speak until he lands in an empty gravel parking lot a few miles out of the valley. When he folds his wings, I glare at him. "You pathetic bastard. You used a fucking child!"

I raise my sword and step back, but he merely laughs and drops his own knife on the gravel.

"You wanna fight me, Knox? Let's fight. No weapons."

I shove my sword into the hard, dry ground and drop my short sword and knives by my feet. When I kick them away, Adam stares at me, his head cocked.

"What?" I ask. "You scared now?"

"Of you?" He rolls his eyes. "Come on, Knox, show me what you've got."

This bastard is dead. Steadying my feet, I watch Adam's every move. The tic of his left eyebrow as he watches me. The sly smirk that dances across his lips. His dark eyes fix on me as though I am *his* prey.

My muscles tense and I clench my fists. Without my powers I'm reluctant to make the first move, and he knows it. The fucking prick knows because he's seen me fight. *Just kill him.* After a deep inhale, I exhale and make my first move. A spin, a kick to the jaw, and a heavy fist that lands on his nose sends him flailing backwards. The unexpected attack fuels his rage and when he leaps to his feet and spins in the air, I'm not fast enough to block him. This time I go down, landing on my ass with a heavy thud.

Adam laughs out loud before his steel toe boot makes contact with my ribs. "Dumb fuck! Get up and fight," he goads as he attempts to kick me again.

This time, I'm faster. I roll to safety and leap to my feet then run at him, slamming his body to the ground, I land on top of him. Punch after punch connects with his jaw, cheeks, and eyes while he struggles beneath me in an attempt to free himself. With my hands firmly gripping his hair above his ears, I lift his head and slam it down onto the gravel. His arms flail wildly as I pound his head down again.

Blood seeps from his split lip and dark bruises mar his face and eyes, but even through the swelling, he still glares at me, and still manages a fucking smirk.

Anger rolls off me in waves and I clench my fists, ready to take my knife and shove it into his skull, but a blow to my head sends me off balance, giving Adam the opportunity to get on top of me. He straddles my chest, his knife at my throat, and his blood dripping from his head and face. A few drops land on my face as an eerie silence hovers. My left arm is stuck beneath Adam's leg, my fist closed around the hilt of my knife.

Adam cocks his head. "Not so strong now."

"Fuck you!"

"I'm going to kill you now, Knox. Then, I'm going to cut your heart out and personally deliver it to your brothers." He drags the knife down from my throat to my chest, tearing the fabric of my t-shirt open so he can slice my skin.

Ignoring the pain comes easy, my focus is on my left arm, waiting for him to move. "Hate to break it to you, *asshole*, but I'm not going to die tonight." *Dumb fucking lies I tell myself.*

"You're not afraid to die?"

"No. But you should be."

The tip of his knife sinks into my flesh and he twists it, causing me to wince as my—now red—blood oozes from my chest. In my struggle to kick out my legs and gain the upper hand, Adam shifts his weight slightly, allowing me to get my right hand free. With a clenched fist, I swing and land a hard hit to his jaw. He merely shakes his head and snarls while forcing the knife deeper into my chest. The moment it hits bone, Adam stops and raises his brow.

My breaths grow heavier with each inhale. Blood pools by my side as Adam continues to cut long jagged lines into my flesh. This is it. My body is failing me, and my strength has waned. There's no way I'll make it back home in time for Flynn to save me.

I tighten my grip on my knife and let my head fall to the side. "Just do it," I tell him. "Kill me."

"Now you wanna die? You really are weak as fuck." He shifts and gets to his knees beside me and works on removing my t-shirt with his knife. Once the fabric is discarded into a bloody heap, Adam continues to cut into my flesh, each slice sending pain searing through my body. "I think I might keep you a while, at least until I get Annie back. Let her watch while I torture you, you think she'd like that?"

I don't reply.

Another cut to my abdomen. Another moan.

"After I'm done with you, I'll find my brother's female. Do you know what I like about killing females?"

No reply.

Another cut. A groan of pain.

"Huh. Not much of a talker now, are you? Well, I'll tell you anyway. Females, when you cut them, they scream so fucking loud. The more they scream, the more I cut, the more blood I spill."

"Just... fuckin'—kill... me."

He extends his feathered wings. "Nah, not yet." He leans down to my face, his voice is quiet, but I hear every word. "First, I want you to watch me kill my niece. Hmm... What's her name again? Georgia. That's right."

I close my eyes and let my memories take me back to the first time I laid eyes on Georgia, and my promise to Roman that I would always protect her. I inhale and summon the remaining shreds of power that flow through my veins, and in one swift movement, I lift my left arm and shove my knife into the base of Adam's skull.

His howl of agony is cut short when I pull out the knife and roll to my side before forcing it through his chest and into his heart. His eyes remain open, wide and staring right at me. Blood pours from the wounds, and dribbles from his mouth.

Slowly, I manage to get to my knees and roll Adam onto his stomach. Using my knife, I hack and cut through the bone and muscle that attaches his wing to his shoulder blade. Pristine feathers covered in blood stick to my hands and forearms, but I don't stop. I continue cutting away at his wings, making sure to remove each feather from the protruding bones. He's not worthy of wings, not worthy of heaven. The bastard isn't even worthy of death.

It's not until I've removed both wings and dragged them away from his body that I realise I'm bleeding profusely. My stomach and chest are a grotesque mess of torn and sliced flesh and raw bleeding wounds. I sway slightly, catching myself on a fence paling a few feet away from where Adam's body lies prone on the gravel.

"Fuck you!" I shout at his corpse. "You'll never touch my family again."

My head spins, and when I fall to the ground, a sharp, stabbing pain pierces my chest.

"Now we're both dead." With one last glance at Adam, I smile and close my eyes.

XXXI
FROM CHAOS COMES HOPE

KNOX

"Haydee, you can't do that." Flynn's voice is in my head, but I can't see him. When I attempt to open my eyes, they remain shut, and I remain in darkness. Am I hallucinating? Is this what mortals feel when they die?

Haydee's voice replies, "Why? They said *you* can't do anything. No one said anything about me." Footsteps track on a hard floor before coming to a halt. In the background of my mind a constant beep plays over and over, but rather than annoy me, it brings a sense of peace.

"Flynn, she has a point. No laws are being broken." That comes from Autumn. *What are they talking about?*

A stinging pain lances through me; I feel it, but my body doesn't react. The voices continue, this time it's Venys. "She loves him, Flynn. Please, let her do this."

"And if it doesn't work?" Flynn sounds sceptical. I know my brother well. Whatever it is they're talking about, he's not going to agree.

"Doc said it needs to happen within the next twelve hours. Come on, Flynn, even he's on board with this, plea—"

"I'll talk to your father," Autumn cuts in. "He'll understand."

The heavy sigh is from Flynn, and I bet the footsteps are as well. When a door slams, there's silence for the longest time. Even the beeping has ceased. There's... nothing.

Time no longer exists.

I'm free falling.

Floating.

Waiting.

Dying.

Darkness reigns, and the chaos I once knew is gone. I'm caught in this blackened void where nothing and no one exists. Memories of my past play in a loop. My childhood, my teen years, the journey to earth where I was seduced by Haydee. The laughter of my brothers. The still air surrounding me is scented with forgotten moments. Crisp winter mornings, ocean waves, and flowers in spring. The scent of Annie's shampoo, her perfume, her... ANNIE!

Open your damn eyes! A flicker of light flashes before me, forcing my eyes to close once more. I focus on each breath that enters my lungs, sucking in fresh, clean air then exhaling. *Try again.* Determination rouses my subconscious and forces me into reality. I blink, letting in tiny shards of light. After another breath, I blink again. My eyes finally open and fix on the ceiling above. I wiggle my fingers and toes. No pain. I take slow, deep breaths and focus on moving my body. I wince when I get to my elbows, but with the pain comes a rush of adrenaline.

"Knox!" The squeal of delight almost deafens me. "Guys, Annie, everyone! He's awake."

I drop my head back and let myself rest against the bed again. When I turn my head, Autumn is standing beside the bed, a huge toothy smile lights up her entire face. She reaches out tentatively to touch my shoulder. "You're awake, finally. We've missed you so much, Knox." She leans down and presses a gentle kiss to my forehead.

"How long's it been?" My voice is husky, and my throat is dry.

Before Autumn gets a chance to answer, another squeal fills the room, followed by a flash of long black hair. The next thing I know, I'm straddled by a gorgeous female. A face I thought I'd never have the pleasure of seeing again. Soft hands cup my cheeks, and tears well in her eyes. I open my mouth to speak, but she leans down and peppers my face with delicate kisses.

"Fuck you!"
Kiss. Kiss. Kiss.
"I fucking missed you."
Kiss. Kiss.
"Don't you dare die on me again, Knox Fallon!"
Kiss. Kiss.

A laugh tumbles out of me, and I hear Clay's voice from the doorway. "I think we'll leave you guys alone for a while. Welcome back, brother." Voices fade and the door closes with a soft click.

"Hey gorgeous," I say, gliding my hands up and down her thighs. "How long was I out?"

She closes her eyes and lets her tears fall. When she opens them, she lies over me and presses her lips to my neck. "You died, Knox. When Flynn found you, you were dead. He cut his arm open right there on the filthy ground and begged you to breathe while his blood dripped into your heart." I lace my fingers through her hair and tug her closer. "God, it was horrible. I couldn't stop screaming. Clay disappeared, and Steel was trying to keep me calm—"

"I'm so sorry," I cut her off. "I had to kill A—"

"Stop. Don't say it. I know everything... about me, about what happened to my family. If you hadn't killed him, I'd be bound to him. It's so much to take in, but I'm learning. I met your Mum and Dad." She lifts her head and looks into my eyes. Her smile is breathtaking. "They love me, Knox."

I cup her cheek and lift my head to press a kiss to her soft, pink lips. "I love you, Annie."

"I love you, too. I guess you're still wondering how long it's been."

"If it's been years, I'm going to freak the fuck out."

She laughs. "Not quite."

Concern weaves its way through my veins and into my heart. How much has changed since I've been gone?

"It's been eight months." Annie traces her fingertip over my lips. I remain silent. "Flynn's blood... it wasn't enough, and the angels—they wouldn't allow a heavenly angel to sacrifice their life for you."

What the hell? A Sacrifice? Someone died to save my life. I clamp my eyes shut, knowing who it was before Annie says the words.

"Knox, it was Haydee. I'm so sorry, babe, I know you loved her, and she loved you so, so much. I met her you know. She said if I don't look after you, she'll come back and kill me." Annie laughs, but quickly turns serious. "Babe," she says as she runs her fingers through my hair. "You have all of Haydee's powers now."

"What the fuck?" I can't have powers. I'm a fallen angel with no wings, it's not possible. "You're serious?"

Annie nods. "You needed a transfusion, and although your brothers were prepared to sacrifice their lives, your father wouldn't allow it."

Thank fuck! I scrub my hands over my face and shake my head. "I don't feel any power yet. Has Doctor Charles been in?"

"Mmm hmm. He said it could take a while, since you were unconscious, but once you're up and moving again your strength and power will increase quickly." Annie's fingers trace over the scars on my chest and abdomen, each feather light touch sends a shiver down my spine. When she reaches my underwear, my cock hardens. "I think it's time for a shower, don't you?" The sassy smirk that dances across her lips pushes me over the edge of reason.

I leap out of the bed with barely a wince of pain, then lift Annie into my arms and head to the shower while she licks and kisses my neck all over.

After a long, hot, and very sexy shower with Annie, we made our way to the dining room for dinner. Seeing the twins and Georgia and Gabe after so long was surreal. They've all grown so much over the past eight months. The twins chatter to one another non-stop, dragging Georgia into their crazy conversations that make little sense to me. For a long time, I sat and just stared at everyone. My brothers, their wives, their children. My entire family was right there, alive and well, and Annie was mine. I couldn't have dreamed of a better outcome.

Flynn informed me that the commander and his father managed to flee the valley, but the rest of the fray were dealt with by my brothers and the police force. Flynn, Clay, and Steel met with the police chief, along with our father to tell them the truth about us. According to Steel it all went well and was sweetened by the fact that our father offered to pay to rebuild the damaged stores, install security in every home, and build a new school with a gymnasium and an indoor swimming pool.

Once I was caught up on everything and shown a thousand photographs of the children from the past eight months, Annie decided I was tired (I wasn't) and needed to go to bed to rest (I didn't).

When morning comes, I gaze out the floor to ceiling window of my bedroom to the mountains in the distance, thankful my life didn't end the night I killed Adam. Thinking about what he did to Annie still sets my blood boiling. She was an innocent victim in all of this and will carry the weight of her sins for eternity. She says she's fine, that it's just part of her story, a life she lived and left behind.

Steel pulled me aside last night and told me that while Flynn was out searching for me, Annie was inconsolable. She was screaming and shouting about killing people and watching them bleed out. Turns out that the moment Adam died, Annie's memories rushed back with a vengeance, the terrifying truths of her childhood spilled into her reality and smothered her light. After a month of our mother visiting Annie and putting her mind at rest, she was finally able to let go of the past and look forward to the future.

While I was lying prone in bed, unconscious, unknowing, life continued without me. The world turned, time ticked by, smiles, love, and laughter were missed. A twinge of resentment seeps into my heart but I quickly push it aside and focus on the here and now.

Delicate fingers trace my cock, followed by a swish of thick black hair that tickles my thighs. The soft, wet heat of Annie's tongue glides up my shaft and she licks the head, swirling her tongue around as her hand strokes up and down. When her mouth envelops my cock, I release a shuddering breath. One hand slides up my chest and using her fingers she tugs on my nipple ring; causing my back to arch.

With my fingers threaded through her hair, I watch her devour my cock until I can barely breathe. "Fuck, baby... never stop..." Damn, it's been too long.

With a pop, she lifts her head and smiles. "I owe you eight months of pleasure; can you handle it?"

I cup her cheek. "Baby, I can take anything you're willing to give."

She raises a brow and a sexy smile plays across her full lips before she opens her mouth and takes my cock once more. Her little moans of pleasure as she sucks cause me to buck my hips frantically, but she doesn't let up, she continues worshipping me, sucking, licking, kissing, and stroking until I explode in pleasure.

"Annie..."

She licks her lips and crawls up beside me, nuzzling into my neck. I kiss her forehead and trace my fingers up and down her spine.

"I love you so much, Knox."

"I love you too, baby. And that was... damn, I don't even words yet."

Lacing her fingers through mine, she brings them up to her lips and presses a kiss to each of my knuckles. I pull her into me, as close as I possibly can without crushing her. As she falls asleep in my embrace, I close my eyes and know that even when we're consumed by chaos and rage, we will find serenity in one another's arms.

THE END

Keep reading for a special three-part epilogue.

EPILOGUE

PART 1

GEORGIA

15 years later

My scream is carried on the wind. "Angel, get down!"

She looks back over her shoulder at me, the long waves of her silky blonde hair fly around her face as she turns and runs for cover. A second later, blue paint splatters across the bark of a fallen tree.

"That was close," Angel says, peeking over the trunk.

I lie still, covered in the branches and leaves Angel and Hope assured me would hide my position. I look through the scope of my paintball rifle, searching for Cael, but he's nowhere to be seen.

There's a noise behind me, then heavy breathing, and a quiet giggle. It's Hope. "Arc's in the tower. Top window on the right."

Glancing at Angel, I watch her balance her gun on the fallen tree. Hope crawls across the mud-covered ground to hide behind the concrete wall a few feet away. When she's in position, we wait. And we wait. The boys are so good at paintball that we rarely win, and they refuse to split up into separate teams. Arc and Cael stick together like they're attached by an invisible thread.

"I see him," Angel whispers. "He's moved to the trees."

I scan the area until I spot Arc hiding in the branches of a tree. Raising my gun slightly, I keep one eye trained on him as I place my finger over the trigger. My heart races, and a rush of adrenaline courses through my veins. "I've got him," I whisper to the girls.

"Take him out," Hope says.

I inhale, and as I exhale, I pull the trigger and... splat! A splatter of red paint covers his chest.

There's a frustrated groan, followed by rustling leaves. "Damn! She got me," Arc yells out as he jumps from the tree and lands on the ground. He jogs over to the waiting area and I spot Gabe and Cael running through the forest.

"Wanna do it?" Angel asks.

"YES!" Hope and I shout in unison.

"On three?" I say.

Together, we count to three, and on three, we jump to our feet and run full speed toward the tower where the boys are hiding. Hope jumps over a boulder and races up the wooden steps of their tower. Angel and I make our way through the forest to attack them from the back of their hideout.

A splash of blue paint hits the ground in front of me, and I freeze. Angel drops to one knee, searching the area, her rifle now slung over her shoulder, and her camouflage machine gun steady in her hands. "There!" she shouts as Gabe runs past in the distance.

At the same time, Angel and I hold the trigger of our guns, peppering the area with red paintballs until finally, we get him.

Gabe rolls across the ground, covered in red paint as he howls with laughter. "Jeez, take it easy girls. It's just a game."

We both giggle as he runs over to Arc. Getting Cael is going to be hard. He's quiet, fast, and he knows every inch of the paintball arena like the back of his hand. I look back at Hope, she's standing in their tower, looking through her scope. When she gives me the go ahead, I reload my gun with another round of paintballs.

Ahead, leaves rustle in the trees and a warm breeze surrounds us. I clamp my eyes shut, focusing only on the sounds. Ahead, above, behind... I'm still learning to harness my powers, so it takes me a few minutes to locate where the heavy breathing is coming from.

"He's behind us..." I whisper to Angel.

Slowly, she turns, and I follow, careful not to make too much noise. Three tall pine trees stand in front of us now, and I know Cael is behind one of them.

I look up to Hope, but she's crouched down by the window of the tower and won't be able to see him. She shakes her head at me, warning me not to move, but Angel nudges my arm and points to the tree in the middle. When I nod, we walk forward, and when we get to the tree, we jump out and pepper Cael with bullets. He screams as he falls to the ground in a ridiculously fake death scene.

We continue to shoot him with paintballs until he's begging us to stop. "Ugh, I hate you all!"

Hope stands and raises her hands in the air. "WE WON!" She leaps down from the tower and we hug each other tight, laughing wildly as the boys pout and wipe paint off their faces.

I pat Arc on the back. "Don't be a sore loser."

He drops his arm over my shoulder. "You're getting better at this, little cuz."

I roll my eyes. "I'm not little," I whine. "I'm fun size."

"Whatever you say, shorty," Cael calls as he runs ahead.

When we get back to the house, Parker is bringing platters of food to the outdoor entertaining area. Cael grabs a handful of nuts and shoves them in his mouth, and Arc does the same.

I scrunch my nose in disgust. "You're both so gross."

Angel and Hope nod in agreement. "You're never going to get a girlfriend, Cael," Hope says.

He shrugs and grabs another handful of nuts, talking while he chews. "You'll see... Besides, maybe I want a boyfriend."

Arc chokes, then coughs and sprays chewed up peanuts all over us.

I step back and wipe my hands over my t-shirt. "Ugh, boys are disgusting."

"You won't be saying that in a few years." Her voice causes a squeal of excitement to leave my mouth before I have a chance to take another breath. When I spin around, I run to her and jump up to wrap my arms around her neck.

"Annie! Oh my god, you're home." I hug her tight, and she kisses my cheek. "I missed you so much." I let her go but grab her hand and squeeze it between mine as she says hello to the others. "Did you have fun?" I ask. "Did you go free-diving? Oh my god, did you swim with sharks? You have to tell me everything."

Annie and Knox left twelve months ago to backpack around the world. They were asked to be a part of ***Rush***, a group of crazy adrenaline junkies who travel the world, searching for the most dangerous activities on the planet. Their first trip was when I'd just turned five years old, and I begged Mum and Dad to let me go with them, of course I had no idea of the dangers back then. I do now, but Dad refuses to let me go until I'm eighteen.

She nods. "Calm down, we've got photos and videos to show everyone. It was amazing, Georgia, the beaches, the oceans..." She smiles a dreamy smile. "And the volcanos, I've never seen anything so beautiful."

"I can't wait til I'm eighteen!" I scan the backyard. "Where's Knox?" I ask.

"Inside seeing the others. You guys were playing paintball?"

I nod and smile. "We won. Girls are the best, as usual."

"Nah ah," Arc says shaking his head. "You got lucky. Next time we'll win."

"Not if Knox is on our team," Hope says.

Cael and Arc narrow their eyes. "That's not fair, no adults allowed."

Angel tilts her head. "That's not even a rule. God, you boys are such sore losers."

The boys ignore her and walk away mumbling about how we must have cheated. When they're gone, I hear Knox, and I smile.

"Georgie girl," he calls.

I slam into him and wrap my arms around his massive middle. "I missed you so much."

He strokes my hair and leans down to kiss my head. "You been good? Nothing wrong?"

I smile bright. Knox is always checking up on me. He checks on the others too, but he's always worried about me, and constantly texting dad to see if I'm okay. Mum says he's been the same since I was born, even though there's nothing at all wrong with me. Well, except for being *"fun size"*. But I don't count that as *wrong*.

"I'm great! We won paintball. Oh, and I've been boxing, I'm so good at it now."

Annie's eyes light up. She's been teaching me boxing, kickboxing, and martial arts since I was just two years old, and I love it. "Come and show me," Annie says.

We head inside where Dad and Flynn are sitting at the kitchen bench. "You won," Dad says. "The boys aren't happy."

I shrug and give him a hug. "Too bad. I'm going up to the gym with Annie and Knox, you wanna come?"

"Is this for fun, or for training?" Dad narrows his eyes; he gets annoyed if I spend too much time in the gym and tells me I need to have hobbies other than training.

"Just for fun, Dad. I want to show Knox and Annie what I've learned."

"Come on then." He ruffles my hair and walks ahead of me, chatting to Knox while they head upstairs.

In the gym, I pull my hair back into a ponytail before I pull on the boxing gloves Annie bought me for my fourteenth birthday. I stand in the middle of the mats as Annie tugs hers on. She jogs over and stands in front of me. "You'll be okay with them all watching?"

My entire family is in the gym now. My parents and my uncles and aunts are standing by the wall, waiting. The boys are sitting on the floor with their legs out in front of them. Hope's sitting on a bright pink exercise ball, bouncing up and down, while Angel sits on one of the exercise bikes, eating a strawberry iced donut. When I smirk at her, she shrugs. "You know you want one."

"Nope. I don't." I nod to Annie. "I'm good to go."

Knox stands against the opposite wall with his arms crossed over his chest. "Watch out, Annie, Georgie girl's been practicing that right hook."

I laugh as me and Annie stand opposite one another and prepare to fight.

When Knox shouts "fight", I start. I plant my feet flat on the floor and steady myself as I raise my hands to block Annie's punches. We don't do full contact, Annie's terrified she'll hurt me. Every time she swings a punch, I block it and continue, swiftly moving my feet to step around her.

She does a spin kick and her foot just passes my nose. The whoosh of air makes me step back quickly before I regain my balance, then I spin and kick, slamming the outside of my foot right into Annie's jaw.

I stop, my eyes wide, shocked I got her, and even more shocked that it was hard, and her lip is bleeding. "Oh my god, I'm so sorry, Annie." I pull my gloves off and throw them on the mat to hug her tight and beg her to forgive me.

"Hey, Georgie, calm down. Sweetheart, it's fine." Logically, I know she's fine. She can't feel the pain, and blood doesn't bother her. But as usual, in the heat of the moment, I panic.

While Annie goes to wash her face, Knox comes over with a training pad. He looks over to Dad. "Has she been getting stronger?" he asks.

Dad nods and laughs as he points to the boxing bag I busted open last week.

"I'd beat her," Cael says. "She's tiny, *and* she hits like a girl."

I roll my eyes and kick his foot. "Shut up, Ca—"

Flynn cuts me off, but he's talking to Cael. "Stop trying to rile her up. I've warned you, mate, if she knocks you out, it's your own fault."

Arc covers his mouth with his hand and leans close to whisper something to Cael. They both laugh, but when Knox glares at them, they finally shut up.

Knox shakes his head. "Cael, this is one fight you *won't* win."

Knox holds the pad and tells me to kick as hard as I can. At first, I don't, because I'm worried I'll hurt him. I've been getting stronger, and I'm not sure just how strong I am now. When I broke the boxing bag, I wasn't even trying. I continue kicking the pad as Knox moves around the arena, and gradually, I go harder. Some of the kicks push him back a little and cause him to lose his balance for a few seconds.

For the past three months, I've had a fire burning inside me. An intense, radiating heat that spreads through my body and sends a rush of adrenaline to every nerve ending. When it happens, I come to the gym to train, desperate to release the energy that's building up inside me. Some days it takes hours to release the pent-up energy.

After a few more kicks, Dad calls out, "Georgia, show him what you can do, sweetheart."

I look at Mum first to gain her approval. They're the only ones who know about my fire. I begged them not to say anything until I was sure I wasn't imagining it. Knox has always said that when my powers finally appear, he'll teach me how to harness them. Mum could, but she says she's not experienced enough to help someone else, and she never uses her powers anyway.

"Come on," Knox says. "What are you waiting for?"

"Okay. I hope you're ready." I clamp my eyes shut and count to five in my head before I spin, then I kick.

I hear one gasp after another right before I hear a massive crash, and a loud thud. When I open my eyes, my entire family are standing there, staring at me. I slowly turn my head to see Knox in the wall. Yes, IN. THE. WALL. It's crushed around him. Broken bricks and crumbling cement all over him. I turn back to everyone, then back to Knox. There's a huge smile on his face as he dusts the debris off himself. "Ah, Roman, I think you need to control your daughter."

Dad laughs and shakes his head. "You and Annie wanted to teach her."

Hope and Angel run over and hug me. "That was freaking amazing," Hope says. "Do it again!"

"Do it to the boys," Angel says, jumping up and down. "Cael first!"

Cael and Arc's eyes widen, and they step back with their hands raised in defence.

Gabe stares at me. "Leave me out of this. I'm always nice to you, Georgie. Favourite cousin, remember?"

With my hands on my hips, I raise my brows. "See, just because I'm small, doesn't mean I'm not strong!"

EPILOGUE
PART 2

KNOX

Annie comes out of the bathroom with a towel wrapped around her hair. "Do you think we should tell them?"

Leaning back on the velvet sofa in our bedroom, I watch her pace the room. "It isn't going to change anything, babe. But if it makes you feel better, I'll get the guys together."

She straddles my lap, wearing only a bra and underwear. With a heavy sigh, she rests her head on my shoulder.

Before we came home from our trip, we stopped in Arcane. There, we met with Lola, Queen of Arcadia, who Haydee discovered was Annie's cousin.

Haydee didn't return to the valley until five years ago. She was furious and said it's the longest it's ever taken her to regenerate, but on the plus side, she was glad I survived the transfusion of her blood. It took me almost two years to come to terms with my new powers. Harnessing fire—I found out—is nothing like harnessing angel light. The power of fire comes from deep in the soul; the place where darkness lies dormant. Releasing the darkness is risky, because with it, comes the chaos and rage that was at one time, my downfall.

It's the same darkness that now resides inside Georgia. Georgia is as much a phoenix as Haydee is, and for that reason alone, Kailey and Roman agreed with me and Annie that allowing her to train regularly in the gym, would help focus her excess energy on something positive. We can only hope she keeps the darkness at bay.

Annie runs her fingers through my hair. "You're worried about Georgie, aren't you?"

"Yeah. It was hard for me to get used to. She's just a kid, you know?"

She nods and presses a kiss to my forehead. "I know. But she has us, and Haydee now too."

I trace my fingertips up and down her spine. "Yeah, sorry, babe. Let's talk about something else. How are you feeling about everything Lola told you?"

"Well..." After a sigh, she continues, "I want to believe her, but it sounds and *feels* so unreal. How do I know she didn't put those memories in my head?" She shakes her head hard as though it will free her from her long-forgotten memories. "But when I close my eyes, there's an ache in my heart and a lump in my throat. It's as though I'm living every moment."

Annie pulls the towel off her damp hair. I pull it over her shoulder and twist the strands around my hand. "Lola's powers are unique. It's why she doesn't leave Arcane. There, she's almost invincible. I know it's a lot to take in, babe, but it's what you've been waiting for. You have the truth now."

After my near-death experience, Annie was content to live the rest of her life not knowing the details that drove her father and Adam to change the course of her life. As the years went by, the mood swings became worse and Annie's desire to fight grew stronger. My brothers were there for her every step of the way, using their power to fight her. There were bloody knuckles and noses, broken bones, and plenty of flesh wounds, but none of us could figure out why—or how—she was still so strong, and still unable to feel pain.

Lola had the answers to all our questions.

We sat in the living room of Lola and Belial's house and listening as Lola used her power to search Annie's memories, all the way back to the moment of her birth.

EPILOGUE
PART 3

ANNIE

one week earlier

The air was thick with a strange, sickly-sweet scent Knox informed me was purity. My senses were assaulted by the angelic clouds that hovered above and caused a wave of nausea to wash over me. My eyes were wide, and my skin tingled as though someone was brushing the softest feathers across my bare flesh. I stared in awe as we followed a neat stone path, lined with brilliant flowers in every colour imaginable. In the centre of each one, puffs of golden dust—pollen—swirled.

Part of me wanted to run and hide. Search for the darkest, dirtiest place possible to conceal the ugliness I carried with me like a weight upon my shoulders. Another part of me, a much smaller part, felt nothing but longing and the intense desire to pack up my life in Ambrosia Valley, and live here among the beauty I never knew existed.

As we walked, Knox took my hand and told me about Lola, Queen of Arcadia, and her husband, Belial. He said they were both angels, and that he'd met them a long time ago. The way his brow creased as he spoke about Belial made me wonder if they had a less than pleasant history.

My thoughts were cut short though when the most beautiful, young girl walked toward us. Long, silky black hair—like mine—reached her slim hips, and her sapphire blue eyes sparkled as she smiled and extended her hand. "Knox, it's lovely to see you. How are your brothers and your family?"

Knox took her hand and bowed his head slightly before kissing the back of it. "It's good to see you too, Lola. My family is great, the children are all growing fast, as you can imagine."

Lola dropped her hand from Knox and turned her focus to me. "You must be Annastasia. I've been looking forward to meeting you. Welcome to Arcane."

For a moment, I stood transfixed on the girl—No. The woman. The freaking queen of one of the heavens. *Damn! There really are seven heavens.* Her pale skin was radiant, and I couldn't look away. "I'm g—good. Good. It's nice to meet you, ah... Queen—"

She cut me off with a laugh. "Oh, just Lola is fine."

I finally managed a smile. "You can call me Annie, if you want... I mean if that's okay." What the hell was I saying?

Lola led us toward a beautiful white house surrounded by large oak trees with bright green leaves and twisted, knobbly branches. She extended a hand and urged us inside. I was surprised to see the inside of the house was fairly normal. It was lavish, like the Fallon Mansion, but on a much smaller scale, and didn't seem like the type of house fit for a queen.

As we sat at the kitchen table, Lola went into the kitchen and flicked on an impressive looking coffee machine. "Belial will be here shortly." She rolled her eyes and shook her head, but a hint of a smirk played on her lips. "He's out with Marcus."

Knox laughed. "Working off his rage?"

Lola laughed with him. "Something like that. He won't cause any trouble, Knox. I've already warned him." I wondered what I was missing and was about to question Knox when a squeal of delight filled the air.

"Ahh... Put me down, Kaleb! Stop... put me down."

The three of us turned our heads at the same time. "Nylah?" Knox said in almost a whisper.

The girl, who was a spitting image of Lola, gave Knox a bright smile. The guy, who looked like he belonged in a heavyweight boxing ring, smirked and dropped Nylah to her feet.

"Ny, Kaleb, you remember Knox, and Annie is his partner. They're from Ambrosia Valley."

"Wow," Kaleb said, sounding impressed. He shook Knox's hand, then mine. "Man, I wanna go there, but Dad won't let me." He pouted and pulled a chair out for Nylah before sitting on the one beside her.

Lola placed a jug of milk and a small jar of sugar on the table, along with a plate of decadent looking choc-chip cookies. Nylah grabbed one and took a bite.

"Are you staying long?" she asked me.

"Um, I'm not sure. We've been gone for a while, so I'd love to get home soon."

"It must be nice being able to go out and do fun stuff." Nylah glanced at her mother, but dropped her head when Kaleb nudged her with his shoulder.

"Ny, you know the rules, honey. And you know your father won't let you leave until you're twenty-one." When Nylah pouted, Lola shook her head and smiled.

"You're brother and sister?" I asked Nylah and Kaleb.

They both let out a loud howl of laughter. "Or not," I said, wincing.

The sound of the front door opening had Kaleb and Nylah jumping to their feet. "We're not related at all," Kaleb said. "Thank fu—"

"Kaleb!" A voice growled from behind us.

"Sorry, Belial." He grabbed Nylah's hand and dragged her from the kitchen, snatching a handful of cookies on his way out. "We need to go. We're meeting Emily at ah..." He looked at Nylah, obviously trying to get her to help him out, but instead, she jumped up and wrapped her arms around Belial's neck.

"Daaaad..." she drew out the word while batting her long, dark lashes. "Can we go to the cliffs, please?"

Belial's eyes went straight to Kaleb who nodded, then shook his head, then nodded again. It was still strange to see people talking to each other using only their minds. I watched Kaleb's face change before he spoke up again. "About nine. The girls were going to stay at my place."

"Pleeeease, Dad."

"Fine. But if I hear you went into the city, you'll be locked in the damn castle until you're thirty."

She pressed a quick kiss to Belial's cheek and waved goodbye as she raced out the front door, Kaleb hot on her heels.

Belial scrubbed a hand down his face. "Never have kids. Especially girls. They'll fuckin' kill you." He extended his hand to Knox, then to me. "Unfortunately, Knox, I've been pre-warned to behave. But if you want to go a few rounds in the arena..."

Lola slapped his massive bicep playfully. "Sit down, you're being ridiculous. There will be no fighting. At all." Belial grabbed Lola around her waist and pulled her into his lap before pressing a kiss to her neck. She fed him a cookie over her shoulder then turned her attention back to me and Knox.

"Okay, let's do this so you guys can get back to your own family." With a nod of agreement from us, Lola began telling me my life story.

She told me I was born in the third heaven to Princess Amalie, her mother's sister, making Lola and I cousins. My mother hadn't been seen for almost a year, which apparently wasn't out of the ordinary for heavenly angels. My father though, had been seen in many places, including right here in Arcane where he would meet with Vandrick, and Adam's grandfather—the old man I despised. She went on to say that at first everyone thought the old man was a normal, mortal human. It didn't take long for them to discover Vandrick had been supplying the old man with pure vampire blood to keep him alive for as long as possible.

A few months later, Vandrick's secret was out, and he was exiled from Arcane along with the old man. No one saw them again. Not long after that, my father, Javier, was asking about them, but would refuse to tell anyone why.

When she reached the part of the story where my father and Adam made a deal, my stomach lurched, and bile rose in my throat. My own father had plunged his angel sword into my mother's heart, then whisked me away. He took me to a filthy, rundown warehouse in Nevermore, a town in the middle of nowhere, where demons and rogue vampires ran rampant.

In Nevermore, my bastard father allowed the old man to inject me with a mixture of vampire and angel blood. The blood kept me strong without the need for breastmilk or food for the first twelve months of my life. But they quickly discovered the side effects. Violent outbursts, an innate craving to kill, and along with the lack of empathy, I lost my ability to feel pain.

But the worst part was, I was obsessed with Adam. I couldn't say no to him, and when I was five years old, he asked me to give him angel wings. The memory of me staring up at Adam with nothing but admiration as pure white wings appear on his back, steals my breath every time I close my eyes.

Adam, the old man, my own father. They each played a part in destroying the life I could have had, and turning me into a little girl who wanted nothing more than to please the boy she believed in. It turned out my childhood dreams were not dreams at all. Thanks to the blood mixture that flowed through my veins, Adam was a reality my young mind craved, and obeyed without question.

The parents I killed were nothing more than pawns in Adam's sick, twisted game. Humans to use and play with while he filled my head with beautiful images of blood, violence, and death.

I pull myself out of the vivid memories, and the ethereal beauty of Arcane, and I tug one of Knox's hoodies over my head before I pull on a pair of black leggings. "I want to tell them," I say to Knox. "Belial said it's possible someone else knows about me. It could put us all in danger. It may not happen, but I know Flynn will feel better if we're prepared."

Knox pulls me into his arms and presses a soft kiss to my lips. "Okay. Let's do it."

I trace my fingertip over his lips. "I love you, Knox. Without you, I would have been lost forever."

ABOUT THE AUTHOR

JULIE ANNE ADDICOTT

ARE YOU READY TO FIND BEAUTY IN BRUTALITY?

Julie Anne Addicott writes across a range of genres including pitch black tragedies, dark and toxic love stories, poetry, and romance filled to the brim with tears, trauma, and tragedy.

Scan here to find the author on social media.

ALSO BY JULIE ANNE ADDICOTT

PARANORMAL ROMANCE

THE CURSE OF THE FALLEN SERIES

A complete, four book paranormal romance series that follows the lives of four cursed, fallen angel brothers on their journey to discover love in the mortal world.

Book 1 – *Flynn & Autumn*
FLYNN – A LUST LIKE NO OTHER

Book 2 – *Steel & Bella*
STEEL – CONSTANT CRAVING

Book 3 – *Clay & Lexi*
CLAY – DEADLY DESIRES

Book 4 – *Knox & Annie*
KNOX – HEARTS WITHOUT CHAINS

DARK & TRAGIC LOVE STORIES

These novels are not romance stories

A Ruin Novel – *Carlie's Story*
LOVE LOST HER WAY

A Ruin Novel – *Tryst's Story*
MY NAME IS TRYST

The House of Machiavellianism – Book 1,
Diablo & Killian
DANSE MACABRE

MM ROMANCE NOVELS

A Hurricane Hearts Novel – Book 1,
Jackson & Lawson
THERE'S ONLY AFTER

The House of Machiavellianism – Book 2,
Salem & Justice
THE DESECRATION OF JUSTICE
*A 20k word short story for the
Shadows in Bloom Anthology
(full story coming 2025)*

Co-written with Ashley Lane
Beckett & Hudson
WAVES
*A 20k word short story for the
I Heard it in a Love Song Anthology*

POETRY COLLECTIONS

Dark poetry with themes surrounding mental illness, suicide, and grief, loss, and love

WHERE MY DEMONS HIDE

BORROWED WINGS & BROKEN DREAMS

GODDESS OF WORDS

CONTENT WARNINGS

Many of Julie Anne Addicott's stories include extremely graphic scenes and themes based on **real life traumatic experiences** of severe child abuse that may be triggering or difficult to read.

These books are suitable for mature adults over the age of 21.

However, if you believe you may be negatively affected by something you read, please take this into account before you purchase and/or read. Sample content and reviews can be found on Amazon. Alternatively, you can reach out to the author for more information through social media or via email.

Content Warning Lists can be found on the author's website (links below) and are updated often.

Please note: These lists will include spoilers and may not include warnings for every instance of triggering content.

My Name is Tryst
https://julieanneaddicott.wixsite.com/jaddicott/general-5

Love Lost Her Way
https://julieanneaddicott.wixsite.com/jaddicott/love-lost-her-way-1

There's Only After
https://julieanneaddicott.wixsite.com/jaddicott/there-s-only-after

Danse Macabre
https://julieanneaddicott.wixsite.com/jaddicott/danse-macabre

The Desecration of Justice
https://julieanneaddicott.wixsite.com/jaddicott/the-desecration-of-justice-1

The Curse of the Fallen Series
https://julieanneaddicott.wixsite.com/jaddicott/the-curse-of-the-fallen-series

HELPLINES, SUPPORT & FURTHER READING

Lifeline Australia
13 11 14
https://www.lifelinesupport.org/

Beyond Blue Australia
Phone: 1300 22 4636
https://www.beyondblue.org.au/

Black Dog Institute Australia
https://www.blackdoginstitute.org.au/

Australian Centre to Counter Child Exploitation
https://www.accce.gov.au/what-we-do/about-us

American Foundation for Suicide Prevention
Phone: 1-800-273-8255
https://afsp.org/

RAINN (rape, abuse and incest national network)
Phone: 800-656-4673
https://www.rainn.org

National Human Trafficking Hotline (USA)
Phone: 1-888-373-7888
https://humantraffickinghotline.org/

Operation Underground Railroad
http://ourrescue.org/

Kids Help Line Australia
1800 55 1800

American Foundation for Suicide Prevention (AFSP)
National Suicide Prevention Lifeline
1-800-273-talk (8255)

Crisis Text Line (USA)
Text talk to 741741

Crisis Services Canada
Call 1.833.456.4566 or text 45645

Samaritans UK
116 123

Childline UK
0800 1111

Made in United States
North Haven, CT
20 June 2025